SMART NUTRIENTS

A Guide to Nutrients That Can Prevent and Reverse Senility

Dr. Abram Hoffer
Dr. Morton Walker

A DR. MORTON WALKER HEALTH BOOK

Avery Publishing Group
Garden City Park, New York

Dr. Hoffer dedicates this book to Clara Hoffer, his mother,
who first alerted him to the value of niacin
in reversing senile changes.

Dr. Walker dedicates this book to Rae Walker, his mother,
who is lively and alert, busy with living,
and sharing herself with others.

FOREWORD

The problem of aging and senility is of almost universal interest among adults. In this book on *Smart Nutrients*, Abram Hoffer, M.D., Ph.D., and Morton Walker, D.P.M., present a large body of valuable information that can potentially help everybody slow down the inevitable aging process and prevent the unnecessary senile syndrome.

In the Huxley Institute-sponsored National Conference in 1972 on Health Care for the Aging, I called attention to the fact that statistical "man," as he ages, may have a slight impairment of hearing, some balding, a little greying of hair, slight impairment of vision, the loss of some teeth, a lessening of heart function, a slight loss of agility, a blunting of memory, a slight loss of sex urge, an increase in imbalance, and a few other changes.

In this book, however, Dr. Hoffer and Dr. Walker are obviously not interested in statistical "man"; they are interested in the aging of *real* people. They are concerned with you and me. The discussions reveal a full appreciation of how different aspects of getting old become real problems in actual life. The two doctors treat the topics of aging and senility in a way that is easily understandable. Anyone who is interested in his or her own welfare during the aging process should read this book and put nutrients to work for his or her benefit.

From my own experience of passing part way through the aging process, I enthusiastically endorse the idea that by providing yourself with *all* the needed nutrients, exercising adequately, and avoiding environmental poisons, it is possible to do marvelous things for one's entire self. This book does not deal with trifling concerns!

Ideally, toward the end of life, we should fall apart all at once and be gone like Oliver Wendell Holmes's "wonderful one-hoss shay," instead of suffering through the diseases of old age. Dr. Hoffer and Dr. Walker have written a book that should help everyone in his or her approach to this ideal. As they make clear, every kind of essential nutrient comes into play in the promotion and prolongation of healthy life. It is a program of living that is well worth following.

Roger J. Williams, Ph.D.

PREFACE

Following many years of clinical experience, I have concluded that senility can, in most cases, be prevented or treated, and that chronic nutritional deficiencies play a large role in causing this disease. With Morton Walker, I decided to present the results of the experience we gained from studying the medical literature and from our own observations.

Dr. Walker and I hope we can dissuade our readers from the sterile view that senility inevitably accompanies aging. Enough is known to prove that senility is preventable. Each one of us who does not avoid senility is simply showing ignorance of the biological factors that allow its onset.

We will present facts and hypotheses about aging and senility that will allow anyone interested in living out life in full possession of his or her mental faculties to do so—or at least to try. But our program must begin as early as possible; the closer one is to senility, the more difficult it is to prevent it.

Our conviction is based upon two kinds of evidence: the first is the accumulated observations made by our professional predecessors and contemporaries in medicine, science, and nutrition, and the second is the recorded observations of nonprofessionals. There are references in the Notes section at the end of the book that document the reports by scientists who have been pioneers in the field of aging.

Since 1954, when I first realized what improved nutrition could do in reversing and preventing senility, I have observed similar beneficial effects in a number of my elderly patients. No one has become senile within my immediate family in the past twenty-five years, even though two had begun to show evidence of senility before they were started on niacin.

In Chapter 1, evidence is outlined for our conclusion that senility is not inevitable, even if the first symptoms have occurred. In Chapters 2 and 3, we describe the aging changes that gradually occur from the stresses of our industrialized society. Chapter 4 contains a discussion of the modern hypotheses to explain the aging process. Because they are hypotheses, this chapter is not carved in stone and probably will be markedly altered as new information accrues.

Chapters 5 and 6 outline why we have concluded that senility is a form of chronic malnutrition; whenever we see a senile man or woman, we visualize the many decades of malnutrition that preceded this unhappy condition. We blame the heavy consumption of food artifacts—junk food—as the source of senile dementia. (In biology, an artifact is an unnatural substance created by an external force.) We believe there will be a steady increase in the incidence of senility in industrialized countries, since the swing toward food artifacts has not been slowed. It is estimated that in a few years as much food will be sold in restaurants and fast food outlets as in supermarkets.

Chapters 7 and 8 describe the vitamins and minerals that appear to be implicated most directly in preventing senility. But good food is not enough; physical fitness is equally important, as discussed in Chapter 10.

We do not claim that all senility can be prevented or reversed. Not every person who appears to be senile is actually senile, as there are several conditions that can produce a similar clinical syndrome. Each of these conditions requires specific treatment. Some conditions are irreversible and will not respond. But our therapeutic program will harm no one and help many, especially if started early. Other pathological conditions must be ruled out, of course, lest total reliance on our program discourage people from seeking other appropriate treatment.

Chapter 9 cites several studies that have proven the beneficial effects of the B vitamin niacin. Among these effects are the ability to stablize cholesterol, decrease the risk of corornary disease, and increase longevity.

We hope that this book will not only light a fire under geriatricians, medical scientists, and nutritionists, but will be followed by a massive research effort to test the whole program on a large scale. Such research won't be needed to convince *us* of the program's value, but to give proof to skeptical physicians who find large studies with statistical tables more impressive.

Meanwhile, since life is short and untreated senility is unrelenting in its march, we suggest you not wait for the decades required to persuade our medical schools and societies. It is your sanity that is at stake while the physician waits for hard clinical evidence.

1. AGING IS INEVITABLE
BUT SENILITY ISN'T

Growing old is just a process of getting tired. Soon I shall doze off, and then fall asleep. How beautiful to stretch oneself out!

—Malcolm Muggeridge

In 1954, Dr. Abram Hoffer and his wife, Rose, had completed plans for a three-month tour of the psychiatric research centers of Europe. The trip came about after the Rockefeller Foundation had awarded Dr. Hoffer's research group a large financial grant. Over a three-year period, the group was responsible for investigating the biochemical basis for schizophrenia. The project was an awesome responsibility, and Dr. Hoffer was eager to begin its development.

Accompanying the foundation's grant, however, was an offer that Dr. Hoffer could not refuse. The philanthropists asked him to tour research centers throughout Europe as their guest and take on the role of "Rockefeller traveling fellow." It was necessary for Dr. Hoffer to make the trip before beginning the new expanded research program, because any information gleaned abroad might be useful in his group's investigations.

As it turned out, this trip played both direct and indirect roles in the formation of a highly successful antisenility nutrition program. A family circumstance provided Dr. Hoffer with a dramatic instance of senility reversal using orthomolecular methods. In orthomolecular medicine, mental diseases or disturbances are believed to be the result of chemical imbalances that, in most cases, are a product of nutritional deficiencies. The first patient for whom he prescribed orthomolecular nutrition for the treatment and reversal of the senile syndrome was his own mother, Clara Hoffer.

A CASE OF SENILITY REVERSAL

During Dr. Hoffer's last visit with his parents before sailing for

Europe, his mother complained to him about how sick she was. Without question, she was having physical and mental problems, including partial loss of vision in one eye, a failing memory, and swollen and painful joints. She had also lost interest in what was going on; forgot names, addresses, and telephone numbers; repeated things she had already said; forgot recent events; had vivid remembrances of her early life; and showed a rigidity in her pattern of living. In short, she was showing signs of senility. The question in Dr. Hoffer's mind was whether he, as a psychiatrist, could provide her with any relief.

Dr. Hoffer had no doubt that his mother was developing the initial characteristics of the senile-dementia syndrome that hits so many older people. He "knew" there was no treatment for it, much as most traditional physicians today "know" that the senile condition is not reversible. In good conscience, however, he felt the need to offer his mother some kind of help, even if it was merely a placebo (an inert substance given for its suggestive effect.)

Previously, Dr. Hoffer had completed two double-blind controlled-comparison experiments with Dr. Humphry Osmond, using placebos, the first such experiments ever accomplished in psychiatry. Dr. Hoffer was quite familiar with the placebo effect, which in England was then called the "dummy" effect. Its success was ascribed to the hope of the patient for a remedy that would alleviate his or her symptoms. In 1954, the science of placebology was just beginning to develop.

A placebo was believed to be more effective if the supposed good effect could be dramatized. This was achieved by a persuasive and charismatic physician, by the proper use of suggestive factors, or by some remarkable property of the "drug" being given. It occurred to Dr. Hoffer that niacin (also known as nicotinic acid or vitamin B3) would be the ideal placebo. It had all the desired properties.

Niacin was quite familiar to Dr. Hoffer, who had been using it for two years with patients and had taken it himself to study its effect. His research staff was enthusiastic about its studies, and some of them were also trying it out on themselves. Niacin was completely safe, but Dr. Hoffer found it did cause a pronounced facial flush that eventually dissipated. Although he did not know it at the time, niacin lowers blood cholesterol and triglyceride levels, which is advantageous for the anti-atherosclerotic effect. Several years before, this B vitamin had also been discovered to be curative for the more common forms of arthritis by William Kaufman, M.D.[1,2]

Dr. Hoffer had no reason to suspect that niacin would be of any value in preventing, treating, or reversing senility. While he did establish that it was exceedingly useful for treating certain types of schizophrenia, Dr. Hoffer's chief reason for giving it to his mother was its placebo effect. He thought she would gain hope from experiencing the niacin flush.

Dr. Hoffer gave his mother a three-month supply with the advice to take one gram after each meal. The possible side effects were carefully outlined, and Clara was prepared for them.

About six weeks later, Dr. Hoffer and his wife received a very cheerful and enthusiastic letter from Clara. She wrote that she was feeling much better and her vision was restored. Neuralgia of the arms and legs, another condition that chronically disabled her, was gone entirely. She said her memory was normal. Her arthritic pains were gone completely, and the four small arthritic bumps on her knuckles, called "Heberden's nodes," were disappearing.

Dr. Hoffer was pleased with his mother's report but frankly was incredulous, and expressed this feeling to his wife. He could not believe his mother was experiencing any kind of real recovery and assumed that the powerful placebo effect had clouded the woman's own assessment of her health. Furthermore, his prior medical indoctrination was that Heberden's nodes never went away.

After arriving home in July 1954, Dr. and Mrs. Hoffer drove to his parents' farm near Hoffer, Saskatchewan, where he had been born and raised. Immediately upon seeing his mother, he realized her mental and physical responses were no placebo effect. Clara was cheerful, relaxed, at ease, and mentally alert. She responded quickly with accurate answers to any questions he asked, and moved with the step of a young woman. The arthritis that had begun to cripple her hands and hips had disappeared. There was no denying that the arthritic condition that had begun to pull her fingers out—the typical ulnar deviation—was no longer present. Her hands were supple, flexible, and free of pain. The little Heberden's bumps had gone away altogether. Her joints were much softer and flatter, and the bony prominences on her fingers were receding back to skin level.

Dr. Hoffer thought long and hard about his mother's mental and physical improvement. He began to suspect that what he "knew" to be the irreversible condition of senility might not be irreversible at all. If just one person responded to the ingestion of niacin, then others would also respond. For although we are all unique biochemical individuals, we are not *that* unique. The only problem was to find out how many others would also respond to niacin, and how the doctor and patient could determine this in advance. Dr. Hoffer investigated niacin over time, with careful studies, and his suspicions were confirmed: Niacin supplementation is a definite antisenility therapy. Dr. Hoffer's conclusion was that this remarkable vitamin should be incorporated as a significant component of any treatment program against senility.

Clara Hoffer remained in good mental health until she sustained a stroke in 1975, and died at the age of eighty-seven. During this interval of twenty-one years, she continued to take regular doses of niacin, ranging from one to four grams per day. Dr. Hoffer had added vitamin C and vitamin E as well as other nutrients (described in Chapter 8) to her antisenility dietary program. Clara maintained an active life for the whole of this time. She participated in all family social activities and wrote her memoirs. In fact, in collaboration with her daughter, Fannie Kahan, Clara published two books, one dealing with her early farm life in Canada, and the other dealing with her husband's agricultural experiences in Europe and Saskatchewan, where he had arrived in 1905 to start farming on a homestead.

Dr. Hoffer is certain that niacin saved his mother from senility, physical weakness, insecurity, and the terrors of living in a nursing home. He testifies that niacin, combined with certain other nutrients, permitted her to age without senility.

There have been other such cases as well. We shall describe them in the chapters that follow, since among them you may find a model of senility reversal that you might be able to match to your own family situation.

SENILITY IS NOT INEVITABLE

It isn't difficult to distinguish an old person from a young person. Throughout life, a variety of changes occur in our bodies that appear to be inevitable. These aging changes reflect biochemical reactions in the cells and anatomical alterations in the organs. The changes don't happen at the same rate in all the organs, and they take place at varying times from one person to the next. Rather striking, in fact, is the way in which individual organs can age before the whole body. Some are aged by the time they are forty years old; others appear young at eighty. Some organs—a kidney or stomach—could probably go on functioning normally for another few decades, but the heart may give out and cause early death.

Aging is inevitable and so is death. The rate at which aging occurs, however, is not highly correlated with age itself as measured in years. It is this flexible relationship—inevitable aging at variable rates of time—that makes this book possible and necessary.

If everyone inevitably aged and deteriorated at the same rate, it would mean that all of us had been programmed in the same way. We might age, deteriorate, and die much like the self-destruct devices so loved by some science fiction novelists. There would be no reason to think that anything could be done to change one's life pattern. But we *can* change our lives and be the masters of our destinies. We have the ability to approach the full life span with alert, creative, memory-filled minds.

Around us we see many people die old, but not senile. Such examples are encouraging, even inspiring. They support our belief that it is possible to prepare a nutritional environment that permits nearly everyone who so wishes to reach the same desirable state, that is, to age without senility. A good deal of evidence exists showing such a nutritional environment is feasible right now, and not in the golden future suggested by medical research scientists.

Our claim is that no one needs to depend just on the variability of the aging process. The information that we supply in this book will permit every reader to take steps to decrease his or her rate of aging. Put to use, our nutritional program will even allow the reversal of some changes that have already taken place.

While this nutritional information won't necessarily make anyone live longer, it will increase the potential for a healthier life expectancy. It will improve the quality of life for people in the more advanced age bracket. Why? How? To illustrate: A youthful individual at seventy is more apt to avoid accidents, such as being run down by a car, than an aged and deteriorated person of seventy, even if for no other reason than that the more active seventy-year-old can dodge out of the path of an oncoming automobile, and have the presence of mind to do so. A non-senile seventy-year-old person can enjoy a fullness of living that is sorely lacking for someone of the same age suffering from senile dementia. We mean to show that senility is not inevitable. Our recommendations, if followed, will ensure that there will be little or no indication of senility at death, no matter the reason or age at which it occurs.

It has been said that "old age can become an expression of human experience. It can be rich, varied, colorful, and in turn enriching; or it can be impoverished, empty, and only serve to emphasize the futility of life." For the elderly of today, reality is too often better described by the latter possibility. With this book, our aim is to transpose it into the former—a journey toward a full life. As the poet John Keats put it:

And like a newborn spirit did he pass
Through the green evening quiet in the sun.

THE RISING INCIDENCE OF OLD AGE AND SENILITY

The import of our message knows no bounds, for the incidence of old age and its associated senility is steadily on the rise. Today we may be living slightly longer, but we are not enjoying healthier lives.

Anyone reaching age forty-five today has no better chance of attaining the age of ninety than he would have had he lived 100 years ago. The major improvements for longevity have taken place in younger people, but there is no corresponding improvement in the health of the elderly. Older people who live longer do so not because they are healthier, but because medicine is more skillful at keeping them alive.

A study by Kraus, Spasoff, Beattie, Holden, Lawson, Rodenburg, and Woodcock (1977) showed that in the United States, 1.2 percent of the age group sixty-five to seventy-four, 5.2 percent of the age group seventy-five to eighty-four, and 20.3 percent of people aged eighty-five and over were in special nursing homes equipped for treating senility. Of the last group, 31 percent were bedfast, 11 percent were chairfast, 74 percent had three or more chronic illnesses, and 71 percent were senile.[3]

Between 1961 and 1971, Canada's population increased by 18 percent. But the population increase in the sixty-five to seventy-four age group was 21 percent; in the seventy-five to eighty-four age group it was 26 percent; and in the eighty-five and over age group, it was 70 percent.

In 1972, 147,000 Canadians lived to be eighty-five or older, while ten times this number attained this age in the United States. *But 70 percent of these elderly Americans were senile.* In 1975, geriatrics occupied one-third of all hospital beds for the acutely ill in the United States, at a cost of $118.7 billion, and during that year, 1.2 million elderly were in nursing homes. One-fourth of the drugs taken in 1975 were consumed by older Americans.

The Office of Human Development of the United States Department of Health and Human Services projects that there will be 71 million old people by the year 2035. One-third will be over seventy-five, and one-tenth will be over eighty-five. By the year 2000, the aged will constitute 20 percent of the national population. In 1987 there were 25 million people in the United States over the age of sixty-five. Right now, one of every nine Americans is a senior citizen who typically can expect to live another sixteen years, according to the Senate Committee on Aging. Social Security records reveal that 10,690 Americans are at least 100 years old. About 75 percent of all Americans now reach the age of sixty-five. Florida leads the states in the percentage of population sixty-five or older with 14 percent. Alaska, Hawaii, and Utah are at the bottom with 7.9 percent.

A total of 3 percent of the population over age sixty-five have psychiatric problems leading to limitation of their activities. The senile are included in this figure. If the same rate continues to apply, we will have 2 million people suffering from senility by the year 2000. Yet this statistic is probably an underestimate since the rate is more likely to increase than to stay the same.

Kraus, Spasoff, and their associates compared two groups of people aged eighty-five or older. One group consisted of those applying for admission to special nursing homes and the other group consisted of those living independently in the community. Certain physical changes forced the first group to apply for admission. Pathological malfunctioning of body systems made it impossible for these people to live alone, or created intolerable circumstances for the people they were dependent on.

One-third of the elderly applicants suffered serious vision and hearing impediments, compared to one-fourth of the independents. One-fifth of the applicants had trouble controlling urinary or excretory functions, while less than one-tenth of the independents experienced these problems. Of the applicants, 67 percent needed help with bathing, 44 percent with dressing, and 25 percent with going to the toilet. None of the independents required any help of this kind. Of the nursing-home applicants, one-third were disoriented with respect to space and time; none of the independents experienced this disorientation. If a similar study were done on people eighty-five and older already in institutions, there would undoubtedly be even more pathology.

Clearly, if we could prevent deterioration of vision and hearing, maintain bowel and bladder control, prevent disorientation, and do away with physical infirmity, society would have almost no applicants for admission to special nursing homes.

We are convinced that a major decrease in senility can be effected even though there will be some for whom this program will not work. Still, we can try. In time, we will approach a state where senility is considered a result of the failure by society to provide a healthy personal lifestyle and proper medical care.

CLASSIFICATION OF AGING DISORDERS

Aging disorders are divided into two basic groups: cerebrovascular disorders and primary degenerative disorders.

Cerebrovascular disorders arise from hypertension, emboli, hemorrhage, thrombosis, and infarctions. Repeated events cause multi-infarct dementia (an infarction is an area of dead tissue in the brain that is caused by oxygen deprivation during a stroke). There is a relationship between the degree of dementia and the amount of infarction. A number of little strokes can have a cumulative effect.

Primary degenerative disorders include the senile dementias, Alzheimer's disease, Pick's disease, Creutzfeldt-Jakob disease, and Huntington's disease. The senile dementias are the subject of this book. There is no nutritional treatment for Pick's and Creutzfeldt-Jakob disease. We will discuss Alzheimer's and Huntington's disease later in this chapter.

What Is Senility?

Senility is the term applied to destructive changes in the functioning cells of the brain. It is a brain disease and a mental disease. Senility is in no way the same as aging. Everybody ages, but only some people become senile. While there are physical changes as well that accompany senility, they are not always present in the brain of the senile person.

In the brain of a young, healthy adult, there are about 12 billion neurons, which are the cells that send nerve impulses through the body. As part of the aging process each day, the brain loses about 100,000 neurons. They get used up and die; most probably this results from the intake of toxic substances. After sixty or more years of losing these irreplaceable brain cells, an uneven pattern develops in the individual's thinking. His mind wanders and he may no longer be able to retain short-term memories. In a word, he becomes senile.

Geriatric specialists estimate that 15 percent of people sixty-five to seventy-five years old and 25 percent of people seventy-five and older are senile, and the number is growing. Scientists generally don't recognize any particular reason for the growing rate of senility. Our claim is that senility results from malnutrition.

The word *senility* is derived from the Latin word *senilis*, meaning *old*. It is a condition characterized by memory loss, particularly for recent events, loss of ability to do simple problems in addition and subtraction, possible decline in vision, and confusion as to where the person is, how he got there, when he arrived, and why he is there at all. There is no specific laboratory test that helps someone diagnose the presence of senility. It is strictly an impressionistic decision made by an objective third party—often a physician.

Some of the newest medical instruments have helped to make a diagnosis of senility. One such instrument is the computerized axial tomogram (CAT scan), which can show a three-dimensional image of a shrunken (senile) brain. The CAT scan alone, however, is not yet considered a verified diagnostic test for senility.

It is important to make an accurate diagnosis for senility because many different health problems can produce symptoms that mimic senility. Some elderly people are falsely labeled senile when their symptoms come from depression, a malfunctioning thyroid gland, pernicious anemia, the effects of drugs such as bromides, or from a variety of other conditions, which may be treatable.

It had been thought for years that hardening of the arteries in the brain was the cause of senility. During the last eight years, research studies have revealed that sclerosis of the brain's blood vessels plays less of a role in the senile condition than had been thought. (Sclerosis is a hardening of tissue that can be caused by many factors.) Senility resulting from arteriosclerosis tends to produce symptoms that worsen episodically. Geriatricians have now changed their thinking and believe the bulk of cases come from senile dementia, a disease more common in women. *Senile dementia* is characterized by the gradual, unrelenting deterioration of the mind. Geriatricians assume the cause is unknown and the pathology irreversible. (We say that neither of these assumptions is correct.)

When senility develops in a forty- or fifty-year-old person, it is then called *pre*senile dementia. Doctors pin a pathological label on the patient in such an age group and call the condition *Alzheimer's disease* or *Pick's disease.* In Alzheimer's disease, shrinkage occurs throughout the brain. In Pick's disease, the changes are more localized. Pathologists have claimed that since at autopsy, Alzheimer's disease is indistinguishable from the shrunken, senile brain, Alzheimer's might be merely the early onset of senility.

Alzheimer's Disease

Alzheimer's disease occurs rarely in persons between ages forty-five and sixty-four (1 per 1,000 population), but is much more common in people over sixty-five (4 percent of all men over age 65). At one time it was defined as a disease that came prematurely, that is, long before one would expect senility; but with the development of diagnostic tests such as the CAT scan, it has been diagnosed more often. Early, middle, and late onset types are described.

Clinically, Alzheimer's disease is characterized by failing memory and later by deterioration of many aspects of the brain's functions. Perceptual difficulties develop, such as being unable to recognize the meaning of things seen; a person looking at the hands of a clock will not be able to determine what time it is. Orientation becomes abnormal and the patient becomes lost in space and time. Patients become more and more dependent and eventually must be watched all the time, either at home or in an institution.

A number of brain changes are associated with this progressive dementia. The brain shrinks. On the CAT scan, spaces show at the surface of the brain; the cortex shrinks away from the skull, most markedly in the frontal region, the forehead. Neurons vanish. Senile plaques (hardened deposits in the brain) are present and neurofibrillary tangles (tangles of nerve cell fibers) appear. The plaques contain elevated concentrations of aluminum. There is a decrease in metabolic activity in large areas of the brain. However, there is no single pathological lesion that is specific to Alzheimer's disease.

There are many similarities between Alzheimer's disease and Down's syndrome. This may be helpful in getting at the bases of both diseases. Down's syndrome is due to the presence of an extra chromosome, or part of a chromosome, number 21. As well as causing characteristic physical and mental changes, this chromosome appears to control the activity of an oxidizing enzyme that contains copper and zinc, called *copper zinc superoxide dismutase*. Down's syndrome patients over age thirty-five develop senile and pathological changes very similar to those of Alzheimer's disease. There is also a genetic relationship between the two diseases. Heston (1982) found a high incidence of Down's syndrome cases among relatives of people with Alzheimer's disease. Out of 3,044 people, 11 cases were found, whereas 4.35 should have been expected, given the incidence of Down's syndrome in the general population. Further, the Down's syndrome cases appeared primarily in the most severely affected families.[4]

The causes of Down's syndrome and Alzheimer's are not known. Medical scientists are looking at the possibility of the presence of chronic viral infections, the possibility of excessive deposition of aluminum, and possible defects in the immune system.

If we assume that both conditions are similar, it is possible that they may be caused by problems with the same chromosome. Since Down's syndrome appears during infancy while Alzheimer's occurs late in life, it is obvious that with Down's syndrome there is a lot of extra chromosome 21, so that it exerts its effect immediately. With Alzheimer's there may be only a slight excess, so little that it might be difficult or impossible to detect. It has been found that chromosomal aberrations occur more frequently in Alzheimer's disease.

There may be a clue in orthomolecular treatment programs developed for Down's syndrome, because if both conditions are similar, what works for Down's syndrome might help Alzheimer's cases if they are caught early. Down's syndrome must involve specific metabolic problems of which the end results are the mental and physical changes. These have been reversed by orthomolecular treatment. If the same biochemical problems, to a lesser degree, are present in Alzheimer's disease, similar biochemical treatment should be even more effective, but it would have to be started early, before there is extensive plaque and neurofibrillary tangle formation.

For over forty years, Dr. Henry Turkel (1975) treated Down's children successfully using orthomolecular methods. He used a combination of vitamins, minerals, and hormones, including thyroid hormone. His patients improved mentally and they lost the typical Down's syndrome facial appearance. With over 600 children treated, he found an 80 to 90 percent improvement rate.[5] Some time ago, Dr. Turkel sent Dr. Hoffer a letter he had received from the mother of a Down's syndrome child. Treatment was started in 1965, when her son was fifteen. His I.Q. was then about 55 and his features were typically Down's. Her letter was written in January 1981. She wrote:

> John continues to do well. Last summer he made a trip to Alaska to see his sister. He paid for the entire trip himself with money he had earned. He made the entire trip by himself except for some help from my nephew who took care of him while changing planes en route both ways. John is a tremendous help to us both physically and financially. None of it would have been possible without you. We appreciate you more every day.

Critics will label this "anecdotal" and demand double-blind experiments. (Dr. Hoffer suggests they first tell us how many Down's syndrome patients have shown this degree of improvement following placebo treatment.) However, even double-blind experiments are not believed.

It was simple to ignore Dr. Turkel, as he was alone in his field and orthodox medical journals would not publish his papers. It was much more difficult to ignore Harrell, Capp, Davis, Peerless, and Ravitz (1981). This group did a double-blind controlled experiment involving sixteen children, five of whom were afflicted with Down's syndrome. The children were given a mixture of vitamins and minerals. In contrast to most vitamin combinations, this one contained ample quantities of niacinamide (vitamin B3) and pyridoxine (B6). Each day these children were given 750 milligrams of niacinamide and 350 milligrams of pyridoxine. However, all but one of the children needed to take thyroid hormone because their body temperatures were low when taken using the Barnes method (this entails taking a temperature reading from under the arm for three consecutive days). All but two were given dessicated thyroid. The children were also placed on an improved diet by reducing sugar and increasing fruit and milk.

There was a significant and substantial improvement in the nutrient group *with thyroid*. Down's children improved most.[6]

This study was not ignored. It was apparently shot down in flames by Smith, Spiker, Peterson, Cicchetti, and Justice (1983). Smith et al. started out by expressing their skepticism. In a letter to the editor of the British medical journal, *Lancet*, they wrote, "It is difficult to understand or speculate how a specific grouping of vitamins and minerals can have such a general beneficial effect on the brain as is claimed, under an almost unlimited number of pathological conditions." They obviously believe nothing can work unless one knows how it works, an interesting example of putting the cart before the horse. Not surprisingly, Smith et al. duplicated Harrell's study by *not* using their protocol. They chose to ignore the change to a low-sugar diet, as well as the administration of dessicated thyroid to children with low body temperatures. They also used one-third less vitamin A than the Harrell study. This duplicate study was used to disprove Harrell, and yet it was not a duplication. Smith et al. correctly concluded, by the evidence of their study, "The study showed that megadoses of this group of vitamins and minerals will not improve the intelligence of children with Down's syndrome."[7]

The entire tone of their letter indicates they believe they have disproved the claim of Harrell and her colleagues. Unfortunately, unwary readers may come to the same conclusion, even though Dr. B. Rimland and Dr. Turkel sought to correct this error.[8,9] However, the rest of the world appears to be less biased against using nutritional therapy. Japan has used Turkel's treatment since 1964 in over eighty government and university hospitals.

Dr. Allan Cott, an orthomolecular psychiatrist, has treated an enormous number of children, many of whom had Down's syndrome. He advises Dr. Hoffer that he has seen dramatic improvements in many Down's children using orthomolecular techniques. In a few children Dr. Hoffer has seen under age seven, the results with good nutrition and supplements have been very good. We agree with Dr. Rimland's conclusion, "The work by Turkel and by Harrell and her colleagues, showing that vitamin and mineral supplementation may help many retarded children, has yet to be refuted."

We have no doubt these positive studies will be corroborated. As nutrient treatment does help Down's, and since Down's patients may show premature aging, it is likely that the same type of treatment can help Alzheimer's.

Remember that the gene that controls the oxidizing enzyme copper zinc superoxide dismutase (CuZnSOD) resides on chromosome number 21. Red blood cells in people with Down's syndrome have increased CuZnSOD activity. This may play a major role in the pathology of Down's syndrome. CuZnSOD activity is increased by 50 percent in platelets, leukocytes, red cells, and fibroblasts. Thus it appears that Down's syndrome is a variant of one of the diseases due to excessive oxidation, perhaps combined with a deficiency of antioxidants. The vitamins and minerals used by Turkel, Cott, and others tend to be antioxidants. But as most Down's children also need thyroid hormone, these nutrients will not work unless the patient is also given thyroid. This is not surprising. No nutritional supplementation will supply thyroid hormone. To expect anything else would be to wish that nutrients could treat hypothyroidism.

After Alzheimer's disease is well established, there is no known treatment. Dr. Hoffer has not been able to treat even one such case successfully out of the twelve or so that he has handled since the early 1980s. They have so far not responded to any combination of nutrients. In one or two cases Dr. Hoffer has been able to retard deterioration, but this is very difficult to judge. In contrast, other senile patients with less well-established disease have shown striking improvement. But it is not usually possible to find the earliest cases because they are always seen first by their family doctors and referred to Dr. Hoffer only after the disease is clearly established. There is one avenue that may hold some promise, however. Dr. Hoffer was beginning to believe there could never be any response in patients with well-established Alzheimer's, until he spoke to a recovered Alzheimer's patient early in 1985, when he was in Auckland, New Zealand. John, about age 70, had deteriorated to a level where he could not speak, nor could he be trusted alone in a city. He would wander away, become lost, and of course could not ask for help. He had been a keen golf enthusiast and had played on many of the world's better golf courses. When well, John's handicap had been seven. Just before treatment started, his handicap was twenty-seven. One of the odd features of his case was that he could still drive from his farm to the golf course and back home again without getting lost.

John was then started on chelation therapy, receiving twenty intravenous treatments of ethylene diamine tetraacetic acid (EDTA) over a period of six weeks. (This therapy involves using an agent such as EDTA to bind with toxic metals in the body, which then excretes them.) Dr. Hoffer conducted an interview with John and his wife one month after his last treatment. If anyone had come into the room during the hour-long conversation, that person could not have detected John had been ill. His perceptions were normal, no thought disorder could be detected, and his mood was normal. His golf handicap had returned to seven. His wife had no doubt what had helped him. Dr. Hoffer and John's wife planned to give him more chelation treatments if he began to relapse.

During Dr. Hoffer's conversation with the couple, he asked John what he remembered of his Alzheimer's condition. John stated he had no recollection of it at all, but that about halfway through the chelation sessions he awoke, or came to. If, in fact, Alzheimer's is like being asleep, a sleep from which one does not awaken, this would explain the entire psychiatric syndrome. Imagine trying to cope with life while asleep, while dreaming. Is Alzheimer's a sleep state filled with dreams and nightmares? During dreams, perception is distorted or difficult to understand, thinking is totally illogical and disturbed, and mood is inappropriate. Is Alzheimer's the best example we have of an oxygen-deprived brain that has, in effect, fallen asleep? If this is what it is, we need to discover how to reestablish aerobic oxidation of cerebral cells.

We do not know of anyone else who has been able to interview an ex-Alzheimer's patient, since there have been no other recoveries. Dr. Edwin Boyle, a medical researcher whose work will be discussed later in this chapter, might have gotten similar results when interviewing patients he had treated with hyperbaric oxygen, but we will never know, because such findings were never recorded.

One recovery does not establish a treatment, but it provides another beacon of hope, as does the recovery of one patient with Huntington's disease. We must try this treatment with as many cases as possible to find out if this one case is a fluke, or if there is a subclass of Alzheimer's victims who are responsive to chelation therapy. The treatment for pre-Alzheimer's syndrome is based on good orthomolecular treatment with special emphasis on antioxidant therapy, combined with thyroid when there is clinical evidence hypothyroidism is a problem. There will probably never be a single treatment for all cases of Alzheimer's. Every lead will have to be pursued.

BIOCHEMICAL DAMAGE AND THE BRAIN

When research into the microscopic anatomy of the brain began, medical scientists believed that senile brains underwent characteristic alterations that could be identified. The pathologists looked for softness of brain tissue, obliteration of cells, and lines of demarcation between viable matter and mush. In some cases, brains from senile people were in fact quite deteriorated, but to a more surprising degree, most senile brains looked normal. There were even plenty of nonseniles who had mushy-looking brains. No relationship could be established between the amount of pathology in the brain and the presence of senility. The theories of the first medical scientists were dashed into nothingness.

If a large chunk of an individual's brain is destroyed by a tumor, a stroke, or a head wound, we would obviously be justified in expecting a major defect in the person's performance. However, these kinds of changes are quite different from those present in a senile person. The senile patient has marked signs of memory loss, an inability to store new information, and certain personality quirks.

We know that there is a dissimilarity between the brain-damaged person and a senile person, but is there any damage in the senile brain? We believe there is—biochemical damage rather than mechanical damage. The basis for our nutritional program to prevent senility is the belief that senile defects are the result of biochemical alterations that have not yet been entirely identified. Only a small portion of the pathology is known. There is some correlation between the degree of biochemical pathology and the degree of senility.

It is reasonable that senile changes in the brain should be different from changes seen in other organs. Some body organs are subject to mechanical wear and tear. For instance, bones bear the entire weight of the body, and eventually become weak and brittle. The heart is in constant motion pumping blood to the other organs, and eventually can become weak. Other organs, such as the liver, kidney, pancreas, and brain, are subject to minor mechanical strain. The only mechanical strain in the brain arises from the unmomentous pulsation of its blood vessels.

Since it is mechanically passive, the brain ought to be one of the last organs in the body to deteriorate. Only ions and molecules are transmitted to and fro across its membranes. Such particles do not wear down tissue. Logically, as long as the molecular state of the brain remains intact, its functioning should remain intact. The biochemical activity of the brain differs entirely from the physical functioning of the other body organs.

Every organ has a special function. The liver is a chemical factory for changing molecules. The lungs place blood in close contact with air so it can eliminate carbon dioxide and take up oxygen. The kidneys purify blood; the bladder stores urine.

The brain has its unique functions as well. It must coordinate all the various components of the body in order for the body to function as a whole and not as a committee of individual parts. The brain must also relate to our two main human environments, the psychosocial and the biophysical. To carry out these very elaborate, intricate functions, the brain must be in direct contact with every section of the body, interpret and react to all the signals speeding to it, and initiate appropriate stimuli to regulate and control the body.

Most of us are unaware of the brain's activity, and luckily so. If we had to pay attention to even a tiny fraction of its activity, we would not be able to function. Some people are disabled simply from being constantly aware of their heartbeat. Feeling heart palpitations can be disconcerting. The basic automatic activity of the brain provides us with stability, which is absolutely essential if we are to live within our psychosocial and biophysical environments.

The second main activity of this remarkable organ concerns our senses. We are aware of seeing, hearing, tasting, touching, smelling, and our body awareness. We know, for instance, how the body is oriented with respect to gravity. Awareness of our external world is mediated through our senses. This is called *perception*. It is more than a matter of having images accurately focused upon the retina, or of recording sound in our ears. All of these signals must be transmitted to the brain and be recognized. Perception is quite a complex phenomenon.

The Demands of Perception

Perception demands recognition and reaction; it also requires thinking. One demand tends to impinge on another. Each thing perceived by the senses is identified as either something trivial to be ignored, or as something that requires concentrated attention. This is a decision the brain usually makes instantaneously, depending upon the person's experience with similar things in the past.

Perception also depends on one's alertness. Many hyperactive children are too alert, too distractable, and apparently are unable to decide what is trivial or not trivial. A slight rustle here or an object there demands their full attention, even if only for a few seconds. Such reactions to distractions may be totally inappropriate. On the other hand, a hyperactive's attention may be so diminished that even an important event such as a car bearing down on the child is ignored. Diminished attention may end such a child's life.

Important or interesting objects or circumstances require reaction. The reaction may vary from giving continuing attention to the phenomenon to fleeing from it in fear. Again, rapid decisions are needed that will be based on past experience as well as on genetically determined behavior patterns.

Failure of the Brain to Function

When the brain fails to function, its failure may affect all four areas of living—perception, thinking, feeling, and behavior. Usually one area will be more affected than others. From such functional changes we derive syndromes. A *syndrome* is an aggregate of signs and symptoms which together constitute the picture of a disease. The syndrome determines which treatment is most appropriate.

A combination of changes in perception and in thinking—including visions, voices, and inappropriate responses—constitute the schizophrenic syndrome. When disturbances in memory, disorientation as to time and place, and confusion are also present, we have the syndrome of delirium. When the main changes are in mood, we are dealing with the neuroses—anxiety, depression, and tensions.

Senility is a very peculiar syndrome consisting of disorientation, changes in memory, and confusion. If changes in perception were present in senility, it would be a delirium; but there are no perceptual changes.

The Hoffer-Osmond Diagnostic (HOD) test, a cardsorting, 145-item questionnaire that identifies and adds up an individual's sensory and time distortions, has been administered to a large number of senile patients.[10,11] Their perceptual disturbance scores are almost invariably low, and they deny the presence of illusions and hallucinations. This has happened so frequently that we must conclude the senile patient does not have perceptual disturbances or paranoid thoughts. When illusions and hallucinations are present, the examiner should consider that either schizophrenia or delirium is present, but this is apparently not the case in senility.

Memory Loss in the Senile Patient

The thinking changes in senility are of a peculiar sort. The main problem is in the area of memory. Furthermore, there is recent evidence that suggests it may be the ability to learn that is altered. It is mainly the ability to remember recent events that is modified. The senile patient may not remember what he had for breakfast, or whether he even had breakfast at all. Nevertheless, he can describe a memorable meal he had eaten many years before.

The ability to "file away" an event so that it can be recalled later seems to be damaged in the senile person. The evidence that points to a learning defect rather than a simple memory defect was first pointed out to the authors by Professor Edwin Boyle, Jr., M.D., when he was research director of the Miami Heart Institute. At that time, he was investigating the effect of hyperbaric oxygen on patients who were becoming senile or who had already had been senile for several years.

Dr. Boyle gave his patients thirty-minute treatments in a chamber containing two atmospheres' pressure of pure oxygen. A large number of senile people were studied in this way, with each receiving the oxygen treatment. They underwent five hyperbaric sessions each week for two weeks. In some cases, senility appeared to be vanquished, and patients formerly hopelessly senile suddenly became normal. They were able to remember not only the past but experiences that had occurred in the present as well. Unfortunately, their senility began to return in several weeks. Each person returned to his pretreatment senility level by the end of a few months. The benefit was only temporary.

The result of this bit of experimentation is of vital importance. It does not suggest that hyperbaric therapy is useless, but that it alone is not the answer to senility. Hyperbaric oxygen will probably provide a useful therapeutic effect when a way is discovered to maintain the patient's overall state of health. Also, the experiment proves that what the senile person learned could still be remembered. It was new learning that had disappeared. This further points to the possibility that it is a biochemical error that creates senility.

We agree with Professor Boyle when he declares that senility is basically a loss of learning ability. Still, in this book, we shall discuss memory loss as the chief happenstance of the condition.

In the beginning, it is not too difficult for a person whose brain is deteriorating to compensate for memory losses. The senile person in the early stages may write important things down or ask others to jog his or her memory. Memory loss remains a minor inconvenience. Since intellect remains unimpaired, one can compensate also by making excuses (except that the statement "I forgot" is not acceptable). The individual can also fabricate—make up events or stories—to satisfy the person to whom he or she is talking. This sort of story-telling is often done skillfully. For this reason, it is essential to have a relative or close friend present who knows the truth. A spouse can readily correct the patient's confabulated or minimized accounts.

It is not unusual for preseniles to admit a few memory problems, but they will also minimize them. A memory problem may wax and wane until it finally becomes irreversibly fixed. It is mandatory for treatment to be started before it is fixed; the longer therapy is delayed, the less significant the results.

Memory loss is not too difficult for the presenile as long as there is no disorientation. However, if an individual becomes lost in time, confused geographically, or fails to recognize himself or others, memory loss becomes impossible to deal with. This gives rise to the trying circumstance of witnessing the senile person wandering away from home, getting lost even in familiar surroundings, or getting hurt on the street.

Senile people also lose themselves in time. The past becomes their life; the present is an irritant; there is no future. They fail to recognize their spouses and children. They relive what happened to them many years before. They are quite helpless psychologically and require shelter, protection, and devoted nursing care.

Although society accepts the inevitability of senility, the authors no longer believe it is as inescapable as death. Our change of mind is based upon what we have seen in the practice of orthomolecular psychiatry. This is direct observable evidence, the only kind admissible in a court of law. It is not hearsay evidence, which is not admissible. Science and medicine have a different attitude than the law toward these two types of evidence. Too often, admissible evidence—that which has been witnessed personally—is disregarded as subjective, while hearsay evidence—that which has been heard from others—is admissible. Perhaps this is why medicine is so frequently embroiled in useless debates. The field of orthomolecular psychiatry has suffered from this peculiar regard for the different forms of evidence. Traditional psychiatry has turned a deaf ear to orthomolecular practices, and the senile have suffered from this disregard.

The proponents of orthomolecular psychiatry depend upon hearsay, too, but they rely much more upon direct personal observation. In most cases, hearsay evidence serves merely to arouse interest. The conclusion that orthomolecular therapy is effective against senility is based entirely on direct personal observations—upon the only evidence admissible by any court. We will present our evidence in the following chapters. You can judge for yourself whether or not senility is reversible.

Henri Louis Bergson, the famous philosopher, has compared the aging process with an hourglass: in the upper part are the good substances; in the lower part, the bad ones. While the first diminishes, the second increases.

We cannot reverse the hourglass, but thanks to several discoveries about nutrient deficiencies and dependencies, we are able to reduce the outflow of the sand to increase the upper part and diminish the lower.

2. NORMAL AGING, PREMATURE AGING, AND PSEUDOSENILITY

> You can't retire from life and you shouldn't. You should use the four great chords of mental health: the ability to love, the ability to work, the ability to play, and the ability to think critically. And if you can achieve this, all with a sense of humor or playfulness, then you're likely to lead a very much more satisfactory life than you otherwise would.
>
> —Ashley Montagu

During the first week of May 1977, a special tribunal of seven appellate court justices ordered the retirement of California Supreme Court Justice Marshall F. McComb. He was declared senile. The tribunal was following the recommendation of the California Commission on Judicial Performance, which had heard evidence of the justice's inability to perform his duties. Charges were first filed against Justice McComb in April 1976.

This Supreme Court Justice's colleagues found that he sometimes fell asleep on the bench, read magazines in court, or did physical exercises while counting aloud, and he walked out of judicial conferences that he described as "talk, talk, talk; squawk, squawk, squawk; yak, yak, yak." Justice McComb had fifty years of judicial service behind him, and the tribunal ruled that it was time for him to retire. His wife was named conservator for her husband after she testified that he could no longer care for himself or his property.[1]

Justice McComb was an example of senility that comes on gradually and accents the peculiarities that have existed in a personality for years but were repressed during earlier years. He had a disease of the brain, but it was not caused by his growing old. It is just that the diseases commonly associated with old age are diseases that require decades to develop, so they usually don't show up in young people. Our society's misconception is that when you're young and get sick, it's labeled "illness," but when you're old and get sick, it's labeled "aging." Sickness and aging, however, are two different states of being.

As we grow older, the 60 trillion cells in our bodies gradually change. Each cell has a limited life, after which it reproduces itself through a process called *mitosis*, or cell division. Then the original cell dies. Thus, at any given second, thousands of your cells may be dying, yet thousands are also being reborn, some faster than others. For example, while fat cells reproduce slowly, skin cells reproduce approximately every ten hours. As mentioned in the last chapter, the notable exception to this constant cell replacement is found in the brain. The moment each of us is born, we have our lifetime maximum number of brain cells, and when these become worn out, they are said never to be replaced. By age 35, each person is losing 100,000 brain cells a day, but because the initial surplus is so great, the loss is scarcely noticeable.

THE POSSIBILITY OF NEURON REPLACEMENT

It is common knowledge that the brain cannot regenerate or grow new neurons, but is this true? A 1984 article in *Science* appeared under the heading "New Neurons Form in Adulthood," with a subheading, "Thousands of neurons are born and thousands more die each day in the brains of birds; the same may be true in other animals, including humans." The story concerned work by Dr. F. Nottebohm and colleagues at Rockefeller University, who found a massive birth and death of neurons in the forebrains of birds well after maturity. Male canaries begin to babble at one month of age. About three weeks later their songs resemble adult songs. By nine months their songs are adult, but they sing only during the breeding season. By late summer, they are not singing, and in the fall they begin to rehearse their new repertoire for the next spring.

Singing is controlled by two specialized areas in the canary brain. HVC neurons respond to sound and RA neurons control the muscles that allow singing to occur. In a bird one month of age,

HVC neurons have one-eighth the volume they reach at maturity. Song learning grows with the increase in the number of neurons. The male hormone, testosterone, stimulates sexual maturity and singing. If testosterone is given to female canaries, it will start them singing. After the breeding season, testosterone levels decrease. HVCs are large in spring, and reduce to half their spring size in fall. There is a direct relationship between the amount of space that the HVC neurons take up and the bird's singing talent. Talented birds have larger HVCs, up to a threefold increase compared to untalented birds. In females that sing, as a result of being given testosterone, HVC increases to double its volume and RA by 53 percent. Also, dendrites branch more and grow larger. (Dendrites are branched extensions of nerve cells that conduct nerve impulses from cell to cell.) Later, Nottebohm was able to prove that the number of HVC neurons doubled in forty-nine days. The new neurons were born in a thin area in the forebrain, the ventricular zone. From there neurons migrated to the HVC area—they were interneurons. This migration required two weeks. During the breeding season, male canaries have about 41,000 neurons in the HVC area. Five months later it decreases to 25,000. There is also an HVC neuron decrease in females. (After all, the females must be able to identify the songs that the males are singing.) In short, in canary brains, and also in budgerigars and ringdoves, neurons die and new ones form in response to need.[2]

In birds, sex hormones are very important. Do testosterone and estrogen play the same role in humans? It is known that brain damage early in life is followed by better recovery than brain damage occurring later in life. Is this due to sex hormone secretion? Nottebohm speculates, "It may be that if neurologists induce [what he calls] 'a prepubertal hormone milieu' in persons with brain injury, they may stimulate the growth of new neurons and neural connections and an enhanced recovery of brain function."

He postulates that the amount of new information gained is limited by the circuitry. "It might be useful to replace components, even at the risk of doing away with existing memories." "Used circuits may have lost their ability to acquire new information." "It may be necessary to replace components which are least functional in order to retain the ability to learn."

Is this the beginning of another hypothesis to explain senility and aging? Perhaps throughout our lives we are continually replacing sets of neurons that are no longer able to function well enough with new neurons that grow and migrate in to establish a new set of interneuronal patterns. As long as repair keeps up with the destruction of neurons, we remain well. If repair falters, which can happen for any number of reasons, the first process to suffer will be new learning and memory. Or does the aging brain sacrifice memory in order to repair areas of the brain necessary for certain vital processes, which, if not repaired, will cause death? If there is a general decrease in ability to repair, grow new neurons, move them into place, and grow new connections, it makes good evolutionary sense to preserve processes essential to life, such as motor activity and cardiovascular function. One can survive without any memory for the recent past, but one cannot survive without physiological function. If this hypothesis is even close to the truth, it would provide support for all treatments that enhance repair mechanisms in the body. It would also offer some hope that using testosterone, and possibly estrogen, carefully in our aging population may stimulate growth of new neurons. The ideal treatment would inhibit the loss of neurons and stimulate the growth of new ones—that is, if our brains are like bird brains in respect to neurons, able to repair components that wear out. But along with regeneration of neurons, there must be stimulation, to force the new neurons to interconnect in the correct patterns. If one were to use estrogen to stimulate new neuron growth in an aging female, it should be done within a stimulating atmosphere. There would be little point in stimulating repair in a nursing home, where life consists of one monotonous day after another. This hypothesis also suggests that sexual activity should be a useful anti-aging activity.

Nottebohm is very cautious in discussing his canary findings; he suggests that because this information is so new, any speculation of what might come out of it is incredibly premature. There is a very wide gap between singing canaries and senile humans, and it will be closed very slowly.

Clinicians are not constrained as are academics. Academics cannot afford to risk being found wrong and so want to be 100-percent sure of their findings before presenting them. They can wait for years, if necessary. But patients who are already showing signs of senility may not have many more years. Our patients are willing to try anything, provided it will not make them worse. If sex hormones might help—even if the idea seems far-fetched—

they should be tried now in aging men and women. We do not need double-blind controlled experiments (unless someone can prove that a placebo will restore memory)—there are no spontaneous recoveries once senility has developed.

THE CHARACTERISTICS OF NORMAL AGING

As you grow older, you may discover some changes taking place in your senses, your energy level, and the functioning of different parts of your body. For instance, your sense of taste and smell will diminish. By age sixty, most people have lost 50 percent of their taste buds, especially if they smoke cigarettes; the ability to smell declines by 40 percent. You may find that your muscles lack tone, especially the facial muscles and those in the back of the arms. Hair and nails start to break more easily and may lack luster. Skin becomes dry and loses its elasticity, taking on a wrinkled appearance. Blood pressure rises, arteries clog, and breathing takes more effort. There are, in fact, a vast number of characteristics that constitute aging. Before describing them, let us add a note of encouragement:

- There exists within each one of us an indefinable "clock of aging."
- There is an excellent chance of discovering the location of this clock, and intervening in its mechanisms to our advantage.
- This can happen within a few decades if the proper emphasis on research is advanced.

Skin Changes

The skin loses its elasticity; a lifted skin fold settles back slowly, rather than immediately regaining its normal position as it had done earlier in life. Elderly skin is dry, wrinkled, and may take on a parchment-like quality. Localized pigmented plaques ("age spots") develop. The skin gets fragile and bruises easily. Yet these changes likely do not to arise solely from aging, but from many years of malnutrition, sun damage, and other factors. Such skin can be restored to its original elasticity and health from receiving proper nutritional treatment.

Hair and nails, which are derived from skin and have similar nutritional requirements, take on specific aging characteristics of their own. The greying of hair takes place either early or late in life, depending on one's genes and blood flow to the scalp. Perspiration glands and oil glands on the head work less efficiently with age, and hair becomes thinner, even when no actual baldness exists. The nails become brittle and form ridges, as well as becoming discolored.

Since the skin is the largest organ of the body, any observer can guess correctly that these outward changes of hair and skin indicate equally major changes in the rest of the body.

Muscle Changes

Muscles lose many fibers, and the fibers remaining in an aged person become weaker in strength. Arms and legs tend to reduce in muscle mass and look thinner. Less muscle mass may also come from an associated decrease in activity.

In the heart muscle, there is an increase in the deposition of a yellow-brown pigment lipofuscin, which is one of the lipochromes. These tiny fat globules make the heart more sluggish in its functioning. Further, the total ribonucleic acid (RNA) usually present in cells varies inversely with the amount of lipochrome. As lipochrome continues to deposit with age, RNA decreases steadily. Even though little is known as to how to reverse these aging changes in the heart, it has been suggested by two Canadian heart specialists, Dr. Wilfrid Shute and Dr. Evan Shute, that vitamin E may be helpful in the reduction of lipochrome deposits. Furthermore, studies with laboratory rats have shown that extra lipochrome is laid down in the neurons of subjects that are deficient in vitamin E. Another report says that magnesium orotate and kavain, a food supplement prepared from kava kava, both prevent the deposition of lipochrome.

Skeletal Changes

The adult skeleton shrinks with age. Deformations due to osteoporosis develop when calcium leaches from bones, leaving them thinner, weaker, and more fragile. Approximately 25 percent of women and 6 percent of men over age sixty-five suffer from this calcium deficiency. It is believed to be a result of a lack of vitamin D_3 and sunlight, along with a calcium deficiency. Geriatrics who seldom leave their rooms are most apt to suffer from osteoporosis, but inadequate exercise is also a major factor.

The skeleton continues to remodel itself in its adaptation to stress. New bone is laid down to reinforce stressed areas and unstressed bone gets reabsorbed. Bones used continually become much stronger; conversely, infrequently stressed bones lose substance. Because of the prevalence of osteoporosis, the elderly are more likely to suffer fractures of the head of the femur, the hips, and the vertebral body from even trivial trauma. Obviously, the best way to prevent osteoporosis is make sure you get enough calcium, vitamin D_3, and exercise.

Astronauts in a weightless environment, as with the elderly who don't exercise, suffer from some osteoporosis. This condition tends to repair itself as soon as normal skeletal stress becomes possible again. The astronauts' experience indicates that calcium can be removed from the bones very quickly and will settle down with associated phosphorus in soft tissues such as the kidney.

Cardiovascular Changes

Aging of the vascular system shows up as an increase in atherosclerotic plaques in the blood vessels. The walls of arteries become inelastic; heart valves become thicker; and increased amounts of fat and connective tissue gather around the heart.

Aging and arteriosclerosis are related, however, only because it takes many years of poor eating habits, including a diet rich in junk foods and high in fat, for arteriosclerosis to develop. Before 1900 there was no association between aging and hardening of the arteries—no doubt because fast food restaurants did not exist. Our observation is that most fast food restaurants serve up heart disease and cancer.

Because of an excess intake of sugar and salt among the elderly (whose taste buds seem to require more flavoring because of their diminished sense of taste), blood pressure tends to increase. For seventy- to seventy-nine-year-old men, the absolute upper limit of normal blood pressure is 205/104. For women in the same age range, it is 215/106. Men between the ages of eighty to eighty-nine have an upper limit of 215/108, and women have 230/110, according to Sir Ferguson Anderson, former professor of geriatric medicine at the Glasgow School of Medicine and past president of the British Medical Association.

We urge lower limits for normal blood pressures in the elderly, and not as an indication for antihypertensive drug treatment, but as a means of reassessing a patient's nutrition and activity status. There is no strong relationship between blood pressure and mortality until blood pressure exceeds 200/120. High blood pressure is a major risk factor for stroke.

Kidney Changes

The reserve capacity of the kidneys tends to decrease to 50 percent of what was once present, but usually there is enough to maintain correct fluid and mineral balance. This is made more difficult for many older people because they drink too little water. About three decades ago, a brief survey of newly admitted senile patients to a mental hospital in Saskatchewan revealed that 25 percent were there as a result of dehydration. These patients had a very low awareness of thirst. They needed only to increase their intake of fluids to get well physically.

The elderly person should make an effort to drink enough water even if he or she isn't thirsty. Zinc deficiency, which causes a decreased sense of taste, may also be responsible for the diminished sense of thirst.

Lung Changes

The lungs' self-cleaning function declines with age. Consequently, an older person's capacity to exchange respiratory gases, such as substituting oxygen for carbon dioxide in the blood, is decreased. When the muscles get weaker, the chest wall becomes less elastic and inspiration is not as deep.

Central Nervous System Changes

By age ninety, symmetrical cerebral atrophy sets in and the brain loses about one-quarter of its weight. The fissures (sulci) on the surface of the brain widen and the brain ventricles slowly enlarge. If there is a sudden enlargement, or more enlargement than would be expected by the regular aging process, it is possible that a blockage of the cerebrospinal fluid, such as hydrocephalus, is present, causing great pressure. Hydrocephalus can be a cause of senility and should be treated surgically by introducing a shunt to allow fluid to drain and relieve brain pressure.

Up to 30 percent of the neurons in a geriatric brain have already been discarded. The extracellular space in the brain vault decreases and senile plaques form.

Alzheimer's disease, a form of early senility, is associated with neurofibrillary changes. They occur first in the hippocampus, a complex structure of the cortical mantie of both cerebral hemispheres that is involved in memory functions. Much later, the changes take place in the neocortex, toward the back of the brain. Giving laboratory animals aluminum salts has reproduced these same kinds of changes.

When senile neurons are examined microscopically using special techniques, they are observed to have lost their normal shape. They become lumpy and gradually have fewer dendrites. Neuromelanins, dark brown pigments derived from noradrenaline and adrenaline, increase in quantity.

With these changes, we would expect malfunctioning of the brain, and this does occur even though the brain has reserve capacity and can compensate for a long time.

Until 1900, it was assumed there was a good correlation between senility and organic brain changes. Between 1930 and 1950, scientists questioned these assumptions. Since then it has become apparent that there is a threshold effect. That is, changes in the brain occur slowly but impairment of function manifests itself once a critical level of pathology is reached. Senility is a result of that pathology.

PREMATURE AGING

Before senility actually sets in, many people in Western industrialized countries undergo premature aging. This is a condition that is, for the most part, neglected by European and North American medicine. This illness does not kill in the obvious way. It cannot be described in a clear manner, and no post-mortem examination indicates its presence. Rather, premature aging is a psycho-physiological disease of our modern civilization manifested by a number of subjective symptoms that are constantly present and commonly accepted. They are influenced by heredity, ecological conditions, style of living, and past diseases.

The Psychophysiology of Premature Aging

When a doctor examines a man of fifty, he may find that the

patient's heart seems like that of a forty-year-old and his mental reactions to be like those of a sixty-year-old, or vice-versa. The unequal functional quality of separate organs seldom is recognized as a form of premature aging.

A man may visit his physician complaining that he is worn out at 5:00 P.M. He needs a couple of drinks to pick him up. His appetite is lost and his bowels are lazy. The slightest physical effort exhausts him. He needs sleeping pills to fall asleep and wakes up without much desire to work. His memory is failing, and he finds the act of sex undesirable. He lives in a constant state of anxiety, and is no longer happy with his life. Even so, the most careful medical examination does not show any organic trouble.

The number of people who look, behave, and feel older than they are is increasing every day. Many start showing these signs in their twenties, and there are so many of them over forty that they attribute their health problems to "getting old." A good proportion of people over sixty, in view of their physical condition, should act and appear far younger than they do, but early debilitation is accepted by them as the natural course of events. Informed people, like Ashley Montagu, whose quote we used to introduce this chapter, say the trick to staying alert, active, and healthy "is very simple—die young as late as possible."[3]

It may seem paradoxical, in this age of unprecedented longevity, to speak of premature aging. The average life expectancy at birth is well over seventy years; never have so many people lived for so long. It is also tempting to minimize the issue by saying that premature aging is better than premature death.

But this is not the whole story. A few decades ago, there appeared an intriguing appendix to the annual World Health Statistic Report, published by the World Health Organization (WHO).[4] Epidemiologists and computer specialists analyzed life-expectancy statistics of thirty-four industrialized countries, dealing not only with life expectancy at birth, but life expectancy at the age of sixty-five.

The difference between the two is, of course, of great importance. Life expectancy at birth increases in a spectacular fashion when childhood diseases are effectively treated or prevented and when major infectious diseases are controlled. Life expectancy at age sixty-five gives different indications, reflecting the advance of the frontiers of longevity against the degenerative or wasting diseases. Today, these degenerative diseases are responsible for the overwhelming majority of "deaths from old age" (although there is no such thing).

The significant aspect of the WHO study is that it showed a man's life expectancy at age sixty-five to be greater in such countries as Greece (79.3 years) and Iceland (80.3 years), than it was in the United States or in most Western European countries. The average life expectancy for both Canadians and Americans was seventy-three years.

Moreover, a comparison with figures recorded by WHO ten years earlier shows that in twenty-three of the thirty-four nations included in the study, the life expectancy of sixty-five-year-old men had decreased, however slightly.

Medicine may have solved many problems regarding the treatment or prevention of specific diseases, but it has not solved the problems created as the human mind and organism try to adapt to an increasing number of relatively sudden alterations away from natural living. These alterations lead to a certain psycho-physiologic syndrome one can label premature aging. The multiple changes in our way of life and our environment created through technology require adaptation. This demand for adaptive activity has been identified as the essence of stress.

The Impact of Stress

Continuous stress and tension are a condition of modern life that can wear out an individual's resistance, and make him or her susceptible to degenerative forces. Usually, when the modern Western worker has succeeded in winning the battle for all the material values of this world, he or she becomes incapacitated by disease and is unable to enjoy them. What good is it to prolong our survival if we are denied the fundamental means to take advantage of the added years? Our society is filled with these "half-invalids" whose contribution to the community and themselves is limited by premature aging.

Stress has been the object of many recent studies and we will discuss it at length in Chapter 6. Here we can provide one inescapable conclusion: The number of stressful events, or stressors, in modern society has been gradually increasing. These varied causative factors all produce essentially the same biologic stress response, the general adaptation syndrome.

There is little reason to doubt that stress has become a major

factor limiting our longevity. Although we know its consequences, or at least some of them, we cannot, nor shall we ever be
able to, avoid stress. As Dr. Hans Selye has pointed out many
times, "Complete freedom from stress is death." We must meet
stress, learn how to cope with it, and attempt to limit its harmful
effects.[5]

One way to overcome constant exposure to stressors is to supply our bodies and minds with optimal nutrition and exercise.
Failing this, we must emphasize the role of the cognitive process
as a major intermediary against many stressors. Your attitude
toward life, your behavioral code, your lifestyle, in short, your
whole personal philosophy, is an essential mediator in the reaction to a stressful situation.

So-called "functional patients" are not well understood by physicians, who hesitate to become involved in the personal problems
that may be the key to a pathologic condition. Even if they recognize the psychic origin of a disease, doctors often resort to the use
of psychotropic drugs, rather than attempting to understand and
eliminate the imbalance that is the origin of the trouble.

Patients have come to expect drugs, surgery, or radiation therapy,
which can be helpful indeed, but which often fail to reach the crux
of the problem. Certainly, none of these can correct premature aging.
Even if the physician takes the time to delve into the personality and
the psychic problems of his patient, his authority in this field is
unclear, and recommendations concerning behavior modifications
are notoriously less acceptable than drug prescriptions.

Nevertheless, the search for psychic equilibrium is an important part of the therapeutic process, in spite of the frustrations it
involves. In our experience, an understanding of the patient (even
if it is never complete) can help the patient help himself. This is
particularly true of the "functional" patient, a patient who suffers
from degenerative disease that precipitates premature aging.

Until biologists and gerontologists discover the "aging factor,"
no miraculous elixir will prevent either the normal aging process
or premature aging. On the other hand, it is commonly observed
that many people look, feel, and behave far younger than their
chronological age indicates. This youth is achieved by a continuous and careful discipline, involving orthomolecular nutrition, a
healthy diet, and exercise. This program is the way to slow down
the aging process—and since the process is often precipitated by
psychic stress, the psyche is a good place to start. This is true

psychosomatic and wholistic medicine. (It cannot be wholistic if it is not psychosomatic.)

PSEUDOSENILITY

Senility is not psychosomatic. The condition is a syndrome that appears in the aging for a variety of reasons. In each case, an attempt must be made to determine the reason for senility and whether it is treatable. Otherwise treatment must be directed at easing the syndrome of disabling symptoms.

"Senility is one of the most serious medical diagnoses that can be given to a patient because the prognosis is so serious and the effectiveness of treatment is not clear," says Leslie Libow, M.D., former chief of geriatric medicine at the Jewish Institute for Geriatric Care in New Hyde Park, New York. "If we value our older people, how can anyone seriously argue that every physician should not do the tests to make sure a treatable cause has not been overlooked?"[6]

Any deteriorating lesion in the brain, whether biochemical or anatomical, will produce a senile-like syndrome—pseudosenility. Treatable diseases of the brain include both disorders in which there is no known anatomical pathology such as an embolism, hemorrhage, or thrombus, and known problems that are present either as a cause or as a complication. In the discussion that follows on the occurrence of pseudosenility, the organic causes of senile-like symptoms such as brain tumors and rare lipid diseases of the brain are not considered.

Depression and Schizophrenia

Depression that occurs in a young or middle-aged person is not usually confused with senility because our society associates senility with old age. However, depression does happen commonly in senile people, and the two problems are often combined. Senility, in fact, may mimic depression so faithfully that the latter will be missed altogether.

Whether there is an apparent psychosocial reason for the presence of depression or not, it must be suspected. A patient prone to depression in the past will have a greater susceptibility to it now. Depression comes on relatively fast, with a lot of complicating irritability attached. Insomnia may also appear.

A substantial number of people are walking around with mild schizophrenia and are able to maintain themselves in the community. Often they are considered slightly odd by neighbors but accepted as eccentrics. As they grow older, unfortunately, these quirks tend to worsen. The double impact of schizophrenia and aging may bring on a senile form of schizophrenia that is difficult to distinguish from outright senility. Schizophrenia in the aged is, therefore, mislabeled as senility, when it is actually a pseudosenile set of circumstances.

In considering the possibility of schizophrenia, the main question is whether schizophrenia was present at any time in the person's past. Also, since a family history increases the probability of the condition, the presence of schizophrenia in first-order relatives is another main diagnostic determinant. It won't be difficult to diagnose the problem of an aged, chronic schizophrenic, but in other cases symptoms of senility are intertwined with the symptoms of schizophrenia.

Malnutrition and Dehydration

Any history of prolonged malnutrition, especially when combined with severe stress, should throw suspicion on nutritional dependency as a cause of pseudosenility. Pseudosenility may even change to true senility from chronic malnourishment, even with the intake of large amounts of food. It is really the quality of food that counts. The most commonly deficient nutrient is niacin (vitamin B3).

The authors believe that most people who become truly senile suffer from many decades of mild to moderate malnutrition, as a result of excessive consumption of *food artifacts*. A food artifact is a component extracted from agricultural produce and recombined into food products that technologists can persuade the public to like, buy, and eat. Food artifacts have very little nutritional value and are a prime cause of obesity in the United States, since they generally offer only calories. You have to eat a lot of these substances to get any nourishment.

Another factor in pseudosenility is chronic dehydration. Our bodies contain 65 to 70 percent water by weight. It is divided into three compartments: (1) blood and lymph, 9 percent of body weight, (2) interstitial, 15 percent, and (3) intracellular, 41 percent. Water, the universal solvent, is essential for every reaction in the body. When fluid intake is too low and excretion via the kidneys and skin is too great, we suffer from dehydration. Deprived of water, most people will die in a matter of days. By this criterion it is more essential than food and less essential than air; we cannot live more than a few minutes without air. Aging people are more vulnerable to dehydration because they drink less fluid, and more often suffer from kidney problems or constipation. Elderly people often suffer from slow, chronic dehydration that is not easily reversed.

Dehydration is often caused by inadequate fluid intake. Many elderly people lose their sense of thirst partially, some completely. They therefore lose one of the most essential signal mechanisms for keeping the body properly hydrated. This loss of sensation may come from zinc deficiency, and is less potentially dangerous if the person knows enough fluid must be taken. A good rule is to take six to eight glasses of fluid per day including soup, juices, and water. But too many people believe that a cup of coffee or tea with each meal will be adequate. Fluid intake must balance loss. If perspiration is excessive or if there is diarrhea, more fluid must be ingested. In hot, dry climates extra fluid is required.

Another cause of dehydration is increased secretion of fluids. This can be caused by excessive intake of mild diuretics such as caffeine or similar compounds in tea, coffee, cocoa, soft drinks, or the use of diuretics to treat hypertension. Many elderly people take these diuretics without realizing the possible consequences.

The physical symptoms of dehydration include significant weight loss, stiff joints, dry scaly skin that loses its elasticity, and marked reduction of secretions. Urine excretion becomes scanty, the secretion of tears declines, and salivation decreases, which makes it difficult to chew and swallow. Perhaps the most serious symptoms are psychiatric: apathy, depression, and confusion. These symptoms are also characteristic of senile dementia.

About thirty years ago, Dr. Humphry Osmond and his clinical staff at Saskatchewan Hospital, Weyburn, observed that about one-quarter of all the elderly patients that were admitted to their mental hospital because they were senile and incompetent became well when they were given fluid and rehydrated. *One-quarter* of their "senile" caseload was caused by dehydration.

Several years ago, Dr. M. Galambos of Valleyview Hospital in Vancouver, British Columbia, reported that a large proportion of senile patients admitted to his ward suffered from dehydration. He had started a rehydration program with vitamin supplementation. It was hospital nursing policy to ensure that each patient consumed at least eight glasses of fluid per day, not counting tea or coffee. He introduced Dr. Hoffer to one patient several months after treatment had been started. The patient had been admitted as senile and when Dr. Hoffer saw him, he was not. Dr. Galambos had found that rehydration was slow, requiring up to one year of treatment. This may seem surprising to most of us, but we have been accustomed only to acute dehydration, which is readily reversed. With chronic dehydration, a number of other changes take place that are not as easily reversed. These include changes in potassium balance and changes in red blood cell formation.

Dr. Hoffer has also seen several elderly patients whose psychiatric state was made much worse by dehydration. One patient, a chronic manic-depressive, became depressed when dehydrated. He concluded he would die and refused to eat or drink. When brought for evaluation he looked like a long-term inmate of a concentration camp. After he was admitted, an intravenous drip was started immediately. His body tissues were so dry he did not convulse when given electroconvulsive therapy, which requires fluid to pass the current. Only after a week of rehydration did he have his first convulsion. That morning, after his first reaction to treatment, he ate breakfast and drank fluid. He recovered from his depression after rehydration.

Organic and Metabolic Diseases

Autopsies reveal that some apparently senile patients have shown little or no visible brain pathology, while other elderly people with a great deal of post-mortem pathology showed no senile symptoms before they died. Expanding lesions in the brain such as hemorrhages, clots, infections, tumors, and other pathology clearly evident from behavior must receive appropriate treatment. To depend only on vitamins, minerals, and orthomolecular nutrition would be the wrong medical care. But these methods should be employed alongside specific medical treatment to improve the quality of the patients' recovery.

Some years ago, Merna Harrington, a woman suffering from a moderate cerebral hemorrhage, was given good immediate and rehabilitative treatment. Over time, she regained most of her normal brain function. One residual symptom did not clear entirely, however, and after two years, it led her into a serious depression. She also suffered from "blocking," a series of interruptions in her logical thinking. The symptoms included trouble with memory, reading, and comprehension. Merna recognized these symptoms and worried about them, but her complaints over these handicaps were responded to by her doctors with the words: "You'll have to live with them." She assumed, correctly, that this meant her physicians would never be able to help her.

Merna was referred for orthomolecular psychiatric care partly because of her depression and partly because she was such a complainer. She refused to accept her previous doctor's prognosis. During our first session, she said the verdict that she would have to live with "blocking" seemed like a death sentence. "If I am forced to go on with this mental disability, I would sooner die," she declared.

Merna was started on three grams of niacin (vitamin B3) and three grams of vitamin C each day. Within three months, most of her disability was gone. It had cleared enough so that she could think clearly, remember recent events with no difficulty, perform her routine daily chores, and live comfortably. While these two vitamins could not have restored dead neurons, they did improve the efficiency of the undamaged portion of the woman's brain, allowing her to compensate more effectively with the brain cells that remained. Merna's depression disappeared as well, so that today she thinks and experiences emotion in a normal way as long as she continues with her orthomolecular nutrition.

There are diseases that are metabolic, or due to hormonal imbalances. Conditions such as Addison's disease, lipodystrophies, and hypothyroidism are included among them.

Subclinical hypothyroidism occurs more frequently than one might imagine. It may be diagnosed early by applying the Barnes technique of measuring surface body temperature under the armpit before arising in the morning. A reading below 97.8°F (36.0°C) when the thermometer is kept in place for ten minutes indicates subclinical hypothyroidism. A better description would be "sublaboratory" hypothyroidism, since the usual laboratory tests are not sensitive enough to pick up every case. The diagnosis is confirmed by the patient's response to small amounts of thyroid extract given over several months. We suspect that many senile people suffer from subclinical hypothyroidism. Every elderly person who complains of feeling tired and cold all the time, and of being chilled easily, should be investigated for thyroid function. Nutrition alone cannot repair dysfunction caused by hormone imbalances.

THE HAZARDS OF GETTING OLD

Dr. Frederick Zeman, who was one of the founders of geriatric medicine in the United States, said: "Disease in old age is characterized by chronicity, multiplicity, and duplicity."

Chronicity and multiplicity, alone or in tandem, won't necessarily create special problems except in terms of the patients' comfort—unless the underlying diseases are not only multiple but serious, in which case they add to the hazards of getting old. Duplicity is the main problem. That is, the family, friends, and physicians who are interested in the elderly person's welfare may be fooled by the pseudosenile symptoms. Communication with the patient will be far from accurate and reliable if he or she is suffering from diminished perceptual faculties—hearing, sight, attention—that have been damaged by the impoverishment of living alone or with a partner who is similarly impaired.

Moreover, just as the immune system is not fully developed in the newborn, it is often damaged in the presenile person. An accurate diagnosis may be difficult to achieve. The diminishing defenses of the body may be at fault.

The elderly person's ability to withstand stress—such as severe environmental alteration, whether internal or external—is decreased. As we mentioned in the last section, subtle or overt depression closely associated with senility can make the individual insensitive to those bodily cues that alert us to the fact that something is going wrong. The symptoms of depression, such as losing weight, lethargy, and weakness, may actually be the symptoms of another underlying disease process, such as cancer.

Sometimes the first step in diagnosis is to ascertain whether depression is drug induced. Reserpine, a drug incorporated into many other medications for a variety of conditions, is one major culprit. The depression may disappear rapidly once the medication is withdrawn. Also, there can be synergistic drug interactions or an inadvertent drug overdose, the result of a patient's taking similar preparations prescribed by different doctors—each unaware of the other's involvement—as well as over-the-counter remedies suggested by the corner pharmacist or friends. These possibilities increase as pseudosenility gets more ingrained. A person may be confused as to dosage times, or take too much of a drug that makes him feel better, on the theory that more is better.

Other hazards of getting old are deteriorating coordination, loss of muscle strength, and osteoarthritis, particularly involving the knees. A misstep can cause a muscular imbalance as the eroded joint gives in and the person topples. Osteoporosis, described earlier in this chapter, makes a fall more dangerous for an elderly person than a younger one. The loss of rigidity in the bone caused by calcium depletion isn't the primary problem. The real danger is the increased porosity, a loss of density in the bone matrix. When the bone twists, the connective tissues lose their cohesiveness, and the bone of an old person breaks like the dried-out limb of a tree. An aged individual may turn awkwardly—twist an arm or leg in the wrong direction—and the stress will be so unusual for that particular area of bone that it will crumble.

A temporary drop in blood pressure can cause a fall. The lowered blood pressure may come from changes in heart rhythm causing quick blockage to the brain and fainting.

Feelings of dizziness among elderly patients are not rare. They also have attacks of nausea; ringing in the ears; decreased hearing; sudden pallor or flushing of the skin; headache; abnormal sensations in the face, trunk, or extremities; difficulty in swallowing or in speech; double vision or other visual disturbances; weakness in the face or hands or legs; loss of consciousness; and a loss of the power of muscle coordination.

Respiratory infection is an acute hazard of old age. The aged often cannot get rid of the secretions; they cough and cough but nothing comes up because they've lost expulsive power. The secretions pile up and it becomes a matter of slow drowning.

Furthermore, secretions tend to thicken because dehydration is so often a part of the picture. And if an old person has ischemic heart disease—a condition that tends to develop in the presence of chronic obstructive pulmonary disease—pulmonary congestion interferes with lung mechanics. It predisposes a person to developing an inability to breathe. Fever and pneumonia may set in quickly. Pulmonary embolism (blood clot in the lung) is always a danger, particularly in senile patients who are immobilized—especially after a leg or pelvic fracture. It is also a danger to those who tend not to exercise.

Tuberculosis can also kill the elderly. It can come on as the result of a lesion that developed in earlier years and was undetected until it broke down in later years.

Abdominal problems such as gallstones, intestinal obstructions, stress ulcers, and cancer are among the main hazards of getting old. Others are leg ulcers, electrolyte imbalances, heart disease, bladder malfunction, and enlarged prostate. Many of these maladies can be responsible for the mental symptoms of so-called "senility." In fact, as we have implied, the greatest hazard of getting old is pseudosenility—being branded as senile when you are not. For example, an elderly woman was misdiagnosed as a case of senile agitation on the basis of her wandering around the house during the night. She had been hospitalized earlier for heart disease and the wandering began as soon as she returned to her daughter's home. What she really had, however, was *orthopnea*, a sense of discomfort when breathing in any but the erect sitting or standing position. The woman was getting up in order to catch her breath. With a change in medical treatment and an improved diet using orthomolecular nutrition, both the nocturnal wandering and the mild confusion that had accompanied it disappeared. Yet pseudosenility had almost marked her as mentally defective for the rest of her life.

Another elderly woman who had what appeared to be senile confusion underwent a medical workup. It revealed a blood hemoglobin of 10.5 grams per 100 milliliters (normal blood hemoglobin for women is 12 to 15), mildly elevated blood pressure, some hardening of the arteries, and some degree of chronic obstructive pulmonary disease. Once she was given treatment to clear up her respiratory function and enough mineral supplementation (especially iron) to push her blood hemoglobin count up to 11.5, her confusion cleared, her thinking improved, and hospitalization for senility was avoided.

A seventy-eight-year-old man was diagnosed as suffering from senility on the basis of extreme confusion. He was hospitalized for mental illness. Fortunately, the old man had a daughter who was genuinely interested in his welfare. She explained that there had been a gradual deterioration over the past year or so that pointed to senility. On the second day of his hospitalization, his laboratory test results were reported. He had a high blood urea nitrogen reading and a urologist was called in as a consultant. The urologist found the man had an enlarged prostate and considerable bladder obstruction. The patient was sent for surgery and, once that had been done, his bladder function improved considerably, his urine output increased significantly, and his blood urea nitrogen went down to near normal levels. Startlingly, the overwhelming part of his confusion cleared, and he no longer acted senile.

His daughter was astonished. Her father hadn't been that alert and clear in his thinking for the prior two years. What was thought to be senility was mostly toxemia from nitrogen retention. His body and brain were being poisoned by his own urine, and a pseudosenile condition had set in. The old gentleman then returned to his daughter's home, and six years later, he died there peacefully at the age of eighty-four with no mental deterioration. Had the diagnosis been left as senile brain disease, he would have been sent to a state hospital and would have died there six years earlier of kidney disease—probably with no one ever realizing what the problem was.

In elderly people, the combination of organ dysfunction and malnutrition can produce the *appearance* of senile confusion. Yet if a patient of fifty-five showed up with that picture, he would be given a good medical workup and the underlying causes would be detected and corrected. If the patient is in his seventies or older, it is all too easy to accept the symptoms of senility at face value and opt for institutionalization because the condition has been labeled "irreversible." This is another one of the hazards of getting old.

Huge medical-care and treatment costs have created a serious ethical problem—where should our resources, which are not unlimited, go? Should we spend $500,000 in providing an artificial heart for a person who can live only a few months or years? The same ethical problem applies to our aging population. Should we be as thorough in investigating an elderly person who can expect another five years as we are in examining a teenage patient who may expect another sixty years of life? This issue was brought to Dr. Hoffer's attention forcefully several years ago. An orthomolecular colleague in New Jersey was charged with abusing the medical system by ordering too many laboratory tests. He had investigated two sisters, each close to age eighty. This investigation included routine laboratory tests, which according to the state agency were excessive. Dr. Hoffer was appearing as an expert witness for his colleague. During her cross-examination, the attorney for the state asked Dr. Hoffer whether this amount of testing could be justified in any old person. Dr. Hoffer, in turn, asked the state attorney whether she believed that because people were old they should not be examined properly. She abruptly dropped the subject. But the question showed that the New Jersey state board believed they could cut costs by withholding tests from people toward the end of their lives.

The authors agree that medical costs should be contained. They can, in fact, be sharply reduced by the application of orthomolecular principles. A little money spent on educating people about how to keep themselves healthy will save enormous sums of money. Too many elderly people find that their life savings are expended in the last few years of their lives. With orthomolecular programs, medical costs over the last five years of life should be only slightly higher than they have been per year over their lifetime.

A Massachusetts physician, Alfred Worcester, wrote:

> The aged, as we must never forget, are always lonesome. They have outlived the preceding, and very likely their own, generation; or, if any survive, only by extra good fortune can there be any more meetings. Their family separations too often have caused the additional loss of their old homes and former neighbors. To the ways and manners of the present, they are not accustomed. They belong to the unforgiving past. They are as strangers in the land.

In the next chapter, we will learn how our society is creating a land full of strangers not only among the very old but also in the younger generations. This comes from a form of malnutrition foisted slyly on us by commercial interests because we are mostly ignorant in the ways of good eating. What is the result? Symptoms that resemble senility, caused by malnutrition.

3. HYPOTHESES OF SENILE PATHOLOGY

There are no diseases of the aged, but simply diseases among the aged.

—Leonard Larson, M.D.

During the golden age of Greece, when the average life expectancy of Greek citizens was little more than eighteen years (reflecting the fact that most people died at birth or in infancy), Pericles delivered his Funeral Oration, the foundation of modern democratic thought, at the age of sixty-nine.

Charlemagne ruled until A.D. 813, and handed over the reins of power to his son when he was seventy-one, at a time when people lived an average of just twenty-two years.

Michelangelo executed the Pietà when he was eighty years old, while the average Italian life expectancy was only thirty-two years.

Goethe was eighty-four when Part II of *Faust* was first published.

Disraeli did not become Britain's Prime Minister until he was seventy, at a time when the average Englishman's life span was forty-seven years.

Sir Winston Churchill was sixty-five years old in 1939, at the beginning of the Second World War, in which he led his people to victory over tyranny. He died January 24, 1965, at the age of eighty-nine, when the average male life span was sixty-seven years.

We can find no senility in the remarkable figures of history. And the antisenility roll call continues with the names of Immanuel Kant, Voltaire, Titian, Mao Tse-tung, Harry Truman, Marshal Tito,

Charles de Gaulle, Queen Elizabeth I, Queen Victoria, Franz Liszt, Plato, Albert Einstein, Buddha, Confucius, Galileo, Copernicus, Archimedes, Thomas Edison, and John D. Rockefeller. Genghis Kahn continued to rule for seven years past our current usual age of retirement. Dwight Eisenhower was sixty-seven when he composed the Eisenhower Doctrine.[1]

The two possible common factors that allowed for continued normal brain function for these historical figures were the inheritance of good genes and the provision of an optimal internal environment. Physicians usually include these two factors when discussing longevity in general and an alert geriatric mind in particular. People who are concerned realize that inheritance plays a role, but there is no way of changing our genes for the better. Since genes require a suitable environment for their expression, however, we *can* try to provide an optimal environment so that even the weakest genes will serve us much better. If one's parents lived long, healthy lives, we can aspire to the same by living in such a way as to avoid certain known risk factors. If our parents' lives were short and marked with illness, we can improve our lives by taking genetics into account, and adjusting our diets and lifestyles accordingly.

Of the remarkable historical figures named above, Sir Winston Churchill is typical of the person whose genes are better than the physiological environment in which he sustains them. His obesity, cigar-smoking, and high consumption of alcohol kept him in a relative hypoglycemic condition, and it is thought that hypoglycemic adults are more vulnerable to brain damage. He suffered a number of small strokes that left him more and more incapacitated as he approached death. It is likely that if Sir Winston had followed a healthier lifestyle, his genes would have had him living well past his 100th year with an active and creative mind.

THE AUTHORS' HYPOTHESIS

Churchill's physical, and possibly also his mental, deterioration represent the classic illustration of a working hypothesis the authors have developed on the cellular cause of senility. According to this hypothesis, *senility is a state of neuron inactivity brought on by anaerobic respiration of the cells.* If aerobic respiration is maintained at its optimum level, no one will become senile. This means that uninterrupted oxygen must be carried to the brain cells by a viable blood supply, that all the respiratory enzymes must remain intact, and that there must always be an adequate amount of glucose in the brain, with no accumulation of anaerobic metabolites. In brief, senility is the inactivation of the brain's built-in health system.

In developing this hypothesis on the pathology of senility, we were confronted with what appeared to be an insolvable problem. We examined the known facts from every angle and considered other hypotheses that exist. Now, when scientists develop a hypothesis, it is not accepted as truth in itself. The function of a hypothesis is to direct research. It is exciting if the scientists are proven right, but even the destruction of a hypothesis will be valuable if their research is done well. Any hypothesis must be grounded in observations that are relevant to the problem. The odds against a hypothesis being proven right are so low that one must not indulge in flights of fancy, where the odds are even lower.

Consequently, we made a number of observations that we used to develop our hypothesis regarding senility. First, we saw the effect reported by Edwin Boyle, Jr., M.D., research director of the Miami Heart Institute, in which hyperbaric oxygen temporarily removed senility, as described in Chapter 1. Second, we knew that a lack of oxygen had the effect of causing cancer. These two ideas, among others, came together to produce the hypothesis stated above.

Otto Heinrich Warburg, one of the world's foremost biochemists, won a Nobel Prize for his basic work with respiratory enzymes and cellular mechanisms. He discovered and characterized certain compounds, called pyridine nucleotide dehydrogenases and flavoproteins, as members of the respiratory chain, and worked out the mechanism whereby the energy released in the oxidation of foodstuffs may be conserved and transferred for use in synthesis and growth. The mechanism of cellular respiration provided the first explanation of the chemical mechanism of enzyme action.

Several years before he died, Dr. Warburg published a review of the problem of cancer. He showed that there was a relationship between anaerobic respiration and cancer growth. When ordinary cells in pure culture are forced to live in an atmosphere that does not have enough oxygen, they switch their respiratory mechanism from one dependent upon oxygen (called *aerobic*), to one not dependent upon oxygen (called *anaerobic*). This change is apparently irreversible. Even more important, the anaerobic cells begin to divide. They are no longer subject to the usual growth controls and eventually become cancerous.

Warburg explained that the malignancy of cancer tissue was correlated with the degree of anaerobic conditions. The less oxygen there was available to the tissue, the more rapid was its growth. Rapid-growing cancer tissues are generally more malignant than slow growing cancer tissues.

Albert Szent-Györgyi (1974), the discoverer of vitamin C, considered that the cancerous state is a reversal to a more primitive state of cellular existence. This occurs because electron flow among protein molecules breaks down and not enough energy is left for the cell to keep division from taking place. In order to remain alive, the cell reverts to an anaerobic form of respiration. It can live in very low oxygen tension, where nontransformed cells would soon die.[2]

Laki and Ladik (1976) reviewed Szent-Györgyi's work and other evidence such as that nerve tumor cells grown rapidly in serum require little oxygen. When serum is withheld, growth stops and oxygen consumption increases. Laki and Ladik supported Szent-Györgyi's work.[3] Low oxygen uptake may be due to less efficient binding of nicotinamide-adenine dinucleotide (NAD), which is made in the body from niacin. The addition of NAD enhances oxidative respiration.

So convinced was Dr. Warburg by his investigations of respiratory enzymes and their mechanisms that he recommended preventive treatment measures to preclude the development of cancer. This included doing everything possible to ensure optimum aerobic conditions in the cells and the tissues. He suggested that everyone ensure optimum oxygen-carrying capacity by keeping hemoglobin levels normal. He also suggested that everyone ensure optimum levels of oxygen-carrying coenzymes such as riboflavin, thiamine, and niacin—all B vitamins. He pointed out that a precancerous condition of the throat known as *leukoplakia* did not become cancerous when patients were given niacin.

The most interesting part of Warburg's report was his theory of dedifferentiation. By *dedifferentiation*, he meant the following: Evolution began with cells that lived without oxygen, in an anaerobic environment. Only later on, did enough oxygen accumulate in our atmosphere to allow cells to develop aerobic respiration. This condition is much more efficient in converting food into energy. More energy is released per gram of food in the presence of oxygen. It is likely that multicellular organisms did not develop until cells became aerobic. While single-celled species had only one function—to divide—multiple-celled organisms demanded that other functions be carried out together in harmony. The main function of anaerobic respiration is cell division. Aerobic respiration permits growth as well as other cellular functions. According to Warburg's theory, the switch back from aerobic to anaerobic respiration brings the cell back to a primitive condition, in which division is its only function. Warburg calls this *dedifferentiation*. Dedifferentiation can bring on uncontrolled cell division among cells still retaining the ability to divide.

What would happen to cells that do not divide, such as neurons? A baby is born with its full complement of neurons. Thereafter, they are lost at a slow pace daily until the individual dies. Neurons as a rule do not regenerate, as pointed out in Chapter 1.

One reason that neurons do not regenerate is that each neuron has a large number of dendrites and long nerves. It is impossible to conceive how such a cell could divide and produce two cells, each with the proper attachments to other cells. Cancers involving nerve cells are exceedingly rare. Neurons do not divide. Dedifferentiation of neurons cannot occur, and therefore cannot cause cancer. In other words, anaerobic respiration of neurons is not there to cause cancer. Then what happens? Since the neurons in the cortex are no longer able to carry on their main function and don't divide, they simply become quiescent (inactive) and the result is senility. This is our hypothesis—*senescence is neuron quiescence*.

THE LACTIC ACID HYPOTHESIS

In 1977, Dr. R.E. Myers reported that the actual cause of damage to the brain that occurs when the blood circulation is shut off is the accumulation of lactic acid; it is not strictly caused by the lack of oxygen. In an experiment he performed, monkeys were not given any food for twenty-four hours and then their ability to withstand a stoppage in blood flow for twelve to fourteen minutes was tested. No detectable damage in the animals was found. Even after twenty-four minutes, the neurologic findings were minimal. Next, the researcher infused glucose into another group of monkeys before causing a new circulatory arrest, and this produced a different picture. After fourteen minutes, the animals developed irreversible changes so extreme that they died or had to be killed. Chemical analyses showed that the amount of lactate in the brains of animals fed glucose had increased to ten times their pre-experiment level, as compared to a mere four-fold increase in the food-deprived animals.[4]

The experiments done by Myers indicate that blood glucose levels should remain at the fasting level, or as close to it as possible, for everyone who wants to avoid senile pathology. This may be achieved by avoiding all free sugar through the use of a hypoglycemic diet. It also seems likely that people who avoid sugar in their diet may have fewer strokes, and if they do have strokes, they will stand a much better chance of surviving with their brains intact. The trick is to avoid processed sugar of any kind. This also means that the hospital administration of glucose solutions should be performed with great care and very slowly, or not at all. Myers concludes:

> These findings direct our attention to a greater concern with the rationale for administering glucose to women in labor—especially those cases where the risk of fetal asphyxia is high. These findings are also relevant to the management of critically ill newborns suffering from respiratory problems and experiencing episodes of apnea. [Apnea is the absence of breathing.]

Women in labor should receive snacks of whole foods, such as seeds, nuts, fresh vegetables, and yogurt. They should not be fed any food artifacts, such as refined carbohydrates like cake, candy, Jell-O, and cola drinks. Depriving mothers-to-be of processed and sugared products might decrease the incidence of infant brain damage from lack of oxygen. This anoxia is one of the causes of learning disorders and hyperactive behavior in children. Hypoglycemic women are more likely to have disturbed infants, and hypoglycemic adults are more vulnerable to senile brain damage for the same reason.

Once again, senility is a state of neuron inactivity caused by anaerobic respiration of the cells. The cells' ability to become active is still there, however, and can be reactivated by increasing the amount of oxygen available (as with hyperbaric oxygen therapy). Unfortunately, medical scientists have no way of permanently maintaining aerobic respiration. Prolonged hyperbaric oxygen therapy would be dangerous, because it tends to increase free-radical concentration. This leads to such harmful effects as premature aging and eventual senility, the very problems we are attempting to avoid. The problem is to provide optimal amounts of oxygen to allow proper aerobic respiration and to protect the body against the oxidative potential of oxygen and free radicals. Any comprehensive anti-senility program must take all of these factors into account.

If we accept the working hypothesis put forth earlier, that senility is dedifferentiation caused by the conversion from aerobic to anaerobic respiration, it follows that any process that reduces the delivery of oxygen to the brain cells, or prevents its utilization, will hasten senility. These factors include lack of oxygen in the air, anemia, circulatory difficulty, and a deficiency of respiratory enzymes in the brain. The most common exposure to decreased atmospheric oxygen occurs during airplane flights. Presenile people therefore ought not be be exposed to decreased oxygen pressure in aircraft cabins for long periods of time.

THE SLUDGING HYPOTHESIS

Another problem is the red blood cells' tendency to adhere to each other—the *rouleoux effect*. When red blood cells stick to each other, like stacked coins in a bank's coin roll, the blood is prevented from flowing freely into the capillaries. Red blood cells travel through capillaries one at a time, delivering the oxygen to surrounding cells. A group of clumped cells is unable to enter. At bifurcations (branchings) of vessels, there will be an uneven distribution of these cells. One branch may get a lot of plasma with few red blood cells, while another may carry too many clumped cells—a situation called sludging. In either case, not enough oxygen is delivered.

Sludging may be seen readily by looking into the eye with an opthalmologist's device called a slit lamp. Small blood vessels in the eye will have no red cells in them if sludging is present. People with marked sludging have certain clinical characteristics. Their faces are pale and puffy due to swelling; their eyes are not alert; they suffer from fatigue, tension, and anxiety. A large number of middle-aged and elderly people have this characteristic clinical syndrome. When they are treated with niacin, they regain their normal facial appearance and color. Dr. Boyle observed that niacin restored the normal homogeneous nature of the blood. The red blood cells once more repelled each other, probably by increasing the electronegative charge on each cell.

Walsh, Melaney, and Walsh (1977) believe that sludging is also a major factor in causing senility. Conditions that bring on sludging, such as diabetes and alcoholism, accelerate the senile symptoms. Moreover, they found that treatment with anticoagulants, which are antisludging medications, was useful in retarding senility.[5] Walsh and Walsh treated forty-nine seniles with the anticoagulant Coumadin. Of this group, 70 percent improved—15 percent of them dramatically. Walsh had given another anticoagulant, Dicumarol, to twenty-four seniles in 1968 with even better results. Even though Dicumarol is more difficult to use clinically, because it produces more side effects, it appears to give a better result.[6]

THE CROSS-LINKAGE HYPOTHESIS

Of the other biochemical hypotheses fashioned to explain aging and senility, we consider the cross-linkage theory proposed by Bjorksten (1960-1971) to be among the most promising.[7,8,9,10,11] This is a very complex explanation of senile pathology. Bjorksten and his collaborators suggested that certain metabolites of molecules in the body, arising from excessive oxidation, combine with two or more long protein molecules to bind them together. An unnatural cross-link forms. The cross-linked protein no longer is able to function normally and cannot be split or hydrolyzed (reacted with water molecules) by enzymes usually present in the body.

This cross-linking is analogous to the vulcanization of rubber. Here, long rubber molecules that float free in solution are bound to each other by other short molecules to form the familiar rubber substance. It is elastic, tough, and can no longer be acted on by natural enzymes. A similar kind of vulcanization effect appears to take place in elderly skin. The largest organ of the body becomes inelastic, brittle, and parchment-like. It is easy to visualize the similarity of senile skin and aged or oxidized rubber.

In this theory of the development of senility, the excessive formation of small molecules that can form cross linkages is the real villain. There are a variety of these highly reactive molecules, including compounds called quinones; chrome indoles such as dopachrome, noradrenochrome and adrenochrome; aldehydes;

and oxidizing ions such as copper. Such substances are synthesized in greater quantity in persons exposed to radiation, to smoking, and to excessive oxygen, or to diseases such as diabetes mellitus. Too much copper in the body and a deficiency of zinc will have the same effect. Perhaps all the toxic and heavy metals (including lead, cadmium, aluminum, mercury, silver, and gold) also do the same.

The long protein molecule that undergoes certain changes to make reactive groups more available for cross-linkage must play another part in senile pathology. Molecules folded into certain configurations may be less likely to be cross-link.

Evidence that free radicals are involved in aging was contributed by Harman (1956, 1962). Free radicals are highly reactive molecules halfway between an oxidized and reduced state. These are especially apt to occur in plasma that is rich in oxygen and in oxidizing enzymes including ceruloplasmin, a protein that transports copper in the blood, and hemoglobin.

Cross-linkage would be particularly harmful in certain tissues such as in blood-vessel walls. Cross-linkage would shorten protein chains, make them inelastic or brittle, and increasingly subject them to failure. Blood vessels must be able to expand and contract in harmony with the beat of the heart, but cross-linkage would not permit that. Also, a cross-linked vessel wall would be less permeable to the transfer of essential nutrients to the cells.[12,13]

Harman and Piette (1966) found direct evidence that oxygen increased the formation of free radicals in the blood from the naturally occurring hormones adrenaline and noradrenaline.[14]

Bjorksten (1968, 1971) aptly summarized the current cross-linkage theory:

> Crosslinking is damaging to the tissues and involves loss of elasticity, reduced swelling capacity, increased resistance to hydrolases and probably enzymes generally, and thus an increase in molecular weight and a tendency toward embrittlement. There is a growing amount of direct evidence and much indirect evidence for postulating the relationship between crosslinking and aging.[15,16]

There are a variety of cross-linking agents present in the living organism, including compounds known as aldehydes, lipid oxidation products, sulfur alkylating agents, quinones, free radicals induced by ionizing radiation, antibodies, polybasic acids, poly-halo derivatives and polyvalent metals. The last four are slow-acting but can also accumulate in the body over time. Sufficient amounts of all these potential cross-linking materials are present in the body to make the changes of aging unavoidable.

According to this hypothesis, programs designed to prevent senility should seek to avoid cross-linkage. This may be done by breaking up those cross-linkages already formed, and by eliminating protein molecules already hopelessly cross-linked. A consistent scheme would include reducing the formation of free radicals by avoiding radiation, cigarette smoke, excessive oxygenation, excessive copper, and other toxic elements, and increasing the availability of antioxidants—such as vitamin C, vitamin E, zinc, and selenium, among others. This scheme would also include eliminating aged protein molecules from the body. Bjorksten is looking for enzymes or other methods for breaking cross-linked molecules into smaller molecules that are easier to eliminate.

We suspect that one of the main functions of skin (and its outgrowths, the hair and nails), is to excrete cross-linked proteins. The body deposits in the skin large molecules that cannot be excreted in the feces or in urine. Human skin grows and wears away, taking with it whatever has been deposited, in the same way that trees get rid of accumulations of minerals by shedding their leaves. The skin is a protein structure, obviously cross-linked, since it is tough but resilient and elastic. It contains more free radicals when exposed to sun and radiation. The result of free-radical activity is obvious; everyone has seen it either on themselves or on others, in the form of suntan, which is the result of free-radical action on molecules such as dopa and other amines.

We have seen increased melanin formation in patients receiving niacin—a few schizophrenics taking the vitamin noticed that their skin, especially on the flexor surfaces (under the armpit, wrist, and on inner aspect of elbow), turned dark brown. However, this is a benign change and after a while, it no longer occurred. The pigmented skin wears away, leaving healthy, normally pigmented skin. This can be accelerated by rubbing wet skin gently. The pigment will rub off easily, much as an old suntan does. The excess free radicals seem to be deposited in the skin for excretion by the skin. We have seen similar changes in the nails. Perhaps the excessive pigmentation characteristic of pellagra (a niacin-deficiency disease) is an attempt by the body to get rid of unusually high amounts of free radicals. Perhaps some cross-linked proteins are also deposited in skin to be eliminated.

THE CHALONE AND ADRENOCHROME HYPOTHESES

Bullough (1973) suggested that stress could delay death by its effect on tissue chalones. A *chalone* is a tissue-specific antimitotic (cell-division inhibiting) messenger molecule present in all mammalian tissues. The antimitotic power of chalones is increased by adrenaline and by a glucocorticord hormone. This is why cells divide more rapidly during sleep, when adrenaline secretion is lower. Bullough postulates that the chalones not only inhibit mitosis but also retard aging. In other words, chalones retard senility by combining these two reactions. In tissues that do not divide (such as neurons), the mitotic process is permanently switched off early in life, and these cells live much longer than cells that divide frequently. By age seventy, however, about 10 percent of all the neurons present at birth have been lost.[17]

Adrenaline is easily oxidized by a compound called adreno-chrome in the test tube, and probably in the body as well. The evidence for this is summarized in *The Hallucinogens*, by Hoffer and Osmond (1967).[18] Adrenochrome is an extremely potent mitotic poison that stops cells from dividing. Most likely the antimitotic properties of adrenaline arise from its conversion into adrenochrome. Adrenochrome is in turn converted into two classes of compounds known as indoles: one, a dihydroxy series, is nontoxic and may have antistress properties; the other, a trihydroxy series (or adrenalutin), is toxic, but in a different way than adrenochrome. The production of adrenochrome requires oxygen. Anoxia, which leads to anaerobic respiration, would therefore shut off the production of adrenochrome and its antimitotic effect. Is this why anaerobic respiration increases the kind of uncontrolled cell division we know as cancer?

Within the past few years adrenaline has been implicated in coronary disease. If this becomes well established, it will provide another explanation for niacin's beneficial effect on heart disease. In a series of reports, Beamish and his coworkers (1981, 1981a, 1981b) showed that heart-muscle tissue takes up adrenaline that is converted into adrenochrome, and it is the adrenochrome that causes fibrillation (rapid contractions of the heart muscle) leading to heart muscle damage and death. They further found that Anturane (a prescription drug used in the treatment of gout) protects against fibrillation induced by adrenochrome and suggest that this is supported by clinical findings that Anturane decreases mortality from heart disease. When the body is under severe stress, as in shock or after injection of adrenaline, a large amount of adrenaline is found in the blood and absorbed by heart tissue. Severe stress is thus a factor in such coronary death whether or not arteriosclerosis is present, but it is likely that an arteriosclerotic heart cannot cope with stress as well. If fibrillation results, it would increase the demand for oxygen to a level that could not be met by a heart whose coronary vessels are compromised.

Niacin protects tissues against the toxic effect of adrenochrome in living organisms. When adrenochrome is given intravenously to epileptics, niacin reverses the EEG changes that the adrenochrome has induced, say Szatmari, Hoffer, and Schneider (1955); according to Hoffer and Osmond (1967), niacin also reverses the psychological changes.

A compound called nicotinamide adenine dinucleotide (NAD) is essential for maintaining appropriate levels of noradrenaline and adrenaline in the synapses, the points where nerve impulses "jump" from one nerve to another. These catecholamines (important nerve transmitters) lose one electron to form an oxidized amine. In the presence of NAD this compound is reduced back to its original catecholamine. If there is a deficiency of NAD, the oxidized adrenaline (or noradrenaline) loses another electron to form adrenochrome (or noradrenochrome). This change is irreversible. Adrenochrome is a synaptic blocking agent, as is LSD. Thus the presence of niacin, which maintains NAD levels, decreases the formation of adrenochrome. It is likely this also takes place in the heart, and if it does, it would protect heart muscle from the effect of adrenochrome, fibrillation, and tissue decay. None of the other substances known to lower cholesterol levels are known to have this protective effect. Niacin thus has an advantage in lowering cholesterol and in decreasing the incidence of fibrillation and heart tissue damage.

Bullough made another interesting suggestion. He pointed out that when a number of different tissues must work together, it is usual for one tissue to act as initiator and pacemaker. If the phenomena we call aging are dictated by the deterioration of nonmitotic tissue, then, he suggests, one of these tissues may play the leading role. The three nondividing tissues are neurons, muscle cells in the heart, and muscle cells in other muscles. The brain must be the initiator and pacemaker of these three. Nervous-system deterioration does lead to muscular deterioration and in turn deterioration of the circulation.

The adrenochrome hypothesis has been tested experimentally by a large number of scientists since it was first reported in 1952. Three major sub-hypotheses have been confirmed: (a) adrenochrome is made in the body, (b) adrenochrome is a hallucinogen, and (c) adrenochrome antidotes are therapeutic for schizophrenia.[19] Moreover, we believe that the quantity of secretion of adrenochrome's oxidation product, *adrenolutin*, affects the clearness of an individual's thinking.[20]

The question arises as to how those persons whose thinking is unclear and those who formulate and project thoughts normally differ biochemically. This can be determined by measuring the amount of adrenolutin present in an individual's blood plasma.[21]

Abnormalities in thinking appear to arise when a person has an adverse reaction to adrenolutin. Such reactions may be triggered by a number of factors, such as cerebral allergies, vitamin dependencies and deficiencies, and other general but severe forms of stress. The essential fatty acids and the prostaglandins are involved.[22,23,24,25] One day all of these factors will be examined and correlated so that we will have a complete picture of what happens when a person is affected by unclear thinking.

Most of the theories of aging and senility—including the cross-linkage theory with its free-radical theory; Bullough's tissue chalone hypothesis; Myers's work on anoxia and lactic acid accumulation; the Warburg and Szent-Györgyi hypothesis on cancer; and Boyle's work with hyperbaric oxygen—involve oxidation. The basic biological problem appears to be to provide optimum amounts of oxygen for oxidation. Too little oxygen may lead to cancer in mitotic tissues, and to senility in nonmitotic neurons; too much leads to physical senility by accelerating free-radical and cross-linkage formation.

Also essential in preventing and combatting senility is providing the body with the right balance of a full range of nutrients, and in forms in which the body can use them to maintain proper functioning of all its cells and organs. In the chapter that follows, we shall consider the devastating effects of nutritional neglect.

4. SENILITY FROM SUBTLE, CHRONIC MALNUTRITION

The cells of our bodies can become unwell and malfunctioning for two general reasons: First, they may be poisoned; second, they may lack a good supply of nourishing food. This nourishing food must be a complex mixture of chemicals (water is one of these "chemicals") in about the right proportions. Included in this food must be about ten or more amino acids, about fifteen vitamins, and a similar number of minerals, all in addition to the fuel—carbohydrate and fat—that our bodies need to run on in the sense that an automobile needs gasoline. All of the food elements enter our body by way of the open mouth, and the health of all the cells of our bodies depends upon whether or not we place within our open mouths the proper kind of food.

—Roger J. Williams, Ph.D.

Getting old is inevitable, but premature senility is not. One day senility will be prevented, and nutrition will be a main factor in that prevention.

Doctors at a National Institute on Aging conference held in Washington, D.C. on June 7, 1978, recommended that the United States government sponsor research on what diets the elderly should follow. The nutrition experts said that too little attention had been paid to the nutritional needs of the elderly, despite the fact that nutrition can play a key role in reducing diseases in old age.

Dr. Robert N. Butler, then director of the National Institute on Aging, said that our entire society stands to benefit by improving the health of the elderly. He noted that more than half of United States health expenditures in 1976 went for the medical care of the 23 million Americans who were sixty-five or over.

"In old age, the composition of the body changes, with lean

body mass being reduced and the proportion of fat increased," said Dr. Robert E. Shank, a professor at Washington University in St. Louis, speaking before the conference. "The elderly usually are advised to eat less than when they were young, but they still require the same amount of nutrients."[1]

E.J. Stieglitz (1949, 1950) wrote that senile changes of the body were primarily due to cellular malnourishment. All of the degenerative diseases have in common the impairment of the nutrition of our body cells. This can be due to any one or any combination of at least four factors:

1. An inadequate supply of food, with a deficiency of essential nutrients.
2. The inefficient distribution of nutrients, because of circulatory impairment.
3. The ineffective utilization of nutrients, due to enzyme deficiencies.
4. An accumulation of harmful metabolic debris, or, as they have been called, "clinkers."

Stieglitz concluded that minor degrees of vitamin deficiencies were present in most people, and he recommended doubling the intake of vitamins, because "wise nutrition is a most powerful tool for the attainment of vigor in later years." What he decided was extraordinary considering that in 1950, the vitamin dependency concept popular today had not yet been developed.[2,3]

We believe that his first factor, a deficiency of essential nutrients, when present for many decades in the form of subtle, chronic malnutrition, is the source of most premature aging and, finally, senility.

We are convinced, moreover, that the first factor, if it persists for a long time, will lead to problems in the third factor, enzyme deficiencies, and later the fourth factor, the accumulation of undesirable products of abnormal metabolism. For a substantial number of people, the inefficient utilization of nutrients alone will render the average diet inadequate.

It is probable that elderly people who live well into old age without becoming senile have been skillful in their selection of food, or they have had digestive systems better able to extract essential nutrients from their food. Droller and Dossett (1959) found that senile patients were low in serum vitamin B12; Kral (1962) also found that malnutrition was a common problem of the elderly.[4,5] These are aspects of aging and senility that have been almost totally ignored by geriatricians. Our contention is that too much money and time has been squandered in looking for psychosocial explanations for senility, and an absolutely inadequate amount has been used to explore the biochemical basis of this degenerative disease. We positively assert that senility commonly arises from subtle, chronic malnutrition that results from the inappropriate application of food technology and the selling of the products of that technology to unwitting consumers.

SOPHISTICATED BUT SIMPLISTIC FOOD TECHNOLOGY

It is easy to understand what good nutrition is if we accept as a basic rule that all animals should eat what the species has adapted to during evolution. Obviously, deer won't be healthy if forced to eat meat, and wolves will die if forced to eat only grass. Other animals, including man, are not so exclusive and can eat various types of food. The important idea is that every species should consume only what it has been adapted to. It is important to understand why this is essential.

All foods must be broken down in the body into their simplest components: proteins into amino acids, carbohydrates into glucose, and fats into fatty acids. This process requires enzymes. If the proper enzymes are not present, the food will be of no value whatever to the creature that consumes it. A dog's digestive tract cannot split grasses. But a ruminant, such as a cow, has a mechanism for storing these complex polysaccharides while they are fermented by microorganisms, which do the basic digestion. In the same way, termites contain in their digestive tract microorganisms that can digest wood. The ability to break down food substances is not enough, however. Even when the food can be broken down, it is still essential that the proportions of proteins, carbohydrates, and fats present are the same or similar to those in the food the species has adapted to, with, of course, adequate amounts of vitamins and essential elements.

The same set of food rules applies to the nutrition of humans. It is unlikely that one could persuade people to vary too far from eating substances they can digest. We don't feed people hay as a staple, no matter how nutritious it is for horses. But today's food technology nevertheless violates the common sense of good nutrition on a grand scale.

Food technology has run rampant, with no controls by nutritionists or physicians. It employs the oldest concepts of nutritional science with the newest methods of food extraction. The old nutrition classifies food in the simplest of terms—proteins, fats, and so forth—and reveals no comprehension of the relationship between cellular and molecular interactions. The old science consists of adding up the individual factors, using such inadequate measures of nutritional requirements as Recommended Daily Allowances (RDAs), which are absolutely meaningless for the individual organism.

On the one hand, food technology is simplistic in its approach to the science of nourishment; on the other, it is highly sophisticated in its techniques for extracting individual food components. The result is a sophisticated but subtle form of chronic malnutrition suffered by some of the world's most affluent citizens.

Thus, the nutritional model followed today, at the end of the twentieth century, is still the nineteenth-century model. We don't have the benefit of eating the whole foods popular in the nineteenth century, however, because modern food technology is refining away the vital wholeness of natural foods and splitting them into separate components. We have labeled these isolated components *artifacts*.

Another nineteenth-century hangover is the industry's approach to toxicology. Individual chemicals are tested to see if they will kill animals, or cause disease such as cancer, and if so, at what dosage level. Quantities below the toxic levels are assumed to be safe. But toxicologists have not been testing combinations of chemicals. Individual chemicals may well be nontoxic, while in combination they can be quite toxic. Nor has anyone tested the combined effect of the dozens of chemicals added all together to our daily food. No one really knows how many chemicals are slipped into our diet. Estimates suggest that several thousand different chemicals routinely become part of the food supply, but it is probably much more.

When any chemical is synthesized or extracted, it carries with it into the final product traces of the chemicals used in its manufacture. It is not practical to produce 100-percent pure material; the cost would be prohibitive. Any additive must therefore carry with it, even if in traces, an imprint of all the chemicals used to make and purify it. But no one has determined the amount of these traces, nor their cumulative effect over a period of thirty or forty years. Probably this will never be done, for scientists would need to test a manufactured food over decades using a constant procedure to ensure that the composition of the food remained the same from the beginning to the end of the experiment.

You could feed test animals a final food product that appears in packages in the store for several generations, but this is seldom done. It would be sensible if manufacturers were required to prove that any product they make is as nutritious as the raw foodstuff from which it was made, on the basis of feeding experiments and not on the basis of chemical composition or RDAs. If a product contained only 70 percent of the food's nutritional value, this would be shown on the labels in large numbers. A pizza pie would list on its label the proportion of each foodstuff used—so much cheese, so much white flour or whole wheat flour, so much sugar, and all the other ingredients—plus one cummulative figure that would allow the consumer to evaluate its contents. Then each purchaser would, at a glance, be able to compare convenience products with natural food.

Ross Hume Hall, Ph.D., a professor of biochemistry at McMaster University Health Center in Ontario, Canada, points out that we need a new science of nourishment. We believe that these new scientists society is searching for are the orthomolecular physicians and nutritionists. They understand both food technology and nutrition. Our present food technologists do not understand nutrition, while our modern nutritionists don't understand how food technology has depleted the nutritional value of our food. Go to any convention of dietitians or establishment nutritionists and you'll see them gorging on assorted junk food and cola drinks supplied gratis by the manufacturers to build goodwill and promote sales among these so-called food experts.

Government agencies that control the industry issue edicts that bear no relation to the real world of modern convenience foods, because they fall back on nineteenth-century nutritional ideas. The deep-fat fried, sugared, white-flour super-doughnut furnishes an excellent example. The doughnut is a mixture of the three most undesirable food artifacts: white flour, pure fat, and pure sucrose (refined sugar). The super-doughnut also contains small quantities of some vitamins. To a person informed on matters of nutrition, it is shocking to be told that two doughnuts plus a glass of milk furnish one-third of the RDA for protein and these vitamins. Yet this has been approved in the United States for school lunch programs. As Hall puts it,

> Thus, a product filled with sugar, chemically manipulated fat, and other artificial ingredients with the wave of a vitamin wand becomes a highly nutritious breakfast. Such nutrition fakery is going to become more prominent as the FDA moves toward approval of vitamin fortification of fabricated foods in general.

Breakfast foods probably represent the worst examples of the conversion of food into food artifacts—junk. A large supermarket may contain over 100 breakfast cereals. The supermarket shopper would think this provides a splendid variety of food with which to balance the diet. But a look at the contents shows these colorful cereals are prepared from just a few grains (rice, corn, wheat), many sugars, corn syrup, synthetic colors, and several chemicals as additional additives. We have, in fact, over 100 different concoctions of flour, sugar, and chemicals. Any health food store providing grains and seeds has a much greater variety of good food, but a much smaller variety of these precooked artificial cereals. Many years ago, the word "ersatz" was used to label a coffee substitute, and it was a derogatory word. The term should be resurrected and applied to all our modern, precooked breakfast cereals—together with a label warning that this ersatz product will be harmful to your health.

Humankind evolved over many centuries, eating a variety of foods that provided certain trophic factors as well as the basic components. Trophic factors are extra nutrients that probably come from the molecular composition of a food, or may be due to chemicals still not identified individually. Trophic factors are removed by processing along with the wide variety of foodstuff also destroyed.

Almost 60 percent of all the calories now consumed by people in North America come from white flour, fat, and sugar—all non-nutritive products. The enormous proliferation of what appears to be food—synthetics—would be impossible without food additives. These are chemicals that do not add any nutritional merit to food. They have made possible the modern supermarket, carrying over 10,000 items made from a few processed materials.

There is an infinite number of product forms—colorful, palatable, stable, easily prepared—but junk. They have no redeeming value. Without the additives, nearly all these junk products would disappear.

The effect of the combination of 1,800 additives with a few processed high-calorie products has never been tested biologically. The food industry is aware that people prefer what appears to be food, but actually is not. Why else would they try so hard to make synthetic foods? One can now buy a synthetic tomato extender that is 50 percent sugar plus synthetic coal-tar-derived dyes (and the trace impurities present in each additive). This product is recommended for making juices, soup, and other convenience items. Even simple substances such as cornstarch are chemically treated to withstand the shock of high temperature processing, and ensure its stability. Cornstarch is no longer a natural starch. There is also imitation honey that appears to be identical to honey, but contains very little real honey.

Government agencies have given up trying to control the quality of food generated by the food-processing industry. Professor Hall described a report in a Canadian newspaper that said Dr. Alex B. Morrison, Chief of Health Protection Branch of Ottawa, eats a highly nutritious natural diet. He even grinds his own wheat to make whole wheat flour. As Professor Hall said:

When it comes to making public recommendations, they fall back on scientific criteria, which in the case of nutrition and safety, are limited. They can, therefore, pronounce quite sincerely, "There's no evidence that such and such food is harmful." Nevertheless when it comes to their own personal life, they make use of their own scientific intuition and personal convictions.

THE DENUTRIFICATION OF THE STAFF OF LIFE

Our last example of the effect of subtle, sophisticated, chronic malnutrition from food technology will be bread—the staff of life. This is a particular hazard for many elderly people who cannot afford a variety of food or cannot chew rougher, healthier food.

Breadmaking first became industrialized when assembly lines for the manufacture of ships' biscuits began in 1833 by the British Admiralty.

Wheat is ordinarily a nutritious food. Each kernel contains everything necessary to start a new plant. Wheat was originally made into flour, either by pounding it or grinding it between large stones. Eventually it was crushed between steel rollers, which made it possible to remove bran and germ leaving a highly refined white flour.

Freshly milled flour is said to be "green" and is not mature. This means that when baked into bread, the cells of the dough are not tough enough to retain gas, so the loaf does not rise as much. It does not produce an even-textured slice. But white flour stored for several months oxidizes. The oxidation gradually strengthens the protein that will form the walls of the gas-holding cells, and the yellow carotene, which the body uses to make vitamin A, is bleached, producing a pure white slice.

A mill that might make 10,000 one-hundred-pound packs of flour a day would require enormous warehouse space to age the flour. The miller, therefore, adds chemicals to the flour that bleach and mature it in a couple of days. For many years, a bleaching and maturing nitrogen trichloride agent called agene was used. In 1946, agene-treated flour was fed to dogs in a medical experiment and produced a form of hysteria in them. Thereafter, agene was banned. Flour is still bleached, however, but with chlorine, chlorine dioxide, and other chemicals. The long-term effect of chlorinating flour has not been examined, but we do know that nitrogen trichloride reacts with an amino acid, methionine, to form methionine sulphoximine, which causes epileptic-like seizures. Chlorine will have the same reaction. Bleaching also destroys both carotene (the precursor of vitamin A) and vitamin E, and it leaves chlorinated residues of amino acids and fats. Other chemicals added to flour, such as potassium bromate, are "improving" or "maturing" agents that have no bleaching effect.

In 1820, the French physiologist, F. Magendie, found that coarse dark bread kept dogs in good health, while feeding them bread made from white flour killed them within two months. The March 11, 1826, issue of the *Lancet* reported, "A dog fed on fine white bread and water, both at discretion, does not live beyond the fiftieth day. A dog fed on the coarse bread of the military, lives and keeps his health." Since then, there has been a vigorous debate between the supporters of whole wheat bread and the supporters of white bread.

As a cereal chemist, Dr. Hoffer was involved for several years on the side of the white bread group. He was a typical food technologist and assumed that in any balanced diet, white bread was as nutritious as whole wheat bread, especially if it was enriched with thiamine, riboflavin, niacinamide, and iron. Since 90 percent of the public seemed to prefer white bread, it seemed appropriate to provide them with what they wanted. Over the past sixty years, white bread has remained the staple for the majority of the population. A small proportion of the population, perhaps 15 percent, were nutritionally aware and consumed only whole-grain breads. In Great Britain, during World War II, white bread did give way to a darker product, but this was a logistical decision, not a nutritional one. By milling darker flour, Britain could import less wheat and could use its ships instead to haul munitions. Sugar was also rationed at that time. Coincidentally, there was a marked improvement in the overall health of the people. That ended after the war, however, when Britons once more had access to all the sugar and white flour they had a taste for.

THE ROLE OF THE FOOD-PROCESSING INDUSTRY

The processing of food can be divided into three phases:

1. The refining of grains and animal products to obtain proteins, fats, and starches.
2. Treatment of the refined product by chemical procedures that change their molecular structure.
3. Fabrication into the final products.

At each stage, chemical additives are used, each carrying its quota of trace impurities, and natural nutrients are lost.

The whole science of food processing is predicated on fooling the public into thinking it is getting nutritional value when it is not. The result is that the degradation of real food into fake food is bringing on early aging and senility.

Most of this degradation previously occurred in fats and starches but proteins are now being destroyed in the same way. The public is becoming aware that sugars and processed starches are dangerous but so far have not been alerted to the equally dangerous protein extenders. The words "protein" and "high-protein food" still carry a connotation of a high-quality, nutritious food, especially for those with hypoglycemia and for vegetarians who want only plant proteins.

Soybeans contain protein and are good high-protein foods, but to the average North American, they taste unpleasant—like soybeans. Soy protein is converted into textured vegetable protein (TVP), and designed to look and taste like chicken, ham, steak, or turkey. This is how it is done: The protein is removed from ground soybean with petroleum solvent, alcohol, and hydrochloric acid. The refined protein is dissolved in alkali, which is then precipitated into an acid bath as filaments. These filament threads are soaked in artificial binders, flavor, and colors. The cemented fibers are mixed with fat and a few minerals and vitamins to simulate the natural meats. They may *look* real, but they are synthetics. Synthetic meats have not been shown to be safe over long-term use. Dr. George M. Buggs, a nutritionist at the University of California, Berkeley, labels them "a nutritional step backwards." These food artifacts are advertised in such a way as to lead the unwary consumer to believe the soy products are as nutritious as the meat they simulate, when in truth they will probably be proven toxic over the long haul.

In 1940, about 20 percent of our food was processed; today that figure is closer to 80 percent. This means that most people depend heavily on food prepared for them by industry. The rapid development of convenience foods and the decreased status of homemakers have played major roles in this shift.

Convenience foods are attractively packaged, can be stored for a long time, require little work and no culinary skill to prepare, and are palatable. The commercial advertising on radio, television, in newspapers and magazines emphasize the wisdom in selecting "Brand A" over any other food. The homemaker is extolled because she knew enough to open up a can of "Brand A" food, not because of her skill in selecting a food that will nourish and keep her family healthy.

Processed food includes everything derived from food but that has been ripped out of food. It is treated and recombined into what appears to be food. Actually it is invariably only a fraction as nutritious (in terms of supporting life) as the original food.

As we implied, white flour is made from the least nutritious portion of the wheat kernel, lacking vitamins and minerals. Similarly, sugar is the least nutritious fraction of the sugar beet or cane—so much so that the word *nutritious* as used here is inappropriate. It is more correct to say that sugar is the most toxic, poisonous fraction of these plants. It is a fraction that provides calories only in the absence of all the essential components of food.

Processed food also contains chemicals that are added to improve certain properties such as color, flavor, and resistance against deterioration. These chemicals add nothing to the nutritional quality and are toxic for many people. There is no requirement that states that foods adulterated with these chemicals must be safe, as would be the case if the same chemical were to be introduced into medicine as a drug. Theoretically, tranquilizers could be introduced into our food if they were shown to prevent oxidation or rancidity. And they might have these properties, indeed, since they are large molecules that can inactivate enzymes, and these enzymes are partially responsible for oxidation of food on the shelf. There is no requirement that states that processed food must be as nutritious as the food from which it was made.

THE DERIVATION OF FOOD ARTIFACTS

Over hundreds of millennia, we have adapted to natural food—food that is alive, such as seeds and vegetables, or food that recently was alive, like meat and fish. There was little deterioration between the time the food was harvested and when it was consumed. Natural nutrition was the pattern followed by hunting and gathering peoples, and remains so even today among those who are still hunters, such as the primitive !Kung people.

With the development of agriculture and cities, it became necessary to feed a population far from where the food was gathered. The supply had to be stored for long periods of time. This did not alter the nutritional quality too much—until modern chemistry created modern food technology. Briefly, this is an elaborate system for converting food into food artifacts. We will present the evidence that this technological change in what we eat is, to a large measure, responsible for our current health crises and for a major increase in senility. But before we can do so, we will outline ways of thinking about food and food artifacts.

Modern food technology developed through chemistry and brought into existence a whole new industry of food processing. In the nineteenth century, chemists discovered that if they subjected food to certain chemical procedures, specific fractions of the food were isolated. Any chemist following the same procedure could isolate the same kind of material. The substances were purified and were found to have particular characteristic properties.

One of these substances is *protein*. Protein consists of long-chain molecules that in turn are made up of a series of small molecules, called *amino acids*. Proteins contain nitrogen.

Another type of material is oily and dissolves in fat solvents more easily than in water. These materials do not contain nitrogen, and are either short- or long-chain hydrocarbons. They are the *lipids* or *fats*.

The third major material is *carbohydrate*, comprised of starch, cellulose and sugars.

Once these substances were isolated and their properties recognized, chemists, and later nutritionists, began to think of foods as just so much protein, fat, and carbohydrate. But in nature, these substances do not exist in pure form; neither do the pure forms of these substances have the properties characteristic of food. In food, we have very complex mixtures of protein, fat, and carbohydrate molecules. These fractions, on the other hand, are food artifacts because they are the products of chemical ingenuity. If these methods had not been discovered, we would know nothing of protein, fat, and carbohydrates, and we would have no food processing industry.

When we swallow food, it is ground, mixed with enzymes, and digested. During digestion, the protein, fat, and carbohydrates are released more or less at the same time, gradually and slowly. The amino acids, fats, and sugars are released slowly and absorbed slowly. Large amounts are not dumped into the blood all at once and do not stress the liver and other digestive organs, but are absorbed in a regulated manner.

Artifacts are not digested in the same way as whole foods are. Protein artifacts have been altered by chemical processing, as have fat artifacts, and the digestion of them is different. Starches and sugars derived from processing are digested too quickly, dumping large quantities of sugar into the blood. Such dumping plays havoc with the pancreas, liver, and the entire digestive apparatus.

Food artifacts can be reconstituted into artifact concoctions that have no similarity to food, and that have not been proven to be nutritious. There are no studies that show corn flakes to be as nutritious as the original corn, for example; nor are there studies that show white flour to be as nutritious as whole wheat flour. On the contrary, there are a large number of studies that prove that artifacts and their combinations are much less nutritious than the food from which they have been extracted.

Whole foods contain vitamins, minerals, enzymes, and other molecules that are essential for health. It is dangerous and naive to assume that every essential nutrient has already been identified. Separate nutrients are also artifacts. In food, vitamins and minerals are bound to, or are component parts of, other food components. They, too, are realized slowly by the body through its digestive system. These extra nutrients are absorbed slowly along with the other food derivatives, with no rapid increases in concentration in the blood, and less loss in the urine as a result of surpassing the renal threshold.

Food seldom contains such a large quantity of any one component that its consumption is dangerous. Thus, it is possible to live on a diet comprised almost entirely of meats. This contains protein and fat. But living on protein alone, free of fat, can be very dangerous. The food industry has now given us textured protein made from vegetable sources to eat; too much of this material will be harmful.

The most dangerous artifacts produced by processing are the carbohydrates, especially the sugars. They actually cause disability and bring on early death.

We must stop thinking of food as protein, fat, or carbohydrates. It is better to think of protein-rich, fat-rich, or carbohydrate-rich *whole* food. For the sake of convenience, we will continue to discuss proteins, fats, and carbohydrates in this book; we must not forget, however, that these are artifacts—not foods—merely capital-producers for the food processing industry.

The food-processing industry has been sensitive to the charge that they produce unhealthy foods. Fortunately for them, they have been able to obtain cover by government-sponsored food guides or rules. Of these, the most pernicious rule is the myth of the balanced diet. It is true that all the nutrients must be provided and that a diet balanced by including various types of foods, such as vegetables, nuts, seeds, fruit, and meat, will be adequate for most people. But this rule, formulated several decades ago, is no longer adequate when so much of our daily intake consists of junk.

A balanced diet consists of a balance of *foods*. You can't balance inadequate *food artifacts* and have a nutritious diet. We have all seen advertisements that claim that an ounce of cereal, eaten with four ounces of milk and some toast, provides a balanced meal. To illustrate the absurdity of this, one could claim that sawdust combined with milk constitutes a nutritious food. Obviously, this kind of advertising is misleading. The addition of some food artifacts, such as junk cereal, can only decrease the nutritional quality of any food with which it is mixed.

Food processors also defend junk food by saying that one does not live on that alone. No one eats only sugar, or white bread, or sugared drinks. But what is not said is that the drift toward junk food, begun some thirty years ago, has become a stampede. So much of our daily intake is junk and, unfortunately, there is not enough food consumed to make up for the nutritional inadequacies of the junk.

It is now possible to have entirely artifact-filled meals, such as Egg Beaters, sausage, artificial tomato catsup, white bread, jam, and Tang for breakfast; artificial hamburgers, potato chips, apple pie, and ice cream and coffee with sugar for lunch; canned soup, canned peas and carrots, steak, canned pears, wine, and tea with sugar for dinner. The only real food in this total litany is the steak, which may be overcooked and covered with artificial flavor enhancers containing glutamate, too much salt, and other spices. Over 90 percent of the menu here is utter junk. Where is our concept of eating a balanced diet then, when many people eat this way?

Today, one-third of all meals in Canada and the United States are eaten away from the home in restaurants, institutions, airplanes, ships, and elsewhere. Soon we will have 50 percent of the public depending on out-of-home dining to assuage hunger. There are not many restaurants that provide real food; most rely heavily on processed convenience items that need only to be heated to get them out of the kitchen to the customer fast.

The result? We are suffering from subtle, chronic malnutrition, not from lack of quantity of food taken into our bodies but from an absence of nutrition in the food we eat. Senility has to be one of the degenerative processes that affect our nerves and arteries as a result of this sort of wrong practice. We affront nature by thinking our food technologists can duplicate her handiwork. The food industry has duped us with its promises of time saved, less work in food preparation, easy recipes, better taste, attractive dishes, varied menus, vitamin fortification, and all the other advertising lies. What we actually buy when we take these products into our homes is premature aging, senility, heart trouble, and other forms of disability—the diseases of degeneration. These diseases of malnutrition amidst affluence and abundance are the topic of our next chapter.

5. THE ROLE OF FOOD ARTIFACTS

Although people insist on examining all the diets of the world looking for one component, such as cholesterol, to blame as a cause of heart disease, they would be doing better to look for the absence of one component, such as vitamin E. Just as it is dangerous to worry only about cholesterol, it is dangerous to worry only about vitamin E. Total nutrition—Supernutrition—is the main concern. Without it, we are predisposed to premature heart disease.

—Richard A. Passwater, Ph.D.

On July 6, 1979, Carol Tucker Foreman, a former head of the Consumer Federation of America and former Assistant Secretary of the U.S. Department of Agriculture, officially proposed a ban on "junk food" covering such items as sodas, chewing gum, frozen desserts, and some candies in the public schools. The USDA had spent almost two years working to define "junk food" and propose the new rule. About 98 percent of the nation's public schools serving federally subsidized lunches were to be affected by the junk food ban beginning January 1, 1980.

At first appearance, it looked as if a victory had been gained by exponents of orthomolecular nutrition and the coauthors of this book. Schoolchildren who wanted to buy non-nutritional snacks and soft drinks from school vending machines or cafeterias would have to wait until the day's last lunch is served under this rule. More than 25.7 million American children would be forced to comply and, theoretically, be saved from early aging and eventual senility because of better nutrition in their formative years. Vending machine operators might be encouraged to offer fruits, vegetables, fruit juices, and nuts instead of "foods of minimum nutritional value," as the Department of Agriculture labels the junk.[1]

In truth, the victory was hollow indeed, for the proposal still permitted most foods with minimal nutritional value. Junk with less than 5 percent of the recommended daily allowance (RDA) of any one of eight basic nutrients would no longer be acceptable. But the full schedule of RDAs are already inadequate, as we've pointed out in prior chapters. Would you permit just 5 percent now of such a low standard? Further, virtually all of this junk is not food, but food artifacts. Food artifacts are derived by food processors who have built a highly lucrative industry through sophisticated technology. They split components from whole foods and sell them separately in the form of protein, fat, and carbohydrate products. Today, that industry is a trillion-dollar operation in Western industrialized countries. So much money and power are not easily turned aside by a mere government edict.

To better understand how food artifacts perpetuate degenerative diseases in our population, we will discuss the separate components—the food artifacts—extracted from whole food. Eating singular components—that is, just protein, fat, or carbohydrate—is a practice quite hazardous to your health. We will explain why.

PROTEIN ARTIFACTS

Protein artifacts, in the form of reconstituted concoctions, were discussed in the last chapter. Proteins, composed of amino acids, are essential for health. Of the twenty amino acids we require, eight cannot be made in the body. These are called the *essential amino acids*. Foods rich in protein are judged to be of high or low quality, depending upon the amount of essential amino acids present. A high-quality protein-rich food will support life and growth better than low-quality protein.

The diet must contain enough protein to maintain repair and growth. This level varies for different individuals. It is best to consume a slight protein surplus to ensure enough at all times, especially when the body is under severe stress. Generally, too little is much more dangerous than too much. For your own body, you must make a decision as to what is the optimal amount. And whenever possible, obtain your protein from a whole food and not from protein artifacts.

FAT ARTIFACTS

Fats are extracted, or pressed, from foods with a high fat content to provide a more concentrated form of energy. One gram of fat artifact provides nine calories of energy, as compared to four calories per gram of protein or carbohydrate. Fats are the main reservoir of energy in animals, which is an advantage since carbohydrates in mass are bulky and rigid. In contrast, fats at body temperature are fluid and yield to movement. If we were to store our excess calories as carbohydrate, we would be more obese and quite stiff—more like a tree or a potato than like an animal. (Plants store energy primarily as carbohydrates.)

Fats are composed of fatty acid molecules of various lengths and with different degrees of saturation. The term saturation refers to the presence of hydrogen. Saturated fats tend to be rigid, like wax, from being fully hydrogenated. Unsaturated fats, which contain less hydrogen, are more fluid. An unsaturated fat can be saturated by adding hydrogen, which is how liquid fats or oils are converted into solid fats like margarine. Enough hydrogen is added to create a compound with the same melting or liquification point of butter.

A variety of fatty acids are required for health, ranging from short-chain acids like butyric acid, to very long-chain acids. The long-chain fatty acids must be in the diet; they are considered *essential fatty acids.*

All natural fats are "cis" molecules. That means there is a constant three-dimensional relationship of the atoms to each other. The enzymes in the body are designed to metabolize these molecules. If these atoms are put together in any other way, they are excreted by the body, because no natural enzymes exist to metabolize them. When liquid fats are hydrogenated, up to 50 percent of the "cis" molecules are converted into something called "trans" molecules. When you consume margarine, up to one-half is not digestible in the body and gets excreted as waste.

Fats are required because they are essential components of our body; they provide a low-bulk, energy-rich source; many metabolic processes, including the absorption of vitamins that are soluble in fat, require the presence of fat. Too little fat may cause a variety of undesirable reactions, and too much fat will cause obesity.

Usually a person can depend upon his or her palate to tell how much fat is needed. Foods too low in fat tend to be less appetizing, and foods too rich in fat tend to be too greasy. The palate is perverted, however, if fats are blended with sugars, as they are, for example, in ice cream. Then huge quantities of fat may be consumed. The optimum amount of fat in the diet varies from individual to individual. Obese and overweight individuals should eliminate all sugars and then cut back, but not eliminate, fat as well as protein.

There are other substances that have fatlike properties, such as cholesterol and lecithin. The idea that too much cholesterol in the diet causes coronary disease is widespread among physicians. This belief has led to the use of low-fat diets, which in itself would cause no harm, but a low-fat diet in most cases leads to an increase in the consumption of carbohydrate artifacts, especially the sugars. If fats were restricted and sugars eliminated, there would be nothing wrong with such a diet, but by focusing almost entirely on fats (cholesterol), the vital role of sugars in causing coronary disease has been overlooked. This may explain why exclusively low-fat diets have been relatively ineffective in lowering the incidence of coronary disease.

The relationship between fats in the food and coronary disease has been examined seriously by Richard A. Passwater, Ph.D., who has concluded that there is no correlation between the fat content of food and cholesterol or triglyceride levels in the blood. Populations who consume a lot of foods rich in fats may be free of coronary disease, and populations on low-fat diets may have as much coronary disease as we do in North America.

A modern program recommended for decreasing the incidence or the possibility of developing coronary disease consists of four changes in one's pattern of living. These are: (1) to relax; (2) to eliminate smoking; (3) to exercise; and (4) to reduce consumption of fat artifacts. All four recommendations are excellent, and we urge every individual to follow them.

The residents of St. Helena, an island in the Atlantic that is a British dependence, either as a result of fate or of geography, observe all four points. They tend to be relaxed compared to other populations. By tradition, they do not smoke much. They are not heavy consumers of fat, and because the island is hilly and there are few vehicles, they get a lot of exercise going from place to place. One would expect that they would have a low incidence of coronary disease.

When Dr. I. Shine, in his book *Serendipity on St. Helena*, examined the population, he found that the incidence of coronary disease was as high as in England.[2] An examination of the data on consumption of sugar showed that the St. Helenian's consumption of sugar was similar to that of an Englishman, about 120 pounds per year. This demonstrates that sugar, not fats, were implicated as a major factor in causing coronary disease on St. Helena. If fat artifacts (like butter and oil) are not heavily implicated, it stands to reason that fat-rich foods might have even less connection. These foods do possess a major defect, however: they are rich in calories and may lead to obesity in those unable to control their food intake.

While it is true that people with high blood cholesterol and/or high blood triglycerides are more apt to suffer from coronary disease, it does not follow that one causes the other. Both are the result of other biochemical problems, probably symptoms of the Saccharine disease, a syndrome described by T.L. Cleave, M.R.C.P., former Surgeon-Captain in the Royal Navy. When blood fats are elevated, the individual is warned that a change in lifestyle, with perhaps the use of specific treatment, is imperative.

Cholesterol and Hardening of the Arteries

Hardening of the arteries is a prominent factor leading to senility. If the hardening occurs in the heart arteries, the heart can't pump blood through the body efficiently, and the brain is especially sensitive to a decreased blood flow. If this reduced flow continues for a long time, there will be deterioration in the brain. A steady loss of brain neurons must lead to organic deterioration of the brain, ending in senility.

Arteriosclerosis in the vessels of the brain will have the same effect as reduction of blood flow everywhere else. There will be a decreased activity in all parts. The human body must be used. If any function is allowed to deteriorate, it will have some effect upon the rest of the body, including the brain.

We have referred to the idea that cholesterol is a cause of arteriosclerosis. Dr. Hoffer was very sympathetic to this idea over thirty years ago. In 1954, he had developed the conviction that niacin was therapeutic for acute or early schizophrenic patients. Dr. Hoffer's research group in Saskatchewan completed the first double-blind experiment ever recorded in psychiatric literature, the testing of nucleotides on acute and chronic schizophrenics. In a second study, testing was done comparing the effects of niacin and niacinamide against a placebo. The three experimental treatments were incorporated into the standard program then current—psychotherapy plus electroconvulsive therapy (ECT). One year after the last patient had been treated, the state of all the patients was examined and recorded. On breaking the treatment code, the research group found that the addition of niacin doubled the one-year recovery rate from the usual natural recovery rate of 35 percent to an unusual 70 percent recovery.

There were no tranquilizers then. Even today, the improvement rate with tranquilizers is not much better than the natural untreated rate. A survey of schizophrenics treated in Massachusetts between 1945 and 1949, when there were no tranquilizers, and another group from 1965 to 1969, when tranquilizers were the only standard treatment, revealed no difference in outcome. If anything, the early group was better off. Apparently, tranquilizers as the main treatment not only did not help them recover, but made the patients more dependent on welfare and other agencies.

In 1954, Professor Rudl Altschul, then chairman of the department of anatomy at the University of Saskatchewan, approached Dr. Hoffer with his discovery that ultraviolet light lowered cholesterol levels in rabbits and in human patients. He was looking for more volunteers to act as subjects, but could not find any physicians who would cooperate with him. In Dr. Hoffer's role as director of psychiatric research, he had access to several thousand patients who might volunteer. Ultraviolet irradiation (like sunlight), as Altschul proposed to use it, seemed not to be harmful and even potentially beneficial, because very few of Dr. Hoffer's patients had much opportunity to be in the sun. In addition, Dr. Hoffer felt that the increased attention focused on the patients because of the research would be psychologically helpful to them. Dr. Osmond, medical superintendent of the mental hospital at Weyburn, Saskatchewan, agreed.

A few weeks later, Dr. Hoffer picked up Altschul at the railroad station and drove to Weyburn, seventy-two miles away. On the way there and back, they discussed their research interests. Altschul had been a neuro-psychiatrist in Prague when he was forced to leave Europe in 1939. He was invited to join the department of anatomy at the University of Saskatchewan as an instructor, and later became chairman of the department. He could not practice medicine because the College of Physicians and Surgeons insisted he intern for one year before they would allow him to practice. Altschul refused to give up his work for the year and switched his interests instead. He became very involved in research on arteriosclerosis, finally becoming an international authority on the subject.

The professor believed that the main factor in the development of hardening of the arteries was a pathological change in the *intima*, the thin layer of cells that make up the inner lining of each blood vessel, that causes it to lose its ability to repair itself. He was also interested in cholesterol levels, since it had been shown that high blood cholesterol levels were associated with increased deposition of arteriosclerotic plaques.

Rabbits normally do not develop hardening of the arteries, probably because of their high consumption of high-fiber food. When rabbits are fed rations very rich in cholesterol, such as eggs, they still do not become ill. If, however, the egg yolk is prepared in a cake and baked, this food then elevates cholesterol levels quickly. The heating process converts a healthy food into a substance that is pathological for rabbits. Having rabbits available with high cholesterol levels, it was possible to try various procedures such as ultraviolet irradiation to lower cholesterol levels.

As Professor Altschul continued to discuss these ideas, Dr. Hoffer became more and more interested in the idea that the intima had lost its ability to heal itself as well. It reminded him of a tissue-healing occurance that he had come across. For many months, Dr. Hoffer had been annoyed by bleeding gums. Many visits to his dentist and large doses of ascorbic acid did not help. The problem apparently was that he had some malocclusion— some of his teeth did not meet head-on. As a result, when he chewed, there was increased pressure and strain between the tooth and socket. He had concluded that his tissues were less able to repair themselves and were beginning to break down, and that there was no treatment except eventually to extract his teeth. About this time, Dr. Hoffer had started to take niacin, one gram, three times per day, to see what the effect would be, both unpleasant (side effects) and beneficial. About two weeks later, he was astonished to realize that his gums no longer bled when he brushed. His gums had become normal, something his dentist confirmed at the next visit. This was such a surprising event Dr. Hoffer could not forget it.

Dr. Hoffer tried to reason why the vitamin had been so helpful and ruled out any placebo effect. He had not expected any improvement; had not taken it for any therapeutic reason; and no one had ever shown that any placebo could cure severe swelling and inflammation of the gums. He eventually hypothesized that the vitamin restored the ability of his tissues, in which his teeth were embedded, to repair themselves.

Niacin's Effect on Cholesterol

When Altschul spoke about repair of the intima, Dr. Hoffer immediately brought up his personal experience with the niacin. It occurred to him that niacin might also restore the ability of the intima to repair itself and thus might prevent or reverse the damage caused by arteriosclerosis. Altschul asked where he could get some, and Dr. Hoffer promised to send him a pound of pure crystalline niacin.

Several months later, Dr. Hoffer received a phone call from Professor Altschul. He was very excited, shouting, "It works, it works!" Hoffer didn't know what he was talking about until Professor Altschul said he had given niacin to rabbits with chronic high blood cholesterol because they were fed cooked egg yolk. Their cholesterol levels promptly became normal.

He asked how he might find patients with high blood cholesterol. Dr. Hoffer offered to do the study at General Hospital, Regina, where he headed the research program for the province. The next day, Dr. Hoffer approached the hospital pathologist, Dr. J. Stephen, and outlined the problem to him. Could Dr. Stephen help locate a number of patients? He agreed to do so. Within a few days, Dr. Stephen had located about seventy patients, all in the hospital.

After their cholesterol levels were measured, the patients were given niacin, one to three grams per day, for two days. Then their cholesterol levels were remeasured. This very quick study and brief series showed that niacin lowered cholesterol in people as well as in rabbits. The higher the pretreatment cholesterol levels were, the greater was the cholesterol decrease. Results of the study were published in 1955 in a paper by Altschul, Hoffer, and Stephen.[3]

The resistance to vitamins at the time was so great that these findings were rejected, with the first public comment appearing in an abstract of the study results in *Nutrition Reviews*. The author was so convinced that niacin could not lower cholesterol—even though he had never tested it—that he incorrectly read the results. By misreading this table, he was able to prove (he thought) that there was no decrease in cholesterol at all. A few months later, Nutrition Reviews published a letter that pointed out this blatant error.

As we have seen, Professor Altschul's main interest was his research program on atherosclerosis, especially its connection with lesions in the innermost layer of arteries. During meetings with Dr. Hoffer, he was told about the properties of niacin, which was theorized then to increase the repair of damaged intima. Professor Altschul demonstrated that niacin lowered cholesterol levels in his rabbits. A sad footnote to this story is that Professor Altschul tried taking niacin himself, but did not like the niacin flush. In the spring of 1963, he discontinued his niacin supplementation, and about nine months later he died of a coronary occlusion.[4]

Since the early study by Altschul, Hoffer, and Stephen, over 1,200 papers have been published confirming their research work. The cholesterol-fighting property of megadoses of niacin is the only one recognized by the FDA, which illustrates that major discoveries often arise from very inexpensive research. Niacin was the first substance ever shown to lower cholesterol levels and triglyceride levels, but because it is a nutrient, not a drug, it has not been widely promoted.

Another compound—this one a drug, Atromid—also lowers cholesterol. It became widely known and used after its discovery. Its parents—large drug companies—continually reminded physicians of its effectiveness by means of colorful, skillfully drawn ads.

We therefore had a situation where a nonphysiological drug, Atromid, which lowers cholesterol and has no other beneficial effect, was used widely; while a natural nutrient, niacin, which has a large number of beneficial properties including the ability to lower blood fat levels, was widely ignored.

Since his early work, Dr. Hoffer has retained an interest in cholesterol metabolism and how it is altered by the vitamin niacin. However, it has become clear that other vitamins and nutritional factors play major roles as well.

Elevated cholesterol levels indicate there is something wrong with the metabolism of the body. If the underlying disease remains unchecked, just lowering cholesterol by interfering with its synthesis, as is done by some drugs, is not good enough. We fully expect that patients whose hypercholesterolemia is controlled by drugs such as Atromid will continue to suffer from the basic disease of which their elevated cholesterol is merely a symptom. In fact, a very large study in the United States showed that just lowering cholesterol did not halt the progress of arteriosclerosis or coronary death. Long-term use of Atromid will keep cholesterol levels down, but has no other beneficial effect, nor is there much evidence that it prevents coronary disease.

In fact, a clinical study in England has proven that Atromid, used as a hypolipidemic, can be detrimental to your health. In this study, it was found that patients given Atromid to reduce cholesterol levels had a much higher death rate than a control group. There was also a higher incidence of gall bladder disease requiring surgery, and of those operated on, a much higher proportion died. As a result, Atromid is still on the market, but it is rarely prescribed. It has even been banned in some European countries. Niacin, on the other hand, is a natural nutrient that is also a safe broad-spectrum hypolipidemic agent.

Niacin will keep cholesterol levels down, but it has so many other beneficial effects that its use is warranted on a routine basis. As a nutrient, it is bound in the long run to be much safer than Atromid. Atromid is a compound not normally found in the body, which therefore has no way of dealing with it. As with most drugs, it acts because of some toxic effect on some enyzmes in the body. This is not the case for niacin. It is not toxic, even though a large quantity of a niacin may cause a niacin flush. This eventually dissipates, with no harmful effects.

The Absent Relationship Between Senility and Cholesterol

Because it is widely believed that food cholesterol and arteriosclerosis are related, it is important to present the existing evidence that food cholesterol and arteriosclerosis are *not* related—the other side of the cholesterol controversy. And if food cholesterol and arteriosclerosis are not related, there can be little relationship between senility and food cholesterol.

In nature, cholesterol does not exist in a pure form but is a component of tissues of the body. It composes a major proportion of the dry weight of the brain and is used by the body to make bile salts, hormones, and vitamin D_3. About 1.5 to 2 grams of cholesterol are made each day by the average person. No one eats pure cholesterol, but we do eat foods containing cholesterol, such as dairy products, eggs, and meats. Nonetheless, food provides only a small proportion of our daily cholesterol requirement; the rest is made in the body. If more is consumed, less is made, and vice versa. For this reason, healthy people who eat just whole food have little to fear.

An excessive intake of sugar and/or of fat can increase cholesterol levels. However, sugar and fat are food artifacts that should not be part of any person's food intake.

It is generally believed that there is a wide range of normal human cholesterol levels, usually between 150 and 250 milligrams (mg) per 100 milliliters of blood. Some laboratories accept even higher levels as normal, a practice we believe to be a serious error. High cholesterol levels indicate there is something seriously wrong with the metabolism, and it must be corrected. When it is corrected, the cholesterol levels will return to normal.

We believe that the normal cholesterol range is 150 to 200 milligrams per 100 milliliters, and that a desirable optimum is around 180 milligrams. Many years ago, Dr. Hoffer studied the effect of niacin on the cholesterol levels of a large number of patients. He found that the amount of change depended upon the original levels. In other words, the more abnormal the problem was, the greater was the corrective response. If cholesterol levels were less than 165 milligrams, they soon rose to that level. Several patients with original cholesterol levels below 120 were at 150, or better, while taking niacin. Cholesterol levels over 165 were decreased, with the highest levels showing the greatest decreases. Dr. Hoffer concluded that it was more accurate to consider niacin a normalizer of cholesterol levels rather than a cholesterol-reducing agent. Practically, this distinction makes little difference, since the vast majority of patients have too much, not too little, blood cholesterol; but the great theoretical significance of this observation has been ignored. Instead of searching for the mechanism by which niacin lowers cholesterol, scientists should have been looking for those aspects of metabolism normalized by niacin.

The idea that food rich in cholesterol causes hardening of the arteries, with consequent coronary disease, has paved the way for the food-processing industries to provide special foods with little cholesterol. A second idea, that polyunsaturated fats will lower cholesterol levels, has created food artifacts high in these fats. Yet both of these approaches, which seemed sound many years ago, have turned out to be incorrect.

Two basic—but incorrect—propositions should be reexamined: First, that foods rich in cholesterol cause arteriosclerosis and coronary disease; and second, that unsaturated fats have beneficial value in preventing heart and vascular disease.

The first proposition would be true if the following statements were true:

- Cholesterol-rich foods increase blood fats to abnormally high levels.
- Abnormally elevated cholesterol levels are a cause of arteriosclerosis.

Extensive research has shown, however, that each statement is mostly wrong. There are many people and groups of people who eat a lot of cholesterol-rich foods and yet have normal or low blood cholesterol levels. Conversely, there are many people and groups of people who eat foods low in cholesterol and have high blood cholesterol levels. The correlation between the cholesterol content of food and cholesterol levels in the blood is so slight that a very large series of patients must be studied in order to find a statistically significant relationship.

The correlation between blood cholesterol levels and coronary occlusions is somewhat closer. This is not surprising, since the fact that the basic metabolic fault that causes both elevated cholesterol levels and coronary disease would ensure such a relationship. In the same way, the two front wheels of a wagon are correlated even if the propulsive power does not come from either one. A correlation does not prove cause and effect, just because a lack of correlation disproves it. The correlation between triglycerides and coronary disease is closer still, indicating that triglyceride levels may be a better indicator of the basic metabolic fault that leads to arteriosclerosis.

Since there is such a low relationship, there seems little point in trying to lower cholesterol levels without doing something about the basic metabolic fault. To give hypocholesterolemic substances while ignoring those factors that are responsible for the problem seems inappropriate. In combination with proper nutrition and essential nutrient supplements, these hypocholesterolemic compounds are valuable.

There is some evidence that the consumption of polyunsaturated fats will lower cholesterol levels. Since these are artifacts, however, all the evidence of the harmful effects of artifacts applies as well. There is no evidence that *foods* rich in these vegetable fats have any significant effect. The American Heart Association has reported there is no conclusive proof that these fats prevent heart disease. They should have made their statement stronger by stating there is a good deal of evidence showing that there is such a slight relationship that it is heavily outweighed by the possible toxicity of polyunsaturated fats.

Diets rich in polyunsaturates have been shown to deplete vitamin E from the body. These fats possess highly reactive double bonds that have an affinity for other atoms. In saturated fats, these reactive bonds disappear. The unsaturated fats are easily oxidized inside and outside the body. In the body, unsaturated fats produce exceedingly reactive free radicals that increase cross-linkages (thereby creating blockages). Vitamin E destroys these free radicals. The consumption of polyunsaturated fats creates an increased demand for vitamin E. The increased production of free radicals is one of the factors that causes premature aging and senility. When heated, these polyunsaturates form toxic polymers that are highly oxidized. Fats or fat-rich foods that are fried too much become much more toxic. Animals fed too many polyunsaturated fats have lost their hair, been stunted, and died early. These fats have also been linked with circulatory sludging. Finally, some data suggest that these fats increase the possibility of cancer, arteriosclerosis, premature aging, and reduced life span.

All the evidence we have referred to reinforces our conclusion that no one need fear whole food, whether it is rich in fat, protein, or carbohydrate. What are to be feared and avoided are the food artifacts, whether they are rich in protein, carbohydrates, or fats. Since there is a relationship between cholesterol and circulatory disease, but no connection of either to food, then it is obvious that there is even less connection to cerebral vascular disorders and to senility. There are many factors causing senility that we should worry about and correct. The consumption of cholesterol-rich food is not among the main ones.

In concluding this section on the cholesterol artifact we have to point out that Dr. Mark D. Altschul rejects the idea that cholesterol causes atherosclerosis. He maintains that hardening of the arteries is due to injury to artery linings resulting from blood flow disturbances. These occur at certain sites determined by the effect of the vessels on flow mechanics. This is a finding that relates to at least four other theories on the formation of atherosclerosis.

When Dr. Hoffer first met Professor Rudl Altschul, with whom the effect of niacin on cholesterol was found, he spoke about this mechanical effect. Professor Altschul's favorite hypothesis was that the inner lining, the intima, of the vessels at stressed areas did not repair itself as well. Dr. Mark Altschul has written that atherosclerosis occurs along the inner side of the curves in the arteries, downstream from where they divide, or branch, and at points where the arteries are rigidly fixed in position by fat or by scar tissue. At these points there is a pulling or lifting effect. In response, these areas thicken, the cells change and increase, and plaque forms into a thick protuberance that spreads in all directions along the lining of the artery. These damaged cells no longer make enough protein for repair, but create fat instead. This is why atherosclerotic plaques are full of cholesterol and other fats, especially the polyunsaturated fatty acids.[5,6]

Factors such as chemical poisons, viral infections, and radiation are harmful to the intima. Common poisons are carbon monoxide and cadmium from smoking, and cholesterol that has been oxidized.

Dr. Altschul's program for avoiding atherosclerosis is:

- Avoid high concentrations of carbon monoxide. Smoke less and keep out of air too rich in auto exhaust.
- Avoid obesity.
- Avoid processed foods containing dried egg yolk or powdered milk. (We would amend this by advising everyone to avoid all food artifacts—junk food.)
- Treat diabetes and high blood pressure.
- Exercise more.

This does not mean that diet and nutrition have nothing to do with heart disease. We have no doubt that good nutrition will decrease the incidence and prevalence of heart disease.[7]

In an article in the *New England Journal of Medicine*, Dr. George V. Mann writes that the use of nutrition to control heart disease has ended. We cannot agree. Dr. Mann has, however, convincingly shown that the use of low-cholesterol diets alone has not been effective. He has nothing to say about junk-free, high-fiber diets, but these have not been examined yet on as massive a scale as the low fat diets have been.[8]

Dr. Mann referred to two studies that showed no relation between diet and blood cholesterol levels, the Framingham study, on 1,000 subjects, and the Tecumseh study, on 2,000 subjects. He also referred to clinical trials where low-fat diets had no effect on coronary disease but in which there was an increase in cancer.

Data showing an increase in consumption of polyunsaturated fats from 10.7 grams per day in 1911 to 24.2 grams per day in 1974 suggest that this did not decrease coronary deaths; but at the same time, total fat intake went up from 125 grams to 158 grams.

CARBOHYDRATE ARTIFACTS

Carbohydrates are primarily suppliers of energy; of the big three artifacts, they are the hewers of wood and the drawers of water. Unlike protein and fats, they are not components of body structures. Nor is much energy stored as carbohydrate. They are digested, absorbed, and rapidly used for the provision of heat and energy for muscle contraction.

Carbohydrates are divided into the simple and complex. Simple carbohydrates are the sugars, such as glucose, fructose, and galactose (monosaccharides), and sucrose or lactose (disaccharides). All the carbohydrates are made from the simplest sugars; when digested, the carbohydrates are broken down into these sugars. They are present in small concentrations in the body. The amount in a person who has not eaten for many hours is around 80 milligrams of glucose per 100 milliliters or less than 1 percent, of blood. But this quantity is essential for life because the cells depend upon glucose for life.

The body has several ways of ensuring that the amount of glucose in blood remains reasonably stable. Unfortunately, the sugar level mechanism will break down when food artifacts are consumed instead of food. Complex carbohydrates are minor components of the body. Liver and muscle tissue can store small quantities of a complex carbohydrate called *glycogen*. Complex carbohydrates are found primarily in plants. They are subdivided into those not digestible by man, such as cellulose, lignin, and wood, and those that are digestible, such as the starches.

As with protein and fat artifacts, starch and sugar do not exist as such in nature. Foods rich in starch, such as potatoes, wheat, or corn, also contain all the other food constituents, such as proteins, fats, vitamins, and minerals. In contrast, pure wheat or potato starch is a pure chemical, as are the sugars.

Carbohydrate-rich foods are safe to eat. Refined artifacts rich in carbohydrate, such as white flour, are less nutritious because so many of the other essential components have been removed. The least nutritious complex carbohydrates are the starches, such as those that are used to thicken gravies and pastries. They are, however, considerably safer than the sugars, for they are digested slowly. The released sugars are absorbed into the blood slowly so that the digestive apparatus, which must maintain steady blood glucose levels, is not swamped.

Indigestible complex carbohydrates have not been given much of a role in human nutrition. They were generally referred to as fiber, and most physicians either ignored them or recommended that they be avoided by patients with peptic ulcers or colitis. Low-residue diets have had a long and dishonorable history in medicine; dishonorable because it was a lack of fiber that was mainly responsible for these conditions. The low-residue treatment merely made the disease worse.

The importance of fiber was emphasized for many years by a few surgeons and physicians, who were rewarded by being considered eccentrics or quacks. Recently, the work of Cleave, Campbell, and Burkitt, and a few others has brought fiber back into consideration. Dr. Burkitt, world renowned for his identification of a type of cancer, has been tireless in promoting the consumption of fiber. More correctly, he has been promoting the use of foods rich in fiber content. The use of fiber alone is about as illogical as using other food artifacts alone.

Fiber serves many functions in the digestive tract. It acts as a carrier for other food components, and slows down the rate of digestion. A coarse fibrous particle is degraded more slowly than a finely ground, fiber-free particle. As a result, the products of digestion are absorbed more slowly.

Fiber acts as a carrier for many substances that are excreted via the gastrointestinal tract such as bile salts, heavy metals, pigments, and many other toxins. By binding these substances, it dilutes them and decreases their chance of harming the interior of the intestinal wall. This is how it protects against the toxic carcinogenic effect of bile salts. Fiber also increases the rate at which the contents traverse the bowel. This decreases contact time between feces and intestinal wall, thus allowing less opportunity for damage to the bowel.

Fiber provides bulk. It binds with several times its weight of water to form a semisolid colloid. This provides some substance for the peristaltic waves to act upon, and increases passage rate. In the absence of fiber, feces become hard and irritating. Passage through the gut is slow and difficult, and defecation becomes painful. The result is constipation. This is a particular problem for elderly people. Laxatives are one of the most common over-the-counter medicines purchased by people over sixty-five. Constipation also causes back pressure on the veins in the abdomen, which can lead to varicose veins and hemorrhoids. Constant straining at stool resulting from constipation will also lead to diverticulitis, an inflammation of the diverticuli (the pouches in the wall of the large intestine), and diverticulosis, a bulging of the muscular layer of the large intestine.

Cleave concluded that consumption of low-fiber food artifacts such as sugar, white flour, and white rice leads to the *Saccharine disease*. The conditions we have briefly described are merely symptoms of this Saccharine disease. There are three main aspects of the condition:

1. *A deficiency of protein that leads to peptic ulcer.* This does not mean that the daily intake of protein is too low, but means that a large intake of food artifacts is so deficient in protein that there is not enough there to bind with the acid released in the stomach. If the only protein-rich meal is at dinner, while during the rest of the day the person consumes copious quantities of coffee, soft drinks, alcohol, and/or sugar, we have a situation where the total protein intake is adequate, but where for most of the day free acid lies in the stomach with no protein to bind it.

2. *A surplus of rapidly digested and absorbed starchy artifacts and sugars.* This leads to obesity, diabetes, coronary disease, and relative hypoglycemia. The latter condition is found in nearly every alcoholic, drug addict, and obese person. It is probably present in 50 percent of our population (40 percent are obese, 5 percent are alcoholic and drug addicts, and 3 percent are diabetic).

3. *A deficiency of fiber that leads to constipation and its consequences such as diverticuli, ulcerative colitis, and even cancer of the bowel.*[9]

The chief villains among the carbohydrate artifacts are the sugars, because they are palatable, inexpensive, and ever-present in food artifacts. It is becoming increasingly difficult to find food artifacts free of sugar, and when they are found, they tend to be more expensive. Thus, pure, unsweetened applesauce is more expensive than the applesauce with sugar added. Sugar-free peanut butter costs more than ordinary peanut butter containing sugar. This is a way of selling sugar at peanut prices and it is an outrage.

The consumption of sucrose (table sugar) has remained fairly constant for the past fifty years. But the consumption of other equally toxic sugars, such as corn syrup and dextrose, has risen markedly. The average North American sugar intake was 136.1 pounds per person in 1990. The Sugar Association, which represents sucrose only, continues to maintain that consumption of sugar (the one it sells) has remained constant. But most people don't realize how much hidden sugar is present in the processed food artifacts they eat. At least 70 percent of all sugars consumed (or 95 pounds out of 136 total consumption) are obtained from processed food artifacts.

Dr. D.M. Hegsted, a professor of nutrition at the Harvard Graduate School of Public Health, stated at a press conference in Washington on January 14, 1977,

> The diet we eat today was not planned or developed for any particular purpose. It is a happenstance related to our affluence, the productivity of our farmers, and the activities of our food industry. The risks associated with eating this diet are demonstrably large.[10]

The yearly consumption of sugars has increased enormously in the past 200 years. There has been a striking increase year by year, except for the periods during the two world wars. The annual per capita consumption of sugar dropped from about 100 pounds to approximately 60 pounds during the first war, and experienced proportionate decrease during the second war. These two periods were marked by a striking improvement in the health of the residents of Great Britain. They became healthier, both physically and mentally. This confounded the psychosomatic theorists who had predicted that there would be a major increase in psychosomatic illnesses, such as peptic ulcer and ulcerative colitis, because of the stress of war.

Since World War II the consumption of sugar has marched steadily upward. It may finally have peaked and taken a downward turn now. The officers of the companies that sell sugar-rich products have become concerned at the drop in per capita consumption of sugar, and have launched campaigns to persuade consumers that not only is sugar harmless, but it is positively beneficial, almost indispensable, for our health. One of their spokesmen, a professor of nutrition from Harvard University, Frederick Stare, said that it would be perfectly safe for the average American to double his or her yearly intake of sugar—this could mean over 250 pounds! The decrease in sugar intake must be credited to the increasing awareness of the public of the harmful effects of sugar. We should aim for a reduction to 60 pounds per person, per year, as an immediate target, and an eventual reduction to under 10 pounds.

In 1977, Senator George McGovern's Select Committee on Nutrition and Human Needs recommended that sugar consumption be reduced by 40 percent, to account for 15 percent of total caloric intake. Actually, the optimum quantity of sugar in the daily diet is zero. Every person should immediately aim for this optimum consumption, if possible. Unfortunately, just a small fraction of the public is aware of the dangers inherent in the overconsumption of sugar.

Sugar is especially harmful to the aged. Decades of sugar consumption make it almost impossible to eliminate it. It tastes good and provides a lot of calories that require little effort to consume. Often, elderly people can't chew fibrous foods and prefer softer, sweeter food artifacts. Sugared tea, white toast, and jam are often the main meal for many elderly people. Whenever we see an elderly, senile person, we immediately visualize many decades of massive sugar consumption. We suggest that senility is one of the consequences of the Saccharine disease.

Let us reiterate, however, that complex polysaccharides (*foods* rich in starch) are nutritious, safe, and important. These include whole-grain cereals, vegetables, and nuts. They must occupy a prominent place in our diets, unless a person is allergic to any of these foods.

The authors believe that all artifacts rich in sugars and starches—in fact, *all* food artifacts—should be labeled with a warning that they will be harmful to your health. Perhaps even a new symbol for slow poison should be developed for sugar, much as the skull is used to denote more rapidly acting poisons.

6. RISK FACTORS

OF SENILITY

Men and women in modern society are wreaking havoc on their physical and mental health and on that of their families and friends. They seem to forget that modern life means great change, and great change is great stress, but it may be good or bad stress. . . .Some people are killed in automobile accidents or by other physical forces of destruction, but stress, though an intangible, can kill just as swiftly and surely.

—Hans Selye, Ph.D., M.D., D.Sc.

An old lady is placed in a municipal nursing home by her children. An executive is named senior vice president of his company. Another loses an important sale. The mother of the bride cries during the wedding ceremony. A child packs for summer camp. A television game-show contestant wins a trip to Acapulco. A shopper in Chicago walks in and out of air-conditioned specialty shops on Michigan Avenue on a hot summer day. A bridge toll taker inhales the exhaust of 550 cars daily as he does his job. A motorcyclist smashes his vehicle into the rear end of a truck and is rushed to the hospital with broken bones, a concussion, and much loss of blood. A soda-fountain worker eats gobs of her ice cream concoctions continuously throughout her working hours.

What do all of these people and situations have in common? Stress. Mental, emotional, thermal, chemical, or physical stress is not itself a disease or an illness. It is part of life, generated by the ever-changing life situations everyone must face. It is not necessarily bad or good. In fact, stress is often the spice of life.

STRESS

Still, stress is viewed today as one of the major and pervasive problems facing the citizens of the industrialized Western countries and Japan. For too many, the stresses they live and work with result in extreme distress and the conditional precursor of many maladies, such as high blood pressure, ulcers, coronary heart disease, depression, suicide, alcoholism, drug addiction, strokes, insomnia, asthma, migraine and tension headaches, kidney disease, cancer, and more. Stress is recognized as a primary risk factor of senility and premature aging as well.

Indeed, stress ranks among the world's highest risk factors for bringing on all kinds of health problems. People in ever-increasing numbers are affected and are being treated for a host of major and minor disabilities that appear to be directly related to the stress conditions under which they live. Ours is a fast-paced, success-oriented society riddled with tension, strain, anxiety, and unnatural, technological alterations in the ecology.

Industry executives and government bureaucrats have begun to look with alarm at the effect stress is having on corporate earnings and the national economy. Estimates by industrialists indicate that the United States alone loses more than $15 billion annually due to stress-related absenteeism, premature death, hospitalization for disease, accidents, resignations, mental illness, and low overall productivity.

What is stress? Doctors and researchers define stress as the response of the body to change—pleasant or unpleasant. If it is unpleasant, an individual may begin to experience physical symptoms, such as pain and gastrointestinal distress, or emotional symptoms, such as anxiety and feelings of inadequacy or insecurity. He or she may become nauseous, irritable, annoyed, hesitant, pessimistic, and even desperate.

In industry, one of the greatest sources of stress in any job is the threat of being fired, laid off, or replaced. According to a United States Congressional Committee report, 1,500 suicides, 1,700 homicides, 25,000 strokes and heart and kidney deaths, 5,500 mental hospital admissions, and 800 deaths from cirrhosis of the liver, occurring over a five-year period, were all associated with a 1.4-percent rise in unemployment in 1970.

Not all stress is job related, of course. Often anxiety develops from a preoccupation with personal affairs: problems with a spouse or with one's children. Financial worries are a major source of stress for people of all ages. These domestic difficulties can cause depression, anxiety, and ultimately physical problems from psychosomatic difficulties.

In one of a series of seminars on stress and how to cope sponsored by Riker Laboratories, Inc., F.C. Goldthorpe, M.D., Manager of Medical Education, explained that stress can be pleasant or unpleasant and that changes caused by stress are not always detrimental, unless the body is unable to handle them. The key, he said, is how the body copes with stress.

Dr. Goldthorpe suggested that each person judge how well he or she was responding to stress. The body has its own alarm system that signals the body to bring the system back to normal. Without a respite from an anxiety-producing situation, a person is in danger of exhaustion and serious illness—even death.

According to some researchers, personality has much to do with how well the body takes stress. People who are aggressive and striving are twice as likely to suffer coronary disease as their counterparts who may be as competent but lack the same obsessive drive for success.

A number of techniques that evolved out of the human potential movement are often taught in workshops to help over-achievers reduce their tendencies toward self-stress. Many of the workshops are devoted to teaching these people "relaxation" exercises, some of which involve stretching out on floors and doing specific tension-relaxation exercises. Another exercise, called "instant relaxation," involves closing the eyes, taking a deep breath, holding it in to the count of five, and exhaling while intoning the word "relax." This exercise is designed to "neutralize" the stimulus causing the stress, at least for the moment.

Fitness programs are also offered in most communities, as a means of easing tension and stress. Some programs include stress-breakers such as mountain climbing and meditation. Others consist of behavioral clinics to teach attendees how to solve personal problems, including how to cope with "midlife crisis."

Another method used to combat stress is to have individuals rate themselves on a "life change and physical ailments" scale, a list that rates by points such stressful events as the death of a spouse (100), marital separation (65), trouble with an employer (23), and so on.

The scale, it has been shown, is an early warning device for detecting oncoming illness. Nearly 90 percent of the people scoring more than 300 points during the twelve-month period that they participated in life change tests experienced a serious health problem. The scale shown in the inset on pages 96–97, developed

The Life Change Scale

If any of these life events occurred to you in the last year, check the "Happened" column and enter its value in "Your Score" column.

Item Number	Item Value	Happened (√)	Your Score	Life Event
1	100	_____	_____	Death of your spouse
2	73	_____	_____	Divorce from your spouse
3	65	_____	_____	Separation from your spouse
4	63	_____	_____	Being assigned a term in jail
5	63	_____	_____	Death of a close family member
6	53	_____	_____	Personal injury or illness (serious)
7	50	_____	_____	New marriage
8	47	_____	_____	Being fired from a steady job
9	45	_____	_____	Marital reconciliation
10	45	_____	_____	Retirement from work
11	44	_____	_____	Change in health of a family member
12	40	_____	_____	Learning that you (or your spouse) are pregnant
13	39	_____	_____	Difficulties with your sexual abilities
14	39	_____	_____	Gain of a new family member
15	39	_____	_____	Readjustment (major) in business
16	38	_____	_____	Radical change in finances
17	37	_____	_____	Death of a close friend
18	36	_____	_____	Change to a different line of work
19	35	_____	_____	Alteration in number of marital arguments
20	31	_____	_____	Taking on a mortgage over $10,000
21	30	_____	_____	Foreclosure of mortgage or loan

Item Number	Item Value	Happened (√)	Your Score	Life Event
22	29	_____	_____	Responsibilities change at work
23	29	_____	_____	Son or daughter leaving home
24	29	_____	_____	Irritating trouble with in-laws
25	28	_____	_____	Recognition for outstanding achievements
26	26	_____	_____	Unemployment or retirement of spouse
27	26	_____	_____	Beginning or ending schooling
28	25	_____	_____	Change in living conditions
29	24	_____	_____	Revision of personal habits
30	23	_____	_____	Trouble with your boss
31	20	_____	_____	New work hours or conditions
32	20	_____	_____	Change of residence
33	20	_____	_____	Change of school or major
34	19	_____	_____	Marked alterations in recreation
35	19	_____	_____	Change in church or club activities
36	18	_____	_____	Major change in social activities
37	17	_____	_____	Taking out a loan or mortgage of less than $10,000
38	16	_____	_____	Change in sleeping habits
39	15	_____	_____	Change in the number of family get-togethers
40	15	_____	_____	Change in eating habits
41	13	_____	_____	Going on vacation
42	12	_____	_____	Year-end Christmas holidays
43	11	_____	_____	Committing a minor violation of the law

Your total score for 12 months is: _____

by Thomas H. Holmes at the University of Washington, School of Medicine in Seattle, may predict if the amount of stress in your life will make you ill.

STRESS PLUS MALNUTRITION

We have no doubt that malnutrition alone will hasten the onset of senility, or that severe unremitting stress will do the same, perhaps by a common mechanism. When they come together in a single elderly person, the combination is devastating to mental and physical health. The result will surely be senility.

Severe physical and emotional stress greatly increases the loss of vitamin C and zinc, both water soluble nutrients. Most likely, there is a similar increased demand for all nutrients when one is under stress, for stress may induce a state of malnutrition just as real as that which follows faulty diet. When both severe stress and malnutrition are combined, the effect is grossly magnified.

A large number of people were exposed to this combination of severe stress and malnutrition between 1935 and 1945, in Europe and the Far East. The concentration and prisoner of war camps of Europe exposed millions of people to monstrous stress from which very few escaped. Those who survived have remained scarred both physically and emotionally.

About 25 percent of the Canadian soldiers held in prison camps died there. In some camps housing American and English soldiers, the death rate may have been higher. When the surviving Canadian prisoners of war (POWs) were released, many were near death, having lost up to one-third of their weight. In camp, they suffered from chronic infections, a variety of deficiency diseases of which scurvy, pellagra, and beriberi were most easily recognized, and severe emotional and psychological shock. Many of these ex-POWs have been studied repeatedly since the end of the war. Stan Sommers collected and published the results of these studies in the *ExPOW Bulletin* over a two year period. Physicians who were prisoners have had no difficulty recognizing the pernicious effect of incarceration, but physicians unfamiliar with the background of the ex-POW and unfamiliar with modern nutrition often fail to recognize why their patients do not get well. These doctors may fall back on the idea that the illnesses are psychosomatic—that they are ill because of psychological conflicts.

The delayed effects of imprisonment have been divided into

two phases. The first is the stage of early aftereffects, which lasted roughly from 1947 to about 1955. The second is the period of delayed aftereffects. The symptom of early aftereffects in young adults is chronic fatigue, which means they find it difficult to work. The delayed effects include premature aging, senility, and early death.

The cardiovascular and nervous systems of ex-POWs were most seriously affected. Every study of the cardiovascular system shows pathology. One study of 10,000 autopsies from Dachau showed that the degree of arteriosclerosis was directly related to the duration of detention at camp. In 50 percent of all ex-POWs, half had residual psychiatric symptoms, the most common of which were fatigue and hypersomnia.

G.W. Beebe (1975) reported in the *American Journal of Epidemiology* that ex-POWs suffered from persistent disease of the cardiovascular system, the gastrointestinal tract, and the eyes; they also developed neuroses.[1] Negsfer (1970), published five years before in the same journal, found that ex-POWs who had been incarcerated by the Japanese suffered a mortality rate 50 percent higher than general U.S. rates for the first ten years following release. Ex-POWs who had been incarcerated in Korea suffered a 40-percent higher death rate, while ex-POWs that were incarcerated in Europe suffered no increase, except for those hospitalized for malnutrition. POWs in European camps were generally not treated as badly as those in Japanese camps. POWs who had been in Korean and Japanese camps were sicker in general; ex-POWs who had been in Japanese camps were especially marked by schizophrenia, anxiety, alcoholism, and arteriosclerotic disease.[2]

These clinical investigations forced the general conclusion that these prison camps induced premature aging—the most characteristic finding. One year at war aged a soldier as much as two years of peace; one year in a camp aged a soldier the equivalent of four years at peace. A POW held by Japan for four years was at age sixty-five as old as a man of eighty-one who had never been in a prison camp. Our own estimate is that one year of living in a prison camp is equal to living five years at home. Life span was decreased ten to fifteen years for war prisoners, and all POWs, irrespective of country of origin, suffered to the same degree. Thus, soldiers who were held as prisoners in World War II are at high risk of turning senile.

A brief quotation from Colonel E.C. Jacobs, M.D., in the *ExPOW Bulletin* for 1978, volume 35, vividly described the combination of malnutrition and stress characteristic of prison camp life:

> The Japanese army had made no preparation to feed, to transport or to house any of the Filipino-American forces. The outcome was a hundred mile "Death March" from Bataan to Camp O'Donnell at Tarlac. This forced march lasted over a period of two weeks and was made essentially without food or water, resulting in the inhumane annihilation of some 17,000 Filipino Americans and the broken bodies of all survivors. Those captives who couldn't keep up were clubbed or bayonetted in full view of the others. During the following forty months of incarceration, another 31,200 prisoners were to succumb to starvation, deficiency diseases, dysenteries, malaria and Japanese indifference and neglect. The survivors were scarred for life, and most of their lives were shortened by many years.
>
> A typical diet varied greatly. It was never adequate, at its best being composed of a poor grade of rice and weeds. A half canteen (about 8 oz. or 160 calories) of polished rice as a thin gruel was given two or three times per day. It contained fine gravel and insects. The weeds were from water buffalo wallows. At worst, no food was given at all.
>
> About once a week, a water buffalo was slaughtered for 5000 to 12,000 prisoners. But after Japanese chefs removed choice cuts for themselves, each prisoner received between 4 to 16 calories of protein.[3]

The daily diet never reached 1,000 calories per day.

In our opinion, our society, even with no war conditions prevailing, affords a similar combination of stress and malnutrition, although admittedly to a lesser degree, and this is a major factor in hastening senility among the older population. How many senile people today had this forced upon them prematurely by the Great Depression of the thirties, when stress was great and many had little food to eat? We will never know unless an attempt is made to do such a retrospective study. Yet we do know that ignorance of what is good nutrition allows similar conditions to continue even now—not out of a lack of abundance, but from lack of nutritional quality in the foods we eat.

DECREASED IMMUNE DEFENSES

Aging may be due in part to a decrease in our immunological defenses. The immune system is comprised of cells that produce antibodies against foreign molecules or invaders, and the antibodies inactivate the invading cells. With age, fewer antibodies are produced, making us more vulnerable to infections and cancer. Autoimmune diseases cause our cells to mistake healthy cells for foreign cells and attack them with antibodies. Autoimmune diseases are degenerative diseases associated with aging.

Slow-acting viruses that require decades for destructive effects to develop may be present. The virus may so alter body cells that they seem foreign and are attacked by antibodies, thus hastening aging.

The brain itself may control aging by its regulation of hormones. Over the past two decades, it has become clear that the pituitary and hypothalamic hormones are involved in brain activity and have an effect upon behavior. Research shows that the behavior of rats becomes abnormal when their pituitary glands are removed. Behavior is also abnormal in rats who have hereditary diabetes insipidus, where vasopressin, an antidiuretic hormone, is not available. Giving the rats adrenocorticotropic hormone (ACTH)—which stimulates the growth of the adrenal gland cortex and its secretion of corticosteroids—or vasopressin restores normal behavior.

In rats whose pituitary glands are removed, behavior becomes normal when they are given fragments of ACTH, lipotropin, and vasopressin that have no hormone properties. Neuroleptic drugs related to ACTH have a short-term effect on behavior. Those related to vasopressin have a long-term effect.

Vasopressin is involved in memory, and, of course, failing memory is a main characteristic of senility. Rats with a genetic defect in the synthesis of vasopressin are inferior in retaining active and passive avoidance behavior—they do not remember as well. Vasopressin appears to promote memory consolidation or retrieval.

De Wied and his colleagues (1977) reviewed the evidence that vasopressin is involved in memory. A single injection of arginine-8-vasopressin increased resistance to extinction of a pole-jumping avoidance response in rats. Smaller amounts placed in the ventricles of the brain were as effective.[4,5]

De Wied concluded, "Findings so far indicate the existence of neuropeptides which affect learning, memory and motivation." Vasopresssin is such a neuropeptide. Other neuropeptides have opiate-like activity and affect sleep, thirst, aggression, and the development of tolerance and physical dependence.[6]

Legros and colleagues (1978) found that blood levels of hormones, including vasopressin, that are produced in the pituitary gland decrease in people after age fifty. They tested the effect of inhaled vasopressin on memory. Twelve subjects were given sixteen international units of vasopressin daily, one puff to each nostril three times per day. Eleven were given a placebo. Those on vasopressin did better on attention, concentration, motor rapidity, and memory tests.[7]

Oliveros (1978) reported that four patients with amnesia responded to vasopressin. One alcoholic patient responded least well. The remaining three, who were suffering from post-traumatic retrograde amnesia (loss of memory of events before the amnesia) and anterograde amnesia (loss of memory of the events that occurred after the amnesia—often including the event that caused it), responded better.[8]

OBESITY AND HYPOGLYCEMIA

Average Americans and Canadians consume over 125 pounds of simple sugars per person per year, and their intake of sucrose—table sugar—has remained constant for the past fifty years. The commercial sugar association makes much of this leveling off in its papers and press releases. What they ignore is that other sugars, such as corn syrup and dextrose, have been consumed at an ever-increasing rate. The latter are usually hidden in foods where they are least expected, such as mayonnaise, soups, crackers, and so on. Most patients placed on sugar-free diets are astonished when they read the labels of boxes and cans. There is an undeniable relationship between the consumption year by year of these toxic levels of sugars and the Saccharine disease. We have already described the manifestations of this disease. Let us now turn to the combined effect of sugar and salt in our diet.

Dr. D.J.R. Rowe (1978) addressed the additive effect of salt and sugar. Canadians and Americans eat an average of 10 grams of salt (one-third ounce) per day, while only about 0.5 grams are required. More than 2 grams per day is dangerous for hypertensives. It is generally accepted that high blood pressure results from a disturbance of the equilibrium between noradrenaline and the sympathetic nervous system, which together regulate the constriction of blood vessels. Also recognized is an increased sensitivity and responsiveness to angiotensin II, a substance in the blood that causes blood vessels to tighten, and noradrenaline in the smooth muscle of artery walls. The latter feature may be associated with excessive sodium intake in predisposed persons. Hypertension and obesity are related to pathological changes in the brain that lead to senility. A number of societies have normal blood pressure that does not increase with age, including the Caracas Indians, Thais, Ethiopians, African bushmen, and Ugandan nomads. They consume one-tenth of the amount of salt that average Americans do.[9]

A recent study showed that in monkeys, either sugar or salt increased blood pressure, but when both were given together, the effect was much greater. Since high blood pressure is an important risk factor for cerebrovascular disease, it must also be a high risk factor for senility.

Excessive sugar consumption is associated with obesity. Obesity can usually be directly related to sugar tolerance, where it causes reactive hypoglycemia (relative hypoglycemia). For this reason, biochemical changes related to obesity may not be unique to the obese condition, but to the high intake of sugars. In our opinion, excessive intake of sugars, obesity, and hypoglycemia are all risk factors for senility, even if blood pressure is not elevated.

Dr. A. Angel (1978) summarized the changes found in the obese. As a result of overeating, adipose mass—made up of large, round fat-containing cells, supported by collagen and fed by many capillaries and sympathetic nerves—increases markedly. These cells are more active in fat metabolism in the obese. Plasma fat concentrations are elevated, with the most common abnormality being an increase in triglycerides. Excess sugar and alcohol drive the liver to make large amounts of fatty acids, which lead to increased triglyceride levels. Low-density lipoproteins (LDLs) are the main cholesterol transport particles in plasma, and they increase in obesity. High-density lipoproteins (HDLs) are made by the liver. They have antiarteriosclerotic properties. Several studies have shown an inverse relationship between plasma HDLs and coronary artery disease. Human adipose cells degrade HDLs in significant amounts.[10]

Obese people have more cholesterol, most of it stored in the fat cells. Daily cholesterol production is increased in proportion to the degree of obesity.

Medical complications of obesity include cardiovascular disease arising from high blood pressure, diabetes, reduced plasma HDL, and hypercholesterolemia. Cerebrovascular disease and stroke occur more often in the obese.

Many people enjoy having a drink in the evening to relax. Often these drinks contain alcohol and possibly a sugar mix. Eventually an individual may use this evening drink to induce sleep, but this is a potent mixture for causing hypoglycemia, a main risk factor for senility.

Dr. S.J.D. O'Keefe and Dr. V. Marks (1977) measured the effect of alcohol mixed with tonic on blood sugar levels in ten young subjects. Each one drank a gin-and-tonic containing one-and-a-half ounces of alcohol (50 grams) and 60 grams of sucrose. This caused more profound hypoglycemia than alcohol alone. The mood changes correlated with blood alcohol and sugar levels were found to be that approximately one hour after drinking, the subjects felt pleasantly inebriated when blood sugar was at its peak; in a few cases, when the alcohol peak occurred after blood glucose began to fall, subjects became depressed.[11]

NUTRIENT DEFICIENCY AND DEPENDENCY

Soon after the vitamin concept was established, early in the twentieth century, nutritionists began to describe deficiency diseases. If the diet lacked thiamine, the deficiency disease beriberi arose; deficiency of niacin caused pellagra; deficiency of vitamin C brought on scurvy; and lack of vitamin D created the condition known as rickets. Much later, it was recognized that some individuals suffer from the same problems because their requirement for the vitamin is so very much greater than normal that even a diet adequate for most people is inadequate for them. This can be called a "relative dependency" since the problem is mainly in the increased requirement for the nutrient and not in the food supply. Of course, there is no sharp line of demarcation and all individuals must be somewhere on a continuum, ranging from those who remain well on quantities that would be inadequate for the majority, to those whose needs may be 100 to 1,000 times greater.

A large number of reactions crop up between the time the nutrient is ingested and its final interaction in the cells. The reason for dependency may reside in any one or more of these reactions, including:

- Destruction or binding of the vitamin in the intestinal tract by certain foods, bacteria, or parasites.
- A defect in the absorptive capacity of the intestine, due to chronic use of laxatives, chronic disease, following surgical removal of portions or genetic or acquired defect in those areas that have a specific absorptive capacity, such as for vitamin B_{12}. For example, inadequate fat intake and malnutrition will reduce the absorption of fat soluble vitamins.
- Before the B vitamins—thiamine, riboflavin, niacin, pyridoxine, and vitamin B_{12}—become functional, they must be incorporated into larger molecules called coenzymes. There can be a block or defect in coenzyme formation reactions. Increasing the amount of vitamin in solution would drive the formation reaction toward synthesis of more coenzyme.
- Vitamins may not be conserved well or may be destroyed too quickly due to oxidation or bacterial degradation.
- There may be an increased destruction due to stress. For example, during any physical or mental stress, there is a marked increase in destruction of vitamin C.

Vitamin dependency may be genetic (inherited) or acquired. The permanent ill health of the ex-POWs previously discussed is an example of a niacin dependency acquired as a result of severe stress and malnutrition. Perhaps they were also made dependent on other vitamins.

Pellagrologists were physicians who specialized in pellagra. Once it was shown that pellagra was cured by niacin, the need for pellagrologists vanished. There are none around today in North America, although there are still a few in India researching this disease. Early pellagrologists were surprised that people with chronic pellagra, who had been ill for short periods of time, required doses of niacin of about 50 milligrams. This huge (for that era) requirement violated the definition of a vitamin as something required in minute quantities. They made no attempt to explain this.

Trace elements are also required in different quantities. There is no scientific reason why there should not be dependencies on zinc or other water-soluble minerals (this would be less probable for metals that can be toxic in large amounts). Since all nutrients are required, one nutrient cannot be more important than another. For any individual, however, the one or more nutrients that he is dependent on will be relatively more important. The rest of the nutrients may be easily available to him in food, but those on which he is dependent will have to be taken in the form of supplements.

Nutrient deficiencies and dependencies play a major role in the development of senility. This means there are as many types of senility as there are dependencies or deficiencies. Grey hair is one of the manifestations of aging. For some people, taking large doses of vitamin E restores their original hair color. Dr. Hoffer's hair began to grey over ten years ago, but to his suprise, 800 IU of vitamin E taken daily over a six month period restored his hair color. For other individuals, other nutrients will do the same, because there is no general relationship of one vitamin to hair color—or to senility.

Some of the vitamins play a more important role than others when taken in orthomolecular doses, but all must be provided in optimal doses. In the chapters that follow, we will describe in detail the various vitamins necessary for an antisenility nutrient formula. You can take nutrients to age without becoming senile.

7. THE ANTISENILITY VITAMINS

If you had three wishes, what would they be?
1. Not to survive my intelligence; in other words, to be able to write effectively and thoughtfully for as long as I live—however long that may be.
2. To cause no sorrow when I leave this life; in other words, to have all those who both love me and survive me to be so glad that I have lived effectively and happily that they will feel no need to mourn.
3. And most of all—to live long enough to see humanity make the crucial decisions for survival; in other words, to die knowing that civilization will survive after all into the 21st century, and for as long thereafter as is possible.

—Isaac Asimov

Martha Bloom, Dr. Walker's mother-in-law, was a woman to whom everyone came for advice. She had great wisdom and strength to support, and serenity to calm, the most anxious friend, neighbor, or family member. People came to the apartment where Martha lived to find answers to their questions, or assistance with their problems. She offered love and caring, and they came to her for advice fulfilling their personal needs.

Martha was a stable force in the lives of the seventeen brothers and sisters of her husband Julius and herself. They all sought the wise counsel that came from her alert mind. Self-educated, but dispensing a homespun philosophy brought from Eastern Europe when she was a very young woman, Martha increased her knowledge by reading the classics and other nonfiction books.

Martha owned a mental storehouse of medical information and used to live in the most natural way possible in an urban environment. She rarely used canned goods but fed her family fresh foods, and cooked delicious meals with plenty of food for anyone who might drop in. Dr. Walker remembers how happy Martha would be with his hearty appetite for her healthy food. She was also an exponent of exercise, the result of which was excellent health for those who followed her example.

The world caved in for Martha, however, when her husband, Julius, in his seventy-second year, was struck by cancer and had a lung removed. For more than a year, she nursed him while he underwent chemotherapy and radiation therapy, but the unrelenting cancer metastasized. Laboring under severe stress, she did everything possible to make Julius well—all to no avail. Julius died and left Martha, at age sixty-seven, to live alone. This stressful event was almost unendurable, and she became ill herself.

Martha's hair turned white that year, and she tried to find comfort in her four children, their children, and the coming of great-granchildren. But over time, stress piled upon stress—in the form of financial worries, fear for her own safety in a city that is an asphalt jungle, the deaths of brothers and sisters one by one, and a lingering, brooding sense of loss that never left her. "I want to be with Julius," she would say, and she meant it.

Worst of all was an attack of hiatus hernia that forced her to adopt an unnatural eating program of soft processed foods she wasn't used to. Hiatus hernia is the rupture or protrusion of part of the stomach through the esophageal opening of the diaphragm. Martha, following her physician's prescription, had to give up the fresh fruits and vegetables she was accustomed to eating. The dead foods—white bread, white rice, softened crackers, and other mushy substances, plus antacid medicines—deadened the symptoms and deadened the brain. The soft diet was another form of stress.

Martha lost weight, had less energy, stopped her regular exercise program of long walks, and began looking to a plethora of doctors for help. Each one gave her a different drug prescription to relieve her various symptoms, treating what they called "old age." Nothing seemed to help, however, and at seventy-five, this formerly active and healthy woman rapidly developed the familiar signs of senility.

At first, senility manifested itself in an inability to put words together during conversations; she forgot the names of her grandchildren; she lost the trend of ideas; she couldn't read words on a page because of rapidly diminishing vision. Even television flashed before her as darkened images that slowly became mere shadows. She slept a great deal and withdrew into herself more and more. She remembered happenings in the distant past but not what she ate for breakfast that same morning—or if she had eaten breakfast at all. Often she actually forgot to eat and began to show the effects of neglect.

Martha's children realized that although it would be a blow to her pride, she could not live alone any longer. She preferred not to give up her home and move in with one of her children, so they hired a nurse to move in with her instead.

In response to new journalistic information relating to ortho-molecular nutrition just filtering in to Dr. Walker (this was before he had met Dr. Hoffer and become familiar with the Academy of Orthomolecular Psychiatry), his wife and one of her sisters sought, and found, an orthomolecular nutritionist. The two sisters took their mother to visit Francis Ferrer, M.D., of New York City. Dr. Ferrer prescribed a wide assortment of nutritional supplements and as-sured them that taking these routinely would help their mother keep her thoughts together.

The nutrients did seem to accomplish their purpose when the daughters managed to get Martha to swallow the capsules and tablets on a regular basis. But she considered any kind of pills to be like the "medicine" she had been against taking her whole life. She fought every swallow. She flushed the supplements down the toilet when her nurse wasn't watching. It was this cantankerous-ness, and the harsh arguments connected with it, that finally forced her nurse to quit.

Martha's children were frantic to find another person to stay with the senile eighty-year-old, but there was no one to be found. They took turns living in their mother's apartment. Mrs. Walker's weekly roundtrip visits from her Connecticut home to Jamaica, New York stretched into overnight stays. The four children had to find a permanent arrangement and while they searched for it, they started giving their mother antisenility nutrients again, even though by now her senile syndrome was very well established.

Indeed, Martha's mind was hardly functioning at all. She could not think rationally or put a few words together in a full sentence. She could not walk alone and fell frequently; she could not dress herself; she could not feed herself; and she made no expression of wants or needs. Very rarely did she comprehend what was said to her. She mumbled in Yiddish, a reversion to her native lan-guage, which she spoke in Russia almost three-quarters of a century before. Lingering in some other time and place, she seemed even beyond remembering recent experiences. She gave no responses to direct mention of certain family occurrences that should have been meaningful.

The children found a place for Martha in an excellent convalescent hospital that catered to her kind of senility. She received the best nursing and medical care that orthodox medicine had available. But the hospital administration was so traditional in its methods that orthomolecular nutrition—using dietary supplementation with vitamins and minerals—was turned down as bordering on "quackery." Although Mrs. Bloom's children were persistent and tried to persuade the authorities to give the nutrients a chance, no one in the hospital would take it upon herself to give her vitamins and minerals on a regular basis. Kind attendants who might have indulged the daughters were too frightened of losing their jobs.

The dietary supplements were abandoned, although Mrs. Walker and her sister believe these supplements would have saved their mother, had they been administered consistently. The nutrients had never been given an opportunity to work. At home, the patient in her mental illness considered those pills poison and refused to swallow them. In the hospital, the authorities regarded nutrients against senility as some kind of black magic. They laughed at nutritional therapy and declared Martha's senility irreversible. No provision could be made at the hospital by her daughters to continue her on dietary supplementation.

At eighty-three Martha finally died under the care of the gentle nurses and astute physicians. One can only wonder why, with all the kind, considerate, and wonderful acts they performed for Martha by keeping her clean, dressing her, spoon-feeding her, and trying to get her to respond to some outside stimulus, they absolutely refused to put a few vitamin pills in her mouth and help her swallow them with a little water. What would have been so wrong with that?

Dr. Walker believes that if any of Martha's children had understood the science of orthomolecular nutrition ten or fifteen years earlier, they might have saved their mother from the living death of senility. She would not have outlived her intelligence.

The nursing hospital in which Martha Bloom died violated the first rule of Claude Bernard, the great nineteenth-century French physiologist, whose research was concerned with the pancreas, the glycogenic function of the liver, and the vasomotor system. Dr. Bernard said that if there is any treatment program that may be of benefit to the patient, and that is not harmful, the physician is obligated to try it.

To paraphrase Claude Bernard's rule, the nutrients should have been used since, as we have seen, substances used for treating senility are even more effective for preventing senility. The treatment of presenility or premature aging is a preventive program since it avoids or slows down any further deterioration of the mind.

The program of nutrition against senility that follows in this and other chapters is derived from our experience with presenile and senile patients, interviews with orthomolecular physicians, and a search of the scientific literature. Because individuals are so variable, we will lay down general rules and descriptions of the various nutrients and merely suggest the desirable dosages. Realize that nutrition is the most important aspect of treatment for the senile, and there is no good substitute for nutritious food. As we pointed out in earlier chapters, the nutritional value of food is largely lost by processing. Consequently, we must suggest supplements in the form of vitamin and mineral tablets, capsules, and powders.

Senility is a disease, not a way of life and not inevitable. In most cases, it is due to chronic malnutrition, for which society, the food industry, and the consumer share the blame.

ORTHOMOLECULAR NUTRITION FOR SENILITY

People should practice orthomolecular nutrition in order to experience optimal health. Orthomolecular nutrition consists of supplementing the diet with substances normally present in the human body. Many of these substances, including vitamins, essential minerals, essential amino acids, essential fats, and others, are obtained exogenously (from outside the body) from foods or dietary supplements. Thousands of others, such as coenzyme Q_{10}, L-carnitine, apoprotein(a), and other proteins are synthesized in the cells of the human body. Optimum health and the best resistance to disease are achieved when all of these substances are present in optimum amounts for body metabolism.

Unfortunately, in Western industrialized society, people seldom ingest the optimal qualities of orthomolecular substances. Our intake of most of the vitamins, for instance, is less than the desired amount, and endogenous (within the body) synthesis of many required substances occurs at less than the optimum rate.

Therefore, taking supplements can lead to an improvement in health. Some regulation of the rates of synthesis and the functioning of macromolecules, such as proteins, can also be achieved.

Evidence indicates that vitamin C insufficiency is a major cause of poor health. The blood level of apoprotein(a) also contributes to causing illness. Moreover, insufficiencies in some other vitamins and many endogenous substances, such as the B vitamins niacin and pyridoxine, and others, cause the body to break down. Measures to achieve the optimum levels of the most important orthomolecular substances can be taken to improve health and control disease. Chief among these are the various vitamins that we shall describe in this chapter.[1] (Table 7.1 is an easy reference table for the daily vitamin doses, and is provided at the end of the chapter on page 125.)

THIAMINE (VITAMIN B₁)

The classical thiamine deficiency state, beriberi, causes psychiatric and neurologic symptoms, which, if they occurred in an older person, can easily be misdiagnosed as senile changes. Thiamine is essential for the metabolism of sugar. When large quantities of sugar are consumed, the body's metabolism tends to increase its own demand for the vitamin. In the same way, alcohol increases the demand for it. Alcohol and sugar have similar biochemical and metabolic effects on the body.

In contrast to carbohydrate-rich foods, which carry thiamine as a component to metabolize the sugar in the whole food, sugar-rich artifacts carry little, or no, thiamine. The consumption of sugar artifacts creates a net deficit in the vitamin economy of the body. It is a condition similar to *Wernicke-Korsakoff syndrome*, a partial destruction of the brain resulting from a lack of thiamine that occurs in chronic alcoholics.

Korsakoff's syndrome was first described by Dr. Korsakoff as being present in people with a long history of alcoholism. It has also been found in people who have not been alcoholic, but there is an unfortunate tendency to consider only alcoholism as a cause. Since early Korsakoff's syndrome is treated with large doses of thiamine, those cases who are not recognized, because the patients are not alcoholics, will not be treated adequately. Dr. W.M. Bowerman (1978) reviewed Korsakoff's original clinical description.[2] He was particularly struck by the association of mental and neurological symptoms. Researchers have concluded that what were considered two syndromes, Korsakoff's and Wernicke's, were in fact one, Wernicke-Korsakoff syndrome. Korsakoff's syndrome emphasized the mental symptoms, and Wernicke's, the neurological symptoms.

The mental symptoms include anxiety and depression, obsessive thinking, confusion, defective memory—especially for recent events, time distortion, irritability, agitation, and sometimes confabulation. These are certainly not unlike the mental changes in the senile person. Wernicke-Korsakoff syndrome can be caused by infection, cerebral hemorrhage, and post-surgical complications.

The symptoms wax and wane, and the patient may cover them up successfully for a long time, but symptoms reappear when stress is placed upon the person. These stressors may be slight or severe and include things such as unusual work, an extra job, accidents, injuries, or surgery. Memory problems are the first to appear. In some, symptoms have been present for many years as a form of minimal brain dysfunction. At times, these patients have had periods of hyperactivity and drive that they found advantageous. Bowerman concludes,

> Not only has alcohol become an artifact because of the prominence of the findings in the alcoholics, but also perhaps because the alcoholic has a pronounced mental and physical response to life's stresses for which he uses alcohol as self-medication. Thus what was thought to be an etiology is rather self-medication for the condition.

It is possible that many senile people are simply examples of Wernicke-Korsakoff syndrome where the additional stresses of age have precipitated another outburst of symptoms. Many seniles do have, to a milder degree, the same symptoms found in alcoholic Wernicke-Korsakoff syndrome.

Thiamine deficiency and/or dependency may be the main cause of this condition. Thiamine is as essential for the metabolism of alcohol as it is for sugar and carbohydrate in general. Since many alcoholics cannot afford to eat and also maintain their alcohol habit, and since alcohol provides calories, there is a decrease in the consumption of food containing vitamins and minerals. Unless an alcoholic makes a special effort to eat very nutritious food (and few do), there inevitably must be a deficiency of all vitamins and minerals.

Regarding this connection, a *New York Times* editorial written by Brandon Centerwall, a medical student at the University of California, San Diego, makes an excellent recommendation. Why not put thiamine in beer, wine, whiskey, and other alcoholic beverages? Wernicke-Korsakoff syndrome can be prevented— simply add the vitamin to all liquor. It is stable, does not change a drink's flavor, and is known to be safe. It therefore seems a logical additive for all alcoholic beverages.[3]

Wernicke-Korsakoff syndrome may also appear in people who are thiamine dependent. Men and women who consume large quantities of refined sugars may be just as vulnerable to the deficiency. If this is an important factor, we can expect to see a significant increase in Wernicke-Korsakoff syndrome among the younger generation when they reach their sixties and seventies, because of the massive consumption of food artifacts that has occurred in the past four decades. We are just beginning to see the children of the first generation of heavy junk-food consumers. This generation may well create a major surge in the incidence of senility in about forty to fifty years. If you want to protect yourself against this, the correct thiamine intake is 250 mg a day, divided into two or three doses.

NIACIN (NICOTINIC ACID OR VITAMIN B₃)

Niacin (known also medically as nicotinic acid) and niacinamide (nicotinamide) are antipellagra vitamins that are incorporated by the body into a coenzyme called nicotinamide-adenine dinucleotide, or NAD. A derivative of vitamin B₃ in nature exists in this coenzyme form, or is bound to the tissues as nucleotides. Sometimes it is so firmly bound the vitamin can't be released in the body. This is the situation with corn, and accounts for the fact that people who subsist on 100-percent corn diets frequently are predisposed to pellagra.

It is likely that the deficiency of any essential nutrient, if continued for a long time, will hasten the onset of senility, but a reduced intake of niacin is especially dangerous. Niacin deficiency seems to be most responsible for a rapid development of the senile syndrome.

NAD participates in a large number of reactions requiring the transport of electrons or oxidation reduction reactions. This is such an important enzyme that the body has developed several methods for ensuring that it is retained. NAD is made from niacin, originating from the amino acid L-tryptophan, and is also made from the vitamin present in food. Finally, when the pyridine molecule is recycled in the body, NAD is split into niacinamide, some of which is converted into niacin, and pyridine is incorporated into NAD. This is called the *pyridine nucleotide cycle.*

When there is too little niacin in food, the deficiency disease pellagra develops. Pellagra is a chronic deteriorating illness that invariably leads to death unless the niacin is replaced. The early stages of pellagra produce depression, anxiety, and fatigue.

For a while, pellagrologists debated whether to include early pellagra among the neuroses. It certainly produces a characteristic neurotic reaction, and later it produces a psychotic reaction—usually a schizophrenic syndrome. If the disease progresses, the clinical syndrome becomes an organic psychosis that, like all organic psychoses, resembles the senile psychoses.

Pellagra, the preterminal disease, is seldom found in our society. The fortification of flour with niacinamide provides most people with just enough of the vitamin to protect them against this. Or does it? Our definition of pellagra depends so heavily on a deficiency of niacin in the diet that if all the symptoms of the disease occurred in a person whose diet contained normal amounts of niacin, no nutritionist or physician would call it pellagra. Furthermore, most physicians and nutritionists simply assume that our diet is so good that even the idea of any substantial proportion of our population suffering from a deficiency is unthinkable.

A proportion of any population requires a higher vitamin intake than the majority of people—to the degree that even a diet that is completely healthy for most would be inadequate in vitamins for them. These people are said to have a vitamin dependency, which we have already mentioned. But to clarify again: *Having a vitamin dependency means that, for this person, there is a relative deficiency of this vitamin.* Pellagra caused by vitamin dependency therefore does not differ in any way from the deficiency disease pellagra—except that the dependent person will be more chronic and will have other metabolic problems of which the niacin dependency is the result.

Dr. Hoffer first realized in 1953 that niacin could help patients with organic brain damage of a milder sort, such as takes place in senility. He and Humphry Osmond had already started experiments using large doses of niacin for treating schizophrenia. Dr. Hoffer was familiar with its use and its relative safety. One day he flew to a small town in Saskatchewan to spend a day examining patients referred to the public health center by local physicians. One of the patients was a middle-aged woman who had completed a program of electroconvulsive therapy (ECT) one month before. She was referred again because her memory was so awful she could not function.

There is no doubt that post-ECT amnesia is a measure of some cerebral pathology. Fortunately, it is transient and very rarely leaves a permanent memory defect, except that the memory of events occurring during the ECT may not return.

In 1953, there was no treatment for post-ECT amnesia, but Dr. Hoffer started the woman on three grams of niacin per day—without any conviction that it would help, but he was certain it would do no harm. When Dr. Hoffer saw her one month later, she was normal. She and her husband reported that one week after starting the niacin treatment, her memory cleared. Since then, Dr. Hoffer has observed that several hundred patients given ECT have much less residual memory defect when they take niacin during, and after, the series of ECT. In most cases, the niacin can then be discontinued unless there are other reasons why it should be used. The memory defect will not come back.

Double-blind experiments are not required to show the antisenility effect of niacin. The original idea for using the type of experiment called "double-blind" arose as a way of dealing with diseases that vary a great deal, such as the common cold or some forms of arthritis. When diseases come and go, one can always say that what appears to be a therapeutic response may simply be a natural recovery. Senility, on the other hand, has a generally progressive downhill course, and no one has reported spontaneous recoveries from it. When a few patients do recover with any treatment, one must accept that the treatment is effective unless further experiments prove the results were not valid. From our experiences alone, we are convinced that niacin is very effective if it is started before the senility is well established. There are a number of factors that may account for the vitamin's antisenility property.

Niacin Lowers Blood Fats, Cholesterol, and Triglycerides

As we have seen, niacin lowers the level of fats in the blood. For most people, at least 3 grams of niacin must be used before there is any significant effect in lowering blood fats. Sometimes as much as 6 grams is required. The slow-release preparations are more effective. In a few experiments, we found that 0.5 grams of slow-release niacin was more effective than 6 grams for the same person. Niacinamide has no such effect. The reason for this difference is still unknown.

Niacin was one of five compounds studied in the $40 million Coronary Drug Project, which involved fifty-five research clinics and 8,341 patients. Two of the compounds, estrogen and dextrothyroxine, were discontinued before the study was completed. The remaining two, niacin and clofibrate, were continued until the termination of the project. About niacin, the investigators concluded, "It may be slightly beneficial in protecting persons to some degree against recurrent nonfatal myocardial infarctions."

Long before this coronary drug study began, Professor Edwin Boyle had placed about 160 similar patients on niacin and followed them carefully for over ten years, giving each one individual attention. Boyle concluded that niacin reduced mortality by about 90 percent.

Professor Rudl Altschul, in his book *Niacin in Vascular Disorders and Hyperlipidemia*, reviewed the evidence that niacin taken over a period of several years could reverse some of the arteriosclerotic pathology in blood vessels.[4]

More recent studies suggest niacin may be valuable in treating heart attacks. Fatty acids can interfere with the ability of the heart to use glucose. They may disturb heart rhythm, leading to arrhythmia, which is potentially fatal. A heart attack is accompanied by an increase in free fatty acids in the blood. Apparently any serious stress can have the same effect. The fatty acids are mobilized from fat depots by the stress-induced secretion of adrenaline. Niacin prevents the release of the fatty acids, although it does not interfere with the release of adrenaline. It stabilizes fatty acids in the cells that store the fat. In one study on ten normal subjects, niacin stopped the interference of fatty acids in heart muscle metabolism. In another study, involving a niacin analogue that also lowered free fatty acids in blood, a similar beneficial effect was observed during heart attacks. Men given this substance within five hours of the onset of a heart attack had fewer serious heart arrhythmias.

Antisludging Effect

Sludging is the term applied to red blood cells that do not float freely in blood but instead adhere to each other, as we described previously. Capillaries are so small that the red cells pass through in single file. When two or more red blood cells adhere or stick to each other, they cannot traverse the capillaries. These capillaries therefore carry plasma only, with no red blood cells. The tissues fed by these capillaries suffer from anoxia (lack of oxygen). If many cells are sludged, large areas of tissues are deprived of oxygen.

Anoxic areas are probably more susceptible to tissue death and small hemorrhages. Preventing sludging should therefore prevent or reverse senile changes caused by sludging.

Niacin apparently acts by increasing the electronegative charge on each cell, making the cells better able to repel each other. Whatever the precise mechanism, there is little doubt that the vitamin has antisludging properties. We have seen many patients whose faces appeared pallid and sickly, who complained of chronic fatigue, memory failure, depression, and anxiety. These are the patients most apt to suffer from sludging. After a few months on niacin therapy, their skin becomes clear, healthy, and regains normal color. At the same time, their fatigue and other symptoms are diminished or gone entirely.

Other Effects

Niacin is an essential component of the coenzyme known as NAD. In persons with a deficiency of NAD, most metabolic reactions would be diminished, and the steady flow of energy to the brain interrupted. Megadoses of niacin probably restore coenzyme function.

Two serious peripheral vascular diseases, chilblains and Raynaud's disease, also respond to varying dosages of niacin. Chilblains is a painful reddening of fingers, toes, or ears following exposure to cold. Raynaud's disease is characterized by intermittent attacks of blanching or blueness of the fingers, often with pain, that are caused by emotional distress or cold. We have seen the beneficial effect of niacin on Raynaud's disease and now consider this an indication for using niacin.

Because these disorders are related to spasms in the blood vessels serving the affected areas, it is likely that niacin's beneficial action comes from its vasodilating property—the same property that causes the niacin flush. Studies with one niacin derivative showed that it increased blood flow in the extremities. In a joint Australian-Scottish study, it was concluded that niacin should be valuable for treating conditions such as Raynaud's disease and chilblains.

William Kaufman, M.D., of Stratford, Connecticut, began to use niacin in gram doses for treating arthritis and found it very effective for most cases. Using a precise method for measuring joint mobility, he developed an index with 100 as the maximum or normal score. Severely arthritic patients had scores below 50. When treated, their scores all increased. For older people, scores generally increased 12 points within two months. For some, they increased 31 points.

Before becoming aware of Kaufman's discovery, Dr. Hoffer had made the same clinical observation in 1954. Since then, most orthomolecular physicians have observed the same beneficial antiarthritic effect.

Niflumic acid, a derivative of niacin, was found to be as effective as endomethacin, one of the widely used drugs for rheumatoid arthritis. A large study done in Norway showed niflumic acid was effective and well tolerated over a long period. At the University of Lund, Sweden, it was found to be as effective in osteoarthritis as endomethacin.

Arthritic limitation of movement accompanied by pain responds particularly quickly to niacin.

The Antisenility Dosage of Niacin

The earlier a person starts on vitamin supplementation with niacin, the lower the required dosage. The recommended dosage should be taken after each meal. We would recommend the following doses for people who do not feel that whole foods alone provide adequate nutrition. From ages twenty to twenty-nine, the recommended dosage of niacin is 100 milligrams; from ages thirty to thirty-nine, 300 milligrams; from ages forty to forty-nine, 500 milligrams; and over fifty years of age, 1000 milligrams. The closer you are to the age of senility, even if you have no symptoms, the more you should be taking preventive measures.

You can start with a low dose and gradually work up, or begin with the full dose, but beware of an initial flush. If the flush is too irritating, you should start with a lower dosage and work up to the larger one slowly over a few weeks. A person needing a higher dosage generally will have the fewest side effects when he begins to use the vitamin.

The optimum dose for niacin is that quantity which is most effective in eliminating symptoms and has few or no side effects. This dose is maintained for life, but it may vary up or down. Each person must become skilled in determining what is the best dosage for himself.

Niacinamide (nicotinamide) may work just as well as niacin if it is started many years before the possible onset of senility. But the closer a person is to developing symptoms, the more important it will be to use niacin, since it works more effectively than niacinamide. The niacinamide dose may be small at first and gradually increase until three to six grams per day are being taken.

Because water-soluble vitamins such as niacin are excreted rapidly, it is best to divide the daily dosage into at least three doses. Ideally, you might take a much smaller quantity every hour, but this is not often practical. The controlled timed-release vitamin preparations drop niacin into the body over an eight- to twenty-four-hour period to reproduce more accurately the slow rate of release of nutrients during the digestion of food. Also, the slow-release tablet minimizes side effects, unless you have an allergy to the material used in binding the slow-release granules.

VITAMIN C

Vitamin C (ascorbic acid) must be listed as an antisenility vitamin, for it has properties that make it particularly valuable for elderly people.

Ascorbic acid maintains the integrity of collagen. Collagen is a major constituent of skin (the largest organ of the body), of bone, and of many other organs. Healthy collagen tissue may resist the invasion of cancer cells better.

Vitamin C has been proven to be a powerful fighter in the immune system. For example, it prevents recurrences of cancer of the urinary bladder, protects against invasion by viruses and bacteria, and reduces the ravages of allergic reactions. Dr. B.V. Siegel (1975) found that ascorbic acid stimulated cells to increase production of interferon threefold. Interferon increases the ability of cells to resist penetration by viruses. In large doses, ascorbic acid has extremely valuable antiviral therapeutic properties. It also reduces allergic reactions because it neutralizes histamine released into the blood.[5]

Vitamin C is also a valuable laxative. Constipation is one of the difficulties often faced by elderly people. The main reason is lack of dietary fiber, but a few elderly patients even on high-fiber diets are constipated until placed upon optimum doses of ascorbic acid. It is much more beneficial than commercial laxatives and is safe. Constipation can be especially damaging, not only for the mechanical reasons described earlier, but because it decreases absorption of nutrients from the gut.

Ascorbic acid prevents and reverses the effects of atherosclerosis, possibly by strengthening the collagen in the arterial walls.

The average healthy person will require one to three grams of vitamin C per day to remain healthy and will require more when ill. Elderly people require triple this dose. We recommend the dosage that just falls short of producing diarrhea. To find that dosage, increase the milligram intake until some diarrhea develops. Then reduce the dose a little.

PANTOTHENIC ACID

Pantothenic acid is one of the B vitamins. It was discovered by Professor Roger Williams over thirty years ago, and it has been ignored for almost as long. Professor Williams reasoned that it might have antiaging properties. He treated mice with this vitamin along with a nutritious diet and found they lived 653 days, whereas the control mice lived 550 days. In human terms, this would be equivalent to an increase in life span from seventy-five to eighty-nine years.

Pantothenic acid is required for normal functioning of the nervous system. In animals, severe deficiency leads to nerve degeneration. This vitamin also maintains the integrity of the immune system. Deficiency decreases the production of antibodies. Pantothenic acid reinforces our defenses against stress by supporting the adrenal glands. It also shows beneficial effects in arthritics. Dr. E.C. Bartin-Wright and Dr. W.A. Elliott of the Rheumatic Clinic at

St. Alfeges Hospital, London, tested 160 arthritics and found that the blood level of pantothenic acid was 69 micrograms per 100 milliliters of blood, which was one-fourth to one-half that of normal controls.

It is prudent to take pantothenic acid as an antisenility nutrient at a dosage of 250 to 750 milligrams per day.

VITAMIN E (TOCOPHEROL)

There are eight vitamin E isomers in nature. Of these, d-alpha tocopherol is the most active biologically. Synthetic vitamin E is the dl form, which is not absorbed as well as the natural form. Vitamin E makes a powerful antioxidant by combining with free radicals, or small, highly active molecules.

Once life forms switched from anaerobic to aerobic respiration, they had to solve a major problem: how to prevent being oxidized (burned) by the oxygen in which they were enveloped. They did this by developing antioxidants. When an apple or a potato turns brown when cut, this is a sign of oxidation. Oxidation must not be allowed to occur in the body. Plants have developed antioxidants, such as vitamin E. Animal tissue must also be protected, and it uses vitamin E as well as vitamin C and glutathione for this purpose. Another antioxidant may be alpha-tocopherylquinone, the main oxidation product of alpha-tocopherol.

The amount of vitamin E required is not agreed upon because there is no clear relationship between vitamin E deficiency and disease in humans. In animals, deficiency of vitamin E causes severe, often irreversible, pathology. In one study on adult men, a diet containing only 5 international units per day showed a marked increase in the rate of destruction of red blood cells after six years. Yet, the daily recommended amount has been lowered from 30 to 15 international units per day. One reason for lowering this estimate was that dietitians were having difficulty in devising a diet that would provide more than 15 international units per day. Horwitt (1976) disagrees with this decision.[6]

Even if 30 international units is adequate to protect us from increased wastage of red blood cells, it is altogether too low for optimum health. Several theories of aging suggest that excessive oxidation may be a cause. It is prudent to assume there is some validity to these ideas and to try to reverse these changes by taking large amounts of vitamin E. Thus Horwitt referred to a study where rats fed vitamin E equivalent to the amount in an average American diet suffered severe lung damage when exposed to 0.1 parts per million (ppm) of ozone for seven days. Rats given six times as much vitamin E were not damaged.

Orthomolecular physicians have been using dosages of 400 international units and upward following the pioneering work of Evan Shute, M.D., and Wilfrid Shute, M.D. These dosages have been severely criticized by many as being unnecessary and even dangerous. Clinical trials of vitamin E as a treatment for coronary disease that were designed to refute the Shutes' work of around 1950 used too little vitamin E for short periods of time. Horwitt points out that it takes a long time to saturate the tissues with vitamin E. He refers to studies that show that vitamin E prolonged blood clotting time.

Vitamin E is the last of the true antisenility vitamins we will discuss at length. The best dose ranges from 800 to 1600 international units per day. This dose can be used immediately or arrived at slowly.

Many physicians seem to think that vitamin E is no better than a placebo. The best evidence against this arises from diseases for which there is no treatment, such as Huntington's chorea. The literature does not reveal that a single patient has ever been cured by having the illness halted and reversed. There are a small number of research papers that continue to report lists of treatments that have failed, but Dr. Hoffer has seen the condition respond to vitamin E.

Huntington's chorea is an inherited disease that appears in about 50 percent of the children of a parent with this disease. The progress of the disease is steadily downhill with a few plateaus, and there have been no recoveries. The disease is also very rare; so rare that Dr. Hoffer had not seen one case between 1945, when he became a medical student, and the time his first patient appeared in about 1971.

This patient had been ill for twenty years and his father had died psychotic in a mental hospital, as had his father's brother. There were five sons, of whom two had chronic Huntington's chorea and resided in nursing homes, hopelessly incapacitated and psychotic. One has died since then.

The patient was the third son in his family to inherit the disease. His weight had gone to 130 pounds from his normal 165 pounds. This was due to his loss of muscle mass. He was physically and mentally ill, and his mind was beginning to change. The young man was overly suspicious, and at the same time indifferent or inappropriately euphoric. He walked with a limp, and was so weak he could not raise his arms over his shoulders. His personal needs, such as eating and dressing, required all his energy, and he had none left for anything else.

The patient was started on a comprehensive program of ascorbic acid and water-soluble B-vitamins, and after six months he appeared to be stronger. In fact, he reported that he was able to work in his garden and could do some repairs on his roof, but he had lost another five pounds. This was an ominous sign, since it indicated the disease was still progressing and muscle tissue was being wasted. At this time, Dr. Hoffer concluded he was really no better.

Dr. Hoffer then started the patient on 800 international units of vitamin E per day. He was aware of the use of vitamin E by veterinarian surgeons for treating muscular dystrophies. One month later, the patient's weight remained steady; after another month, he had gained four pounds; within four months, he weighed 137 pounds, and that was not fat. The man's muscles were rapidly regenerating and when last seen, he had been nearly well for over two years. His weight has remained at about 135 pounds. His wife stated that the only sign of any residual disability was that he walked with a slight limp when he was very tense.

Huntington's disease is a cerebral degenerative disease that mimics the worst aspects of senility. Vitamin E was an important factor in halting this disease, and if it can be so effective in halting the progress of such a serious disease as Huntington's disease, there can be no basis for the belief it is an inert substance. This is the first case of the condition recorded where the disease has been brought under control.

Of course, vitamin E is also one of the most valuable substances in controlling cardiovascular disease. There have been several studies that prove taking at least 100 international units of vitamin E a day can considerably lower the risk of heart attacks.[7,8]

OTHER VITAMINS

Other vitamins, although not specifically antisenility factors, will be needed if there are special indications. These include vitamin A, if there are special problems with the skin or eyes; vitamin D_3, if there are problems with calcium metabolism; vitamin K, if

Table 7.1 Recommended Doses of Antisenility Vitamins

Vitamin	Age	Recommended Daily Dosage
Thiamine	All ages	250 mg/day in divided doses
Niacin	20–29	100 mg after each meal
	30–39	300 mg after each meal
	40–49	500 mg after each meal
	50+	1000 mg after each meal
Pyridoxine	All ages	500 mg/day
Pantothenic Acid	All ages	250 to 750 mg/day
Vitamin C	All ages	1 to 3 grams/day
	65+	3 to 9 grams/day
Vitamin E	All ages	800 to 1600 IU/day

bruises develop too easily; and folic acid and vitamin B_{12} if blood levels are low. Any one of these may be required in optimum doses.

Pyridoxine (vitamin B_6) is such an important nutrient that it seems only prudent to use it as a supplement. It is involved in a large number of vital metabolic reactions. Up to 500 milligrams per day should be taken—more if there are clinical indications of pyridoxine dependency.

In addition, a healthy balance of minerals must be maintained in the body. These, together with other important elements of a sound nutritional program, will be considered in the following chapter.

8. DIETARY MINERALS AND OTHER ASPECTS OF GOOD NUTRITION

> No life could develop if minerals were excluded. They provide structural and functional support, and for each element there exists an optimum quantity that furnishes maximal support for a cell. Nature already furnishes these optimum quantities so that minimal amounts of energy are needed to either increase or decrease amounts inside a cell. Any quantity less than the optimum would eventually lead to a deficiency state, and cellular malfunction might express itself in some obvious manner.
>
> —Abram Hoffer, M.D., Ph.D.
> and Morton Walker, D.P.M.

"Charlie Smith and the Fritter Tree," was televised on October 9, 1978, by the Public Broadcasting Service. It showed the life story of 136-year-old Charlie Smith, and Mr. Smith was around to see it.[1] The film traced his life from the time he was taken from Africa when he was twelve years old and was put aboard a slave ship for bondage in Texas, until his freedom in 1863, because of the Emancipation Proclamation. It depicted him as a cowhand, an outlaw who rode with Jesse James, a bounty hunter, a fruit picker, and finally a grand old storyteller.

For most of his life, Charlie Smith rode the range on his horse as a cowpoke. He hustled those longhorn steers and ate their trail dust pushing them on to market. The secret of the cowboy's longevity is probably the very dust he found distasteful. There are many minerals in it.

Of the six nutrients that our bodies need—minerals, vitamins, water, protein, carbohydrates, and fats—dietary minerals have the power to keep us young and rejuvenate our bodies. Minerals are actively engaged in strengthening the nervous system, growing new hair, normalizing the heartbeat, providing energy, improving thinking power, overcoming fatigue, building a dynamic memory, and sparking our other metabolic processes.

A mineral imbalance will alter one's disposition. In a mineral-deficient person, you will see signs of forgetfulness, easy fatigue, lack of incentive, lackluster skin and hair, a short temper, nervous tension, defeatism, depression, vengefulness, and even suicidal tendencies. In fact, if anyone has a shortage of just one mineral, he can expect that his system will begin to weaken and lose its efficiency, with disease eventually setting in.

There are two categories of dietary minerals: major minerals and trace minerals. Major minerals are needed in large amounts by the body. Trace minerals get their name from the fact that they are found in very minute amounts (traces) in the body and may be toxic in larger quantities.

Taking minerals in regulated amounts through foods rich in minerals or mineral supplements will ensure a long life. Among other things, minerals have the ability to regulate the flow of bodily fluids. The delicate internal water balance needed for all mental and physical processes is necessary for good health. The flow of liquids (blood and lymph) brings the cells oxygen and nutrition and empties them of wastes. The minerals draw these substances into and out of our cells by the law of mass action, in which areas with a heavier concentration of minerals will always draw water from the areas with a lighter concentration of minerals. In this way, concentration is equalized between the fluids inside and outside of the cells as an ongoing body process.

The bodily fluids, solutions of water and dissolved mineral salts, hold the cells in electrolyte balance. The mineral salts each generate a tiny electrical charge, either positive or negative. Each cell is similar to a minute electrical battery, with both positive and negative polarities receiving the electrolytic solution containing the essential chemicals and minerals it needs. Give the cells the minerals they need, and they will give you long life and good health.

PARTICULAR DIETARY MINERALS
REQUIRED BY THE ELDERLY

We are not aware of studies that link any particular mineral to senility, but certain ones are more necessary for the elderly. Rather than acquire your supply of minerals from supplementation, we recommend that you get them from eating an abundance of fresh fruits and vegetables, nuts, and grains. Fresh foods contain many more minerals in a natural balance than processed foods. If fresh foods are not available, homeopathic cell salts may be purchased in a health food store. These are also available in the form of a combination tablet containing twelve mineral salts. Or you may wish to take chelated minerals. A *chelated mineral atom* is an atom that is surrounded or enclosed by a larger protein molecule. The chelation process changes the positive ionic (electrolyte) charge to a negative ionic charge, making it more acceptable through the villi of the intestines into the blood stream, where it can be used easily and efficiently by the body.

Of the fourteen major and trace minerals necessary for life, three in particular are recommended to reduce the effects of aging. They are calcium, magnesium, and zinc.

Calcium

Calcium is the most abundant mineral in the body; the bones and teeth hold 99 percent of it. Osteoporosis and periodontal disease, both manifestations of calcium deficiency, are common in the elderly. Osteoporosis may appear as early as age twenty-five, but it is more common in women toward the end of life. In the Sudan, where calcium intake may exceed two grams per day, periodontal disease and spinal bone disease are rare.

The recommended dosage of calcium supplement is one gram a day, but Dr. Hoffer advises that twice as much for an older person would be better. Herta Spencer, M.D., of the Veterans Administration Hospital in Hines, Illinois, suggests 1200 milligrams per day. The United States Government's recommended daily allowance (RDA) is only 800 milligrams a day. Dr. Spencer also found that aluminum antacids, even in small doses, can damage bones by causing the loss of both calcium and magnesium.

Magnesium

Magnesium, an essential mineral, occurs in the body in appreciable quantities. The adult body contains about twenty-five grams, 70 percent of which is combined with calcium and phosphorus in the bone salt complex. Magnesium aids in the absorption of calcium. It is one of four mineral ions that must be in balance in extracellular fluids so that the transmission of nerve impulses and muscle contraction can be regulated.

The National Research Council of the United States recommends a daily magnesium intake of 350 milligrams for the adult male and 300 milligrams for the adult female. Since the average American diet rarely provides anything near this inadequate RDA, this dosage should be tripled. Otherwise, a deficiency of magnesium will show up as symptoms of senility, including mental confusion, disorientation, apprehensiveness, muscle twitching, tremors, and blood vessel clots.

Zinc

Zinc, a trace metal, is extremely important in the synthesis of RNA, DNA, and protein, and is essential in maintaining an adequate blood level of vitamin A. There are seventy known enzymes that contain zinc. One of these breaks down a molecule called superoxide, which accumulates in sites of inflammation of rheumatoid arthritis. In one study, sixteen elderly patients were able to take 220 milligrams of zinc sulfate three times a day with minimal side effects. If any diarrhea occurs, lower doses, or a different form of the mineral, such as zinc gluconate may be used.

Zinc salts are water soluble and thus easily lost from the body. Unlike iron, which can be conserved, zinc has to be taken every day as do vitamins. We consider zinc an important antisenility mineral because a deficiency in elderly people can cause a confused state, which may be mistaken for senility. A lack of zinc causes a disorder of taste and smell resulting in reduced food consumption. In men, zinc in adequate doses decreases the probability of prostate enlargement.

The average zinc content of a mixed diet is between 10 and 15 milligrams. Since this mineral is relatively nontoxic and such an important mineral, we recommend a dosage of 45 milligrams per day for the older person.

Some people will require a dosage range of 30 to 100 milligrams per day of zinc gluconate or 200 to 660 milligrams of zinc sulphate. The higher doses are necessary for special needs, such as a deficiency in taste or smell, chalky white areas on the nails, or prostate trouble.

THE NUTRIENT CONTENT OF FOODS

It is always best to acquire all of the daily allotment of nutrients you need from the nutritional quality of foods eaten. We have, therefore, supplied a listing of the vitamin and mineral content of many foods to help you tailor your eating to your specific dietary needs. Use the listing to identify foods that are good sources for the particular vitamin or mineral you are interested in.

While the values given in these lists can be useful in comparing nutritional content in foods, the absolute values for food nutrients will vary, depending on such factors as the condition of the soil where the food was grown (or what type of nutrition an animal received), the amount of processing or refining, and the method of preparation.

The serving size of each food in the lists has been standardized to 100 grams. This was done to provide a more appropriate comparison between the relative amounts of nutrients in foods and allows them to be ranked from highest to lowest. Remember, however, not all foods are consumed in 100-gram quantities, especially if they are highly concentrated, like kelp, dulse, wheat germ, and brewer's yeast. Such foods often appear at the top of the list, indicating that they are concentrated nutritional sources. To get an idea of what 100 grams of a food represents, it may be helpful to consider what it is equivalent to in common measurements. A 100-gram serving size is approximately equal to any one of the following:

- about ⅜ cup fluid measure
- about ¼ cup dry measure
- 3¼ ounces of milk or yogurt
- slightly more than 1 cup leafy vegetable
- ¾ cup root vegetable
- 5½ ounces nuts, seeds
- ⅔ cup sliced fruit
- ½ cup cereal grain, uncooked
- 7 tablespoons cooking oil
- 5 tablespoons honey, molasses

The following lists indicate the amounts of important nutrients available in 100-gram portions of various foods.

Vitamin A (Carotene)

IU per 100-gram portion (3½ oz)	Food Source	IU per 100-gram portion (3½ oz)	Food Source
50,500	Lamb liver	2,000	Green onions
43,900	Beef liver	1,900	Romaine lettuce
22,500	Calf liver	1,750	Papayas
21,600	Peppers, red chili	1,650	Nectarines
14,000	Dandelion greens	1,600	Prunes
12,100	Chicken liver	1,600	Pumpkin
11,000	Carrots	1,580	Swordfish
10,900	Apricots, dried	1,540	Whipping cream
9,300	Collard leaves	1,330	Peaches
8,900	Kale	1,200	Acorn squash
8,800	Sweet potatoes	1,180	Eggs
8,500	Parsley	1,080	Chicken
8,100	Spinach	1,000	Cherries, sour red
7,600	Turnip greens	970	Butterhead lettuce
7,000	Mustard greens	900	Asparagus
6,500	Swiss chard	900	Tomatoes, ripe
6,100	Beet greens	770	Peppers, green chili
5,800	Chives	690	Kidneys
5,700	Butternut squash	640	Peas
4,900	Watercress	600	Green beans
4,800	Mangos	600	Elderberries
4,450	Peppers, sweet red	590	Watermelon
4,300	Hubbard squash	580	Rutabagas
3,400	Cantaloupe	550	Brussels sprouts
3,300	Endive	520	Okra
2,700	Apricots	510	Yellow cornmeal
2,500	Broccoli spears	460	Yellow squash
2,260	Whitefish		

Vitamin A from animal source foods occurs mostly as active, preformed vitamin A (retinol), while that from vegetable source foods occurs as pro-vitamin A (beta-carotene and other carotenoids) that must be converted to active vitamin A by the body to be utilized. The efficiency of conversion varies among individuals; however, beta-carotene is converted more efficiently than other carotenoids. Green and deep-yellow vegetables, as well as deep-yellow fruits, are highest in beta-carotene.

Vitamin E (Tocopherol)

IU per 100-gram portion (3½ oz)	Food Source	IU per 100-gram portion (3½ oz)	Food Source
216	Wheat germ oil	3.0	Bran
90	Sunflower seeds	2.9	Asparagus
88	Sunflower seed oil	2.5	Salmon
72	Safflower oil	2.5	Brown rice
48	Almonds	2.3	Rye, whole
45	Sesame oil	2.2	Rye bread, dark
34	Peanut oil	1.9	Pecans
29	Corn oil	1.9	Wheat germ
22	Wheat germ	1.9	Rye and wheat crackers
18	Peanuts	1.4	Whole wheat bread
18	Olive oil	1.0	Carrots
14	Soybean oil	0.99	Peas
13	Peanuts, roasted	0.92	Walnuts
11	Peanut butter	0.88	Bananas
3.6	Butter	0.83	Eggs
3.2	Spinach	0.72	Tomatoes
3.0	Oatmeal	0.29	Lamb

Vitamin D

IU per 100-gram portion (3½ oz)	Food Source	IU per 100-gram portion (3½ oz)	Food Source
500	Sardines, canned	50	Liver
350	Salmon	50	Eggs
250	Tuna	40	Milk, fortified
150	Shrimp	40	Mushrooms
90	Butter	30	Natural cheeses
90	Sunflower seeds		

Vitamin K

IU per 100-gram portion (3½ oz)	Food Source	IU per 100-gram portion (3½ oz)	Food Source
650	Turnip greens	17	Whole wheat
200	Broccoli	14	Green beans
129	Lettuce	11	Pork
125	Cabbage	11	Eggs
92	Beef liver	10	Corn oil
89	Spinach	8	Peaches
57	Watercress	7	Beef
57	Asparagus	7	Chicken liver
35	Cheese	6	Raisins
30	Butter	5	Tomatoes
25	Pork liver	3	Milk
20	Oats	3	Potatoes
19	Green peas		

Vitamin B_1 (Thiamine)

IU per 100-gram portion (3½ oz)	Food Source	IU per 100-gram portion (3½ oz)	Food Source
15.61	Brewer's yeast	.73	Millet
14.01	Torula yeast	.72	Wheat bran
2.01	Wheat germ	.67	Pistachio nuts
1.96	Sunflower seeds	.65	Navy beans
1.84	Rice polishings	.63	Heart, veal
1.28	Pine nuts	.60	Buckwheat
1.14	Peanuts, with skins	.60	Oatmeal
1.10	Soybeans, dry	.55	Whole wheat flour
1.05	Cowpeas, dry	.55	Whole wheat
.98	Peanuts, without skins	.51	Lamb kidneys
.96	Brazil nuts	.48	Lima beans, dry
.93	Pork, lean	.46	Hazelnuts
.86	Pecans	.45	Lamb heart
.85	Soybean flour	.45	Wild rice
.84	Beans, pinto and red	.43	Cashews
.74	Split peas	.43	Rye, whole grain

.40	Lamb liver	.30	Pork liver
.40	Lobster	.25	Garlic, cloves
.38	Mung beans	.25	Beef liver
.38	Cornmeal, whole ground	.24	Almonds
		.24	Lima beans, fresh
.37	Lentils	.24	Pumpkin and squash seeds
.36	Beef kidneys		
.35	Green peas	.23	Brains, all kinds
.34	Macadamia nuts	.23	Chestnuts, fresh
.34	Brown rice	.23	Soybean sprouts
.33	Walnuts	.22	Peppers, red chili
.31	Garbanzos	.18	Sesame seeds, hulled

Vitamin B$_2$ (Riboflavin)

IU per 100-gram portion (3½ oz)	Food Source	IU per 100-gram portion (3½ oz)	Food Source
5.06	Torula yeast	.35	Soy flour
4.28	Brewer's yeast	.35	Wheat bran
3.28	Lamb liver	.33	Mackerel
3.26	Beef liver	.31	Collards
3.03	Pork liver	.31	Soybeans, dry
2.72	Calf liver	.30	Eggs
2.55	Beef kidneys	.29	Split peas
2.49	Chicken liver	.29	Beef tongue
2.42	Lamb kidneys	.29	Brains, all kinds
1.36	Chicken giblets	.26	Kale
1.05	Veal heart	.26	Parsley
.92	Almonds	.25	Cashews
.88	Beef heart	.25	Rice bran
.74	Lamb heart	.25	Veal
.68	Wheat germ	.24	Lamb, lean
.63	Wild rice	.23	Broccoli
.46	Mushrooms	.23	Chicken, meat and skin
.44	Egg yolks		
.38	Millet	.23	Pine nuts
.36	Peppers, hot red	.23	Salmon

.23	Sunflower seeds	.22	Rye, whole grain
.22	Navy beans	.21	Mung beans
.22	Beet and mustard greens	.21	Beans, pinto and red
		.21	Blackeyed peas
.22	Lentils	.21	Okra
.22	Pork, lean	.13	Sesame seeds, hulled
.22	Prunes		

Vitamin B₃ (Niacin)

IU per 100-gram portion (3½ oz)	Food Source	IU per 100-gram portion (3½ oz)	Food Source
44.4	Torula yeast	6.4	Beef kidneys
37.9	Brewer's yeast	6.2	Wild rice
29.8	Rice bran	6.1	Chicken giblets
28.2	Rice polishings	5.7	Lamb, lean
21.0	Wheat bran	5.6	Chicken, meat & skin
17.2	Peanuts, with skins	5.4	Sesame seeds
16.9	Lamb liver	5.4	Sunflower seeds
16.4	Pork liver	5.1	Beef, lean
15.8	Peanuts, without skins	5.0	Pork, lean
13.6	Beef liver	4.7	Brown rice
11.4	Calf liver	4.5	Pine nuts
11.3	Turkey, light meat	4.4	Buckwheat, whole grain
10.8	Chicken liver		
10.7	Chicken, light meat	4.4	Peppers, red chili
8.4	Trout	4.4	Whole wheat grain
8.3	Halibut	4.3	Whole wheat flour
8.2	Mackerel	4.2	Mushrooms
8.1	Veal heart	4.2	Wheat germ
8.0	Chicken, meat only	3.7	Barley
8.0	Swordfish	3.6	Herring
8.0	Turkey, meat only	3.5	Almonds
7.7	Goose, meat only	3.5	Shrimp
7.5	Beef heart	3.0	Haddock
7.2	Salmon	3.0	Split peas
6.4	Veal		

Pantothenic Acid (a B Vitamin)

IU per 100-gram portion (3½ oz)	Food Source	IU per 100-gram portion (3½ oz)	Food Source
12.0	Brewer's yeast	1.4	Lentils
11.0	Torula yeast	1.3	Rye flour, whole
8.0	Calf liver	1.3	Cashews
6.0	Chicken liver	1.3	Salmon
3.9	Beef kidneys	1.2	Camembert cheese
2.8	Peanuts	1.2	Garbanzos
2.6	Brains, all kinds	1.2	Wheat germ, toasted
2.6	Heart	1.2	Broccoli
2.2	Mushrooms	1.1	Hazelnuts
2.0	Soybean flour	1.1	Turkey, dark meat
2.0	Split peas	1.1	Brown rice
2.0	Beef tongue	1.1	Wheat flour, whole
1.9	Perch	1.1	Sardines
1.8	Blue cheese	1.1	Peppers, red chili
1.7	Pecans	1.1	Avocados
1.7	Soybeans	1.1	Veal, lean
1.6	Eggs	1.0	Blackeyed peas, dry
1.5	Lobster	1.0	Wild rice
1.5	Oatmeal, dry	1.0	Cauliflower
1.4	Buckwheat flour	1.0	Chicken, dark meat
1.4	Sunflower seeds	1.0	Kale

Vitamin B$_6$ (Pyridoxine)

IU per 100-gram portion (3½ oz)	Food Source	IU per 100-gram portion (3½ oz)	Food Source
3.00	Torula yeast	.81	Soybeans, dry
2.50	Brewer's yeast	.75	Chicken liver
1.25	Sunflower seeds	.73	Walnuts
1.15	Wheat germ, toasted	.70	Salmon
.90	Tuna	.69	Trout
.84	Beef liver	.67	Calf liver

.66	Mackerel	.30	Kale
.65	Pork liver	.30	Rye flour
.63	Soybean flour	.28	Spinach
.60	Lentils, dry	.26	Turnip greens
.58	Lima beans, dry	.26	Peppers, sweet
.58	Buckwheat flour	.25	Beef heart
.56	Blackeyed peas, dry	.25	Potatoes
.56	Navy beans, dry	.24	Prunes
.55	Brown rice	.24	Raisins
.54	Garbanzos, dry	.24	Sardines
.53	Pinto beans, dry	.24	Brussels sprouts
.51	Bananas	.23	Elderberries
.45	Pork, lean	.23	Perch
.44	Albacore	.22	Cod
.43	Beef, lean	.22	Barley
.43	Halibut	.22	Camembert cheese
.43	Beef kidneys	.22	Sweet potatoes
.42	Avocados	.21	Cauliflower
.41	Veal kidneys	.20	Popcorn, popped
.34	Whole wheat flour	.20	Red cabbage
.33	Chestnuts, fresh	.20	Leeks
.30	Egg yolks	.20	Molasses

Folic Acid (a B Vitamin)

IU per 100-gram portion (3½ oz)	Food Source	IU per 100-gram portion (3½ oz)	Food Source
2022	Brewer's yeast	180	Kidney beans
440	Blackeyed peas	145	Mung beans
430	Rice germ	130	Lima beans
425	Soy flour	125	Navy beans
305	Wheat germ	125	Garbanzos
295	Beef liver	110	Asparagus
275	Lamb liver	105	Lentils
225	Soybeans	77	Walnuts
220	Pork liver	75	Spinach, fresh
195	Bran	70	Kale

65	Filbert nuts	38	Whole wheat flour
60	Beet and mustard	33	Oatmeal
	greens	32	Dried figs
57	Textured vegetable	30	Avocado
	protein	28	Green beans
56	Peanuts, roasted	28	Corn
56	Peanut butter	28	Coconut, fresh
53	Broccoli	27	Pecans
50	Barley	25	Mushrooms
50	Split peas	25	Dates
49	Whole wheat cereal	14	Blackberries
49	Brussels sprouts	7	Ground beef
45	Almonds	5	Oranges

Vitamin B_{12} (Cobalamin)

IU per 100-gram portion (3½ oz)	Food Source	IU per 100-gram portion (3½ oz)	Food Source
104	Lamb liver	2.0	Eggs
98	Clams	2.0	Whey, dried
80	Beef liver	1.8	Beef, lean
63	Lamb kidneys	1.8	Edam cheese
60	Calf's liver	1.8	Swiss cheese
31	Beef kidneys	1.6	Brie cheese
25	Chicken liver	1.6	Gruyere cheese
18	Oysters	1.4	Blue cheese
17	Sardines	1.3	Haddock
11	Beef heart	1.2	Flounder
6	Egg yolks	1.2	Scallops
5.2	Lamb heart	1.0	Cheddar cheese
5.0	Trout	1.0	Cottage cheese
4.0	Brains, all kinds	1.0	Mozzarella cheese
4.0	Salmon	1.0	Halibut
3.0	Tuna	1.0	Perch, fillets
2.1	Lamb	1.0	Swordfish
2.1	Sweetbreads		

Biotin (a B Vitamin)

IU per 100-gram portion (3½ oz)	Food Source	IU per 100-gram portion (3½ oz)	Food Source
200	Brewer's yeast	24	Sardines, canned
127	Lamb liver	22	Eggs
100	Pork liver	21	Blackeyed peas
96	Beef liver	18	Split peas
70	Soy flour	18	Almonds
61	Soybeans	17	Cauliflower
60	Rice bran	16	Mushrooms
58	Rice germ	16	Whole wheat cereal
57	Rice polishings	15	Salmon, canned
52	Egg yolk	15	Textured vegetable protein
39	Peanut butter	14	Bran
37	Walnuts	13	Lentils
34	Peanuts, roasted	12	Brown rice
31	Barley	10	Chicken
27	Pecans		
24	Oatmeal		

Choline (a B Vitamin)

IU per 100-gram portion (3½ oz)	Food Source	IU per 100-gram portion (3½ oz)	Food Source
2200	Lecithin	223	Lentils
1490	Egg yolk	201	Split peas
550	Liver	170	Rice bran
504	Whole eggs	162	Peanuts, roasted
406	Wheat germ	156	Oatmeal
340	Soybeans	145	Peanut butter
300	Rice germ	143	Bran
257	Blackeyed peas	139	Barley
245	Garbanzo beans	122	Ham
240	Brewer's yeast	112	Brown rice

104	Veal	42	Green beans
102	Rice polishings	29	Potatoes
94	Whole wheat cereal	23	Cabbage
86	Molasses	22	Spinach
77	Pork	20.5	Textured vegetable
75	Beef		protein
75	Green peas	15	Milk
66	Sweet potatoes	12	Orange juice
48	Cheddar cheese	5	Butter

Inositol (a B Vitamin)

IU per 100-gram portion (3½ oz)	Food Source	IU per 100-gram portion (3½ oz)	Food Source
2200	Lecithin	150	Grapefruit
770	Wheat germ	130	Lentils
500	Navy beans	120	Raisins
460	Rice bran	120	Cantaloupe
454	Rice polishings	119	Brown rice
390	Barley, cooked	117	Orange juice
370	Rice germ	110	Whole wheat flour
370	Whole wheat	96	Peaches
270	Brewer's yeast	95	Cabbage
270	Oatmeal	95	Cauliflower
240	Blackeyed peas	88	Onions
240	Garbanzo beans	67	Whole wheat bread
210	Oranges	66	Sweet potatoes
205	Soy flour	64	Watermelon
200	Soybeans	60	Strawberries
180	Peanuts, roasted	55	Lettuce
180	Peanut butter	51	Beef liver
170	Lima beans	46	Tomatoes
162	Green peas	33	Eggs
150	Molasses	13	Milk
150	Split peas	11	Beef, round

Vitamin C (Ascorbic Acid)

IU per 100-gram portion (3½ oz)	Food Source	IU per 100-gram portion (3½ oz)	Food Source
1300	Acerola	36	Turnips
369	Peppers, red chili	35	Mangoes
242	Guavas	33	Asparagus
204	Peppers, red sweet	33	Cantaloupes
186	Kale leaves	32	Swiss chard
172	Parsley	32	Green onions
152	Collard leaves	31	Beef liver
139	Turnip greens	31	Okra
128	Peppers, green sweet	31	Tangerines
113	Broccoli	30	New Zealand spinach
102	Brussels sprouts	30	Oysters
97	Mustard greens	29	Lima beans, young
79	Watercress	29	Blackeyed peas
78	Cauliflower	29	Soybeans
66	Persimmons	27	Green peas
61	Cabbage, red	26	Radishes
59	Strawberries	25	Raspberries
56	Papayas	25	Chinese cabbage
51	Spinach	25	Yellow summer squash
50	Oranges and juice		
47	Cabbage	24	Loganberries
46	Lemon juice	23	Honeydew melon
38	Grapefruit and juice	23	Tomatoes
36	Elderberries	23	Pork liver
36	Calf liver		

For certain nutrients, there are few food sources that contain appreciable quantities. In these cases we list those foods that are best sources, rather than relative nutrient amounts.

Vitamin B17 (Amygdalin)

Foods containing more than 500 milligrams per 100-gram portion:

Wild blackberries	Apple seeds	Cherry seeds
Elderberries	Apricot seeds	Nectarine seeds

Peach seeds
Pear seeds
Plum seeds
Prune seeds

Fava beans
Mung beans
Bitter almonds
Macadamia nuts

Bamboo sprouts
Alfalfa leaves

Foods containing between 100 and 500 milligrams per 100-gram portion:

Boysenberries
Currants
Gooseberries
Huckleberries
Loganberries
Mulberries
Quince

Raspberries
Alfalfa sprouts
Buckwheat
Flax seed
Millet
Squash seed
Mung bean sprouts

Garbanzo beans
Blackeyed peas
Kidney beans
Lentils
Lima beans

Foods containing below 100 milligrams per 100-gram portion:

Commercial black-
   berries
Cranberries
Black beans

Peas
Lima beans
Sweet potatoes,
   yams

Cashews
Beet tops

Para-aminobenzoic Acid (PABA) (a B Vitamin)

Good sources include:

Mushrooms
Liver
Bran
Cabbage

Sunflower seeds
Wheat germ
Oats
Spinach

Whole milk
Eggs

Pangamic Acid (Vitamin B_{15})

Good sources include:

Apricot kernels
Yeast
Liver
Rice bran

Corn grits
Wheat germ
Sunflower seeds
Pumpkin seeds

Oat grits
Wheat bran

Bioflavonoids (Vitamin P)

Good sources include:

Grapes	Black currants	Peppers
Rose hips	Plums	Papaya
Prunes	Parsley	Cantaloupe
Oranges	Grapefruit	Tomatoes
Lemon juice	Cabbage	
Cherries	Apricots	

Calcium

IU per 100-gram portion (3½ oz)	Food Source	IU per 100-gram portion (3½ oz)	Food Source
1093	Kelp	118	Whole milk
925	Swiss cheese	114	Buckwheat, raw
750	Cheddar cheese	110	Sesame seeds, hulled
352	Carob flour	106	Ripe olives
296	Dulse	103	Broccoli
250	Collard leaves	99	English walnut
246	Turnip greens	94	Cottage cheese
245	Barbados molasses	93	Spinach
234	Almonds	73	Soybeans, cooked
210	Brewer's yeast	73	Pecans
203	Parsley	72	Wheat germ
200	Corn tortillas (lime added)	69	Peanuts
		68	Miso
187	Dandelion greens	68	Romaine lettuce
186	Brazil nuts	67	Dried apricots
151	Watercress	66	Rutabaga
129	Goat's milk	62	Raisins
128	Tofu	60	Black currants
126	Dried figs	59	Dates
121	Buttermilk	56	Green snap beans
120	Sunflower seeds	51	Globe artichokes
120	Yogurt	51	Dried prunes
119	Beet greens	51	Pumpkin and squash seeds
119	Wheat bran		

50	Cooked dry beans	22	Asparagus
49	Common cabbage	22	Winter squash
48	Soybean sprouts	21	Strawberry
46	Hard winter wheat	20	Millet
41	Oranges	19	Mung bean sprouts
39	Celery	17	Pineapple
38	Cashews	16	Grapes
38	Rye grain	16	Beets
37	Carrots	14	Cantaloupe
34	Barley	14	Jerusalem artichokes
32	Sweet potatoes	13	Tomatoes
32	Brown rice	12	Eggplant
29	Garlic	12	Chicken
28	Summer squash	11	Orange juice
27	Onions	10	Avocado
26	Lemons	10	Beef
26	Fresh green peas	8	Bananas
25	Cauliflower	7	Apples
25	Lentils, cooked	3	Sweet corn
22	Sweet cherries		

Magnesium

IU per 100-gram portion (3½ oz)	Food Source	IU per 100-gram portion (3½ oz)	Food Source
760	Kelp	160	Wheat grain
490	Wheat bran	142	Pecan
336	Wheat germ	131	English walnut
270	Almonds	115	Rye
267	Cashews	111	Tofu
258	Blackstrap molasses	106	Beet greens
231	Brewer's yeast	90	Coconut meat, dry
229	Buckwheat	88	Soybeans, cooked
225	Brazil nuts	88	Spinach
220	Dulse	88	Brown rice
184	Filberts	71	Dried figs
175	Peanuts	65	Swiss chard
162	Millet	62	Apricots, dried

58	Dates	24	Cauliflower
57	Collard leaves	23	Carrots
51	Shrimp	22	Celery
48	Sweet corn	21	Beef
45	Cheddar cheese	20	Asparagus
41	Parsley	19	Chicken
40	Prunes, dried	18	Pepper, green
38	Sunflower seeds	17	Winter squash
37	Common beans, cooked	16	Cantaloupe
		16	Eggplant
37	Barley	14	Tomato
36	Dandelion greens	13	Cabbage
36	Garlic	13	Grapes
35	Raisins	13	Milk
35	Fresh green peas	13	Pineapple
34	Potatoes with skin	13	Mushrooms
34	Crab	12	Onions
33	Bananas	11	Oranges
31	Sweet potatoes	11	Iceberg lettuce
30	Blackberries	9	Plums
25	Beets	8	Apples
24	Broccoli		

Phosphorus

IU per 100-gram portion (3½ oz)	Food Source	IU per 100-gram portion (3½ oz)	Food Source
1753	Brewer's yeast	457	Pinto beans, dried
1276	Wheat bran	409	Peanuts
1144	Pumpkin and squash seeds	400	Wheat
		380	English walnuts
1118	Wheat germ	376	Rye grain
837	Sunflower seeds	373	Cashews
693	Brazil nuts	352	Beef liver
592	Sesame seeds, hulled	338	Scallops
554	Soybeans, dried	311	Millet
504	Almonds	290	Barley, pearled
478	Cheddar cheese	289	Pecans

267	Dulse	51	Okra
240	Kelp	51	Spinach
239	Chicken	44	Green beans
221	Brown rice	44	Pumpkin
205	Eggs	42	Avocado
202	Garlic	40	Beet greens
175	Crab	39	Swiss chard
152	Cottage cheese	38	Winter squash
150	Beef or lamb	36	Carrots
119	Lentils, cooked	36	Onions
116	Mushrooms	35	Red cabbage
116	Fresh peas	33	Beets
111	Sweet corn	31	Radishes
101	Raisins	29	Summer squash
93	Milk	28	Celery
88	Globe artichoke	27	Cucumber
87	Yogurt	27	Tomatoes
80	Brussels sprouts	26	Bananas
79	Prunes, dried	26	Persimmon
78	Broccoli	26	Eggplant
77	Figs, dried	26	Lettuce
69	Yams	24	Nectarines
67	Soybean sprouts	22	Raspberries
64	Mung bean sprouts	20	Grapes
63	Dates	20	Oranges
63	Parsley	17	Olives
62	Asparagus	16	Cantaloupe
59	Bamboo shoots	10	Apples
56	Cauliflower	8	Pineapple
53	Potato, with skin		

Sodium

IU per 100-gram portion (3½ oz)	Food Source	IU per 100-gram portion (3½ oz)	Food Source
3007	Kelp	1428	Dill pickles
2400	Green olives	1319	Soy sauce (1 tablespoon)
2132	Salt (1 teaspoon)		

828	Ripe olives	47	Yogurt
747	Sauerkraut	45	Parsley
700	Cheddar cheese	43	Artichoke
265	Scallops	34	Dried figs
229	Cottage cheese	30	Lentils, dried
210	Lobster	30	Sunflower seeds
147	Swiss chard	27	Raisins
130	Beet greens	26	Red cabbage
130	Buttermilk	19	Garlic
126	Celery	19	White beans
122	Eggs	15	Broccoli
110	Cod	15	Mushrooms
71	Spinach	13	Cauliflower
70	Lamb	10	Onions
65	Pork	10	Sweet potatoes
64	Chicken	9	Brown rice
60	Beef	9	Lettuce
60	Beets	6	Cucumber
60	Sesame seeds	5	Peanuts
52	Watercress	4	Avocado
50	Whole milk	3	Tomatoes
49	Turnips	2	Eggplant
47	Carrots		

Potassium

IU per 100-gram portion (3½ oz)	Food Source	IU per 100-gram portion (3½ oz)	Food Source
8060	Dulse	640	Figs, dried
5273	Kelp	604	Avocado
920	Sunflower seeds	603	Pecans
827	Wheat germ	600	Yams
773	Almonds	550	Swiss chard
763	Raisins	540	Soybeans, cooked
727	Parsley	529	Garlic
715	Brazil nuts	470	Spinach
674	Peanuts	450	English walnuts
648	Dates	430	Millet

416	Beans, cooked	214	Eggplant
414	Mushrooms	213	Peppers, green
407	Potatoes, with skin	208	Beets
382	Broccoli	202	Peaches
370	Bananas	202	Summer squash
370	Meats	200	Oranges
369	Winter squash	199	Raspberries
366	Chicken	191	Cherries
341	Carrots	164	Strawberries
341	Celery	162	Grapefruit juice
322	Radishes	158	Grapes
295	Cauliflower	157	Onions
282	Watercress	146	Pineapple
278	Asparagus	144	Milk
268	Red cabbage	141	Lemon juice
264	Lettuce	130	Pears
251	Cantaloupe	129	Eggs
249	Lentils, cooked	110	Apples
244	Tomatoes	100	Watermelon
243	Sweet potatoes	70	Brown rice, cooked
234	Papaya		

Iron

IU per 100-gram portion (3½ oz)	Food Source	IU per 100-gram portion (3½ oz)	Food Source
100.3	Kelp	4.7	Almonds
17.3	Brewer's yeast	3.9	Dried prunes
16.1	Blackstrap molasses	3.8	Cashews
14.9	Wheat bran	3.7	Beef, lean
11.2	Pumpkin and squash seeds	3.5	Raisins
		3.4	Jerusalem artichokes
9.4	Wheat germ	3.4	Brazil nuts
8.8	Beef liver	3.3	Beet greens
7.1	Sunflower seeds	3.2	Swiss chard
6.8	Millet	3.1	Dandelion greens
6.2	Parsley	3.1	English walnuts
6.1	Clams	3.0	Dates

2.9	Pork	0.8	Pumpkin
2.7	Cooked dry beans	0.8	Mushrooms
2.4	Sesame seeds, hulled	0.7	Bananas
2.4	Pecans	0.7	Beets
2.3	Eggs	0.7	Carrots
2.1	Lentils	0.7	Eggplant
2.1	Peanuts	0.7	Sweet potatoes
1.9	Lamb	0.6	Avocado
1.9	Tofu	0.6	Figs
1.8	Green peas	0.6	Potatoes
1.6	Brown rice	0.6	Corn
1.6	Ripe olives	0.5	Pineapple
1.5	Chicken	0.5	Nectarines
1.3	Artichokes	0.5	Watermelon
1.3	Mung bean sprouts	0.5	Winter squash
1.2	Salmon	0.5	Brown rice, cooked
1.1	Broccoli	0.5	Tomatoes
1.1	Currants	0.4	Oranges
1.1	Whole wheat bread	0.4	Cherries
1.1	Cauliflower	0.4	Summer squash
1.0	Cheddar cheese	0.3	Papaya
1.0	Strawberries	0.3	Celery
1.0	Asparagus	0.3	Cottage cheese
0.9	Blackberries	0.3	Apples
0.8	Red cabbage		

Copper

IU per 100-gram portion (3½ oz)	Food Source	IU per 100-gram portion (3½ oz)	Food Source
13.7	Oysters	1.1	Beef liver
2.3	Brazil nuts	0.8	Buckwheat
2.1	Soy lecithin	0.8	Peanuts
1.4	Almonds	0.7	Cod liver oil
1.3	Hazelnuts	0.7	Lamb chops
1.3	Walnuts	0.5	Sunflower oil
1.3	Pecans	0.4	Butter
1.2	Split peas, dry	0.4	Rye grain

0.4	Pork loin	0.2	Whole wheat
0.4	Barley	0.2	Chicken
0.4	Gelatin	0.2	Eggs
0.3	Shrimp	0.2	Corn oil
0.3	Olive oil	0.2	Ginger root
0.3	Clams	0.2	Molasses
0.3	Carrots	0.2	Turnips
0.3	Coconut	0.1	Green peas
0.3	Garlic	0.1	Papaya
0.2	Millet	0.1	Apples

Black pepper, thyme, paprika, bay leaves, and active dry yeast are also high in copper.

Manganese

IU per 100-gram portion (3½ oz)	Food Source	IU per 100-gram portion (3½ oz)	Food Source
3.5	Pecans	0.16	Carrots
2.8	Brazil nuts	0.15	Broccoli
2.5	Almonds	0.14	Brown rice
1.8	Barley	0.14	Whole wheat bread
1.3	Rye	0.13	Swiss cheese
1.3	Buckwheat	0.13	Corn
1.3	Split peas, dry	0.11	Cabbage
1.1	Whole wheat	0.10	Peaches
0.8	Walnuts	0.09	Butter
0.8	Fresh spinach	0.06	Tangerines
0.7	Peanuts	0.06	Peas
0.6	Oats	0.05	Eggs
0.5	Raisins	0.04	Beets
0.5	Turnip greens	0.04	Coconut
0.5	Rhubarb	0.03	Apples
0.4	Beet greens	0.03	Oranges
0.3	Brussels sprouts	0.03	Pears
0.3	Oatmeal	0.03	Lamb chops
0.2	Cornmeal	0.03	Pork chops
0.2	Millet	0.03	Cantaloupe
0.19	Gorgonzola cheese	0.03	Tomatoes

0.02	Milk	0.01	Beef liver
0.02	Chicken breasts	0.01	Scallops
0.02	Green beans	0.01	Halibut
0.02	Apricots	0.01	Cucumbers

Cloves, ginger, thyme, bay leaves, and tea are also high in manganese.

Zinc

IU per 100-gram portion (3½ oz)	Food Source	IU per 100-gram portion (3½ oz)	Food Source
148.7	Fresh oysters	1.7	Haddock
6.8	Ginger root	1.6	Green peas
5.6	Ground round steak	1.5	Shrimp
5.3	Lamb chops	1.2	Turnips
4.5	Pecans	0.9	Parsley
4.2	Split peas, dry	0.9	Potatoes
4.2	Brazil nuts	0.6	Garlic
3.9	Beef liver	0.5	Carrots
3.5	Nonfat dry milk	0.5	Whole wheat bread
3.5	Egg yolk	0.4	Black beans
3.2	Whole wheat	0.4	Raw milk
3.2	Rye	0.4	Pork chops
3.2	Oats	0.4	Corn
3.2	Peanuts	0.3	Grape juice
3.1	Lima beans	0.3	Olive oil
3.1	Soy lecithin	0.3	Cauliflower
3.1	Almonds	0.2	Spinach
3.0	Walnuts	0.2	Cabbage
2.9	Sardines	0.2	Lentils
2.6	Chicken	0.2	Butter
2.5	Buckwheat	0.2	Lettuce
2.4	Hazel nuts	0.1	Cucumber
1.9	Clams	0.1	Yams
1.7	Anchovies	0.1	Tangerines
1.7	Tuna	0.1	String beans

Black pepper, paprika, mustard, chili powder, thyme, and cinnamon are also high in zinc.

Chromium

The values listed below show the total chromium content of these foods, and do not indicate the amount that may be biologically active as the Glucose tolerance factor (GTF). Those foods marked with an * are high in GTF.

IU per 100-gram portion (3½ oz)	Food Source	IU per 100-gram portion (3½ oz)	Food Source
112	Brewer's yeast*	11	Scallops
57	Beef round	11	Swiss cheese
55	Calf's liver*	10	Bananas
42	Whole wheat bread*	10	Spinach
38	Wheat bran	10	Pork chop
30	Rye bread	9	Carrots
30	Fresh chili	8	Navy beans, dry
26	Oysters	7	Shrimp
24	Potatoes	7	Lettuce
23	Wheat germ	5	Oranges
19	Peppers, green	5	Lobster tails
16	Hen's eggs	5	Blueberries
15	Chicken	4	Green beans
14	Apples	4	Cabbage
13	Butter	4	Mushrooms
13	Parsnips	3	Beer
12	Cornmeal	3	Strawberries
12	Lamb chop	1	Milk

Selenium

IU per 100-gram portion (3½ oz)	Food Source	IU per 100-gram portion (3½ oz)	Food Source
144	Butter	89	Apple cider vinegar
141	Smoked herring	77	Scallops
123	Smelts	66	Barley
111	Wheat germ	66	Whole wheat bread
103	Brazil nuts	65	Lobster

63	Bran	18	Beef liver
59	Shrimps	18	Lamb chop
57	Red swiss chard	18	Egg yolk
56	Oats	12	Mushrooms
55	Clams	12	Chicken
51	King crab	10	Swiss cheese
49	Oysters	5	Cottage cheese
48	Milk	5	Wine
43	Cod	4	Radishes
39	Brown rice	4	Grape juice
34	Top round steak	3	Pecans
30	Lamb	2	Hazelnuts
27	Turnips	2	Almonds
26	Molasses	2	Green beans
25	Garlic	2	Kidney beans
24	Barley	2	Onions
19	Orange juice	2	Carrots
19	Gelatin	2	Cabbage
19	Beer	1	Oranges

Iodine

IU per 100-gram portion (3½ oz)	Food Source	IU per 100-gram portion (3½ oz)	Food Source
90	Clams	11	Cheddar cheese
65	Shrimp	10	Pork
62	Haddock	10	Lettuce
56	Halibut	9	Spinach
50	Oysters	9	Green peppers
50	Salmon	9	Butter
37	Sardines, canned	7	Milk
19	Beef liver	6	Cream
16	Pineapple	6	Cottage cheese
16	Tuna, canned	6	Beef
14	Eggs	3	Lamb
11	Peanuts	3	Raisins
11	Whole wheat bread		

Nickel

IU per 100-gram portion (3½ oz)	Food Source	IU per 100-gram portion (3½ oz)	Food Source
700	Soybeans, dry	25	Carrots
500	Beans, dry	24	Eggs
410	Soy flour	22	Cabbage
310	Lentils	20	Tomatoes
250	Split peas	20	Onions
175	Green peas	18	Potatoes
153	Green beans	16	Beef
150	Oats	16	Apricots
132	Walnuts	16	Oranges
122	Hazelnuts	15	Cheese
100	Buckwheat	15	Watermelon
90	Barley	14	Lettuce
90	Corn	13	Apples
90	Parsley	12	Whole wheat bread
38	Whole wheat	12	Beets
35	Spinach	12	Pears
30	Fish	8	Grapes
27	Cucumbers	8	Radishes
26	Liver	6	Pine nuts
25	Rye bread	6	Lamb
25	Pork	3	Milk

Molybdenum

IU per 100-gram portion (3½ oz)	Food Source	IU per 100-gram portion (3½ oz)	Food Source
155	Lentils	100	Spinach
135	Beef liver	77	Beef kidney
130	Split peas	75	Brown rice
120	Cauliflower	70	Garlic
110	Green peas	60	Oats
109	Brewer's yeast	53	Eggs
100	Wheat germ	50	Rye bread

45	Corn	24	Lamb
42	Barley	21	Green beans
40	Fish	19	Crab
36	Whole wheat	19	Molasses
32	Whole wheat bread	16	Cantaloupe
32	Chicken	14	Apricots
31	Cottage cheese	10	Raisins
30	Beef	10	Butter
30	Potatoes	7	Strawberries
25	Onions	5	Carrots
25	Peanuts	5	Cabbage
25	Coconut	3	Whole milk
25	Pork	1	Goat's milk

Vanadium

IU per 100-gram portion (3½ oz)	Food Source	IU per 100-gram portion (3½ oz)	Food Source
100	Buckwheat	10	Cabbage
80	Parsley	10	Garlic
70	Soybeans	6	Tomatoes
64	Safflower oil	5	Radishes
42	Eggs	5	Onions
41	Sunflower seed oil	5	Whole wheat
35	Oats	4	Lobster
30	Olive oil	4	Beets
15	Sunflower seeds	3	Apples
15	Corn	2	Plums
14	Green beans	2	Lettuce
11	Peanut oil	2	Millet
10	Carrots		

The following foods contain large amounts of sodium chloride, added during processing, and should generally be avoided:

Canned or frozen vegetables	Packaged spice mixes
Cured, smoked, or canned meats	Bouillon cubes
	Canned fish

Commercial peanut butter
Potato chips, corn chips,
  pretzels, etc.
Luncheon meats
Salted nuts

Salted crackers
Canned or packaged soups
Processed cheeses
Commercial salad dressings
Meat tenderizers

OTHER ASPECTS OF GOOD NUTRITION

Good nutrition must take into account four main principles:

1. Avoid all food artifacts.
2. Avoid foods to which you have an existing allergy.
3. Eat in such a way as to minimize the response to allergenic foods, to prevent the creation of new allergies.
4. Eat food that is palatable and follow the daily eating pattern that you find most comfortable.

The harmful effect of consuming food artifacts has already been discussed. Obviously, the degree of harm depends upon the quantity of artifacts eaten. When rats are fed nutritious food to which more and more sugar is added, the degree of harmfulness, as measured by their growth, increases. The rate of growth diminishes as the amount of sugar added goes up. The same rule applies to food artifacts. Without question, the fewer food artifacts you eat, the less harm you do to your body.

We suggest that the proportion of food artifacts be brought down as much as possible. Reduce it to at least 20 percent of your total caloric intake. This means that all the calories provided by junk (sugar, white flour, etc.) should not exceed about 400 calories per day—a diet that will greatly increase the amount of food fiber. If you have a problem with constipation (fewer than two bowel movements a day), even with the extra fiber, you should increase your fiber intake by adding bran, alfalfa tablets, or any other high-fiber food. Remember, foods adulterated by flavors, colors, and any other chemicals that have not been shown to be safe are also food artifacts.

Single and multiple food allergies are exceedingly common, something an experienced clinical ecologist can spot immediately. Adults who have bags under their eyes that vary in color from normal flesh tones to dark, almost black, are allergic people. Some people have large half-moons under their eyes. Even children can be affected. Usually allergy-prone people have some puffiness under the eyes. These surface blemishes are commonly ascribed to fatigue and lack of sleep. While fatigue does intensify the eye circles, it is not the true cause.

You should suspect two classes of foods (and food artifacts) as being allergens. These are the staple foods and artifacts that are eaten nearly every day, such as cereals, dairy products, sugar, and foods (and/or artifacts) that you dislike, or of which you are inordinately fond. A dislike for a certain food may have arisen years ago before from an unpleasant reaction to it. The reason for the dislike may have been forgotten, but not the dislike itself. These foods present no problem since they are not eaten. If, however, they are introduced into the diet again for any reason, they may make you ill.

This kind of reaction has happened with a small proportion of patients who have been placed on a hypoglycemic diet by their physicians, or who have adopted such a diet on their own. For example, in order to follow a rigorous diet that calls for frequent eating of high-protein foods, an individual may increase his milk intake, when previously he had avoided milk. After going on the hypoglycemic diet, such a person may have felt much better for many months, but eventually became ill again, experiencing depression and anxiety. This coincided with the reappearance of a milk allergy, an allergy linked to a past dislike of the milk.

One of our patients obeyed the rules of the hypoglycemic diet by eating a beef steak with each meal. He became more and more distressed until an allergist found he was allergic to beef. As soon as he eliminated beef from his eating program, he recovered.

Any food or food artifacts of which one is extremely fond should be looked upon with suspicion. It is possible to be addicted to them based upon a chronic allergy. We have seen patients consume forty cups of coffee with sugar each day, 120 ounces of soft drink, a loaf or more of white bread, or twelve glasses of milk.

To learn about your allergic addiction, it might be a good idea to make a list of all the foods you would not dream of doing without, and avoid them for about four weeks. You will be surprised by how much better you will feel once you've gone through the two-week withdrawal period. This may be very intense, but it is not quite as extreme as "cold turkey" withdrawal from heroin or morphine.

Although it may seem to contradict the rule we have just

discussed, our advice is to eat only palatable foods. Before, we were discussing not palatability, but inordinate longing or craving for certain foods. Palatability is food enjoyment. It is important to enjoy what you eat, not only for the pleasure derived from it, but because it improves the ability of the digestive tract to digest and assimilate food.

Palatability served us well as long as we had only whole food to eat. It was only after food artifacts came about that our palate became perverted. So we cannot depend solely on taste; we should use our intelligence to select nutritious foods. It is surprising, though, how soon we develop a liking for whole natural foods again. Many people who have scoffed at whole wheat bread as animal fodder have been amazed at how tasty it became after they stopped eating white bread. What was formerly a delicious arti- fact now becomes a pallid, gooey substance—consumed with discomfort.

If the above suggestions are followed, the ravages of senility will be held in abeyance for much longer periods than would otherwise be the case. It is even possible that people who follow these practices all their lives may require no, or very few, nutrient supplements.

There is another important advantage to following a whole- food-only, allergy-free, palatable diet: It will decrease the damage that will ensue if you should suffer a stroke or a cardiac arrest. Dr. R.E. Myers reported that the real cause of damage to the brain during stoppage of circulation was the accumulation of lactic acid in the brain. This depended upon the amount of glucose found in the brain immediately prior to the stoppage. This study by Meyers has been cited before, but its importance causes us to emphasize it again.

Meyers found that monkeys starved for twenty-four hours before circulatory arrest was produced and could withstand up to twenty-four minutes before brain damage was found. In humans, it is generally accepted that four to six minutes of stoppage of blood to the brain produces irreversible brain damage.

If animals deprived of food were infused with glucose imme- diately before the circulatory arrest, they suffered severe and permanent brain damage after only fourteen minutes. Myers found that when glucose was present, there was much more lactic acid in the brain. Normal lactate levels are three micro- moles per gram of tissue. After ten minutes of circulatory arrest in food-deprived monkeys, lactate increased to eleven micromoles; when they were given a glucose infusion, it went up to thirty micromoles.[2]

The work by Myers suggests that the amount of brain damage following cirulatory arrest depends upon the amount of sugar in the blood. If a patient is receiving an infusion of 5 percent glucose in saline, as is commonly given in a hospital, circulatory arrest is more apt to cause severe brain damage. For this reason, as well as others, glucose infusions should be used with great care and administered very slowly.

But there is another, perhaps even more important, matter. People who follow the basic rules of good nutrition are much less apt to have elevated blood sugar levels after meals. A person who has been on food artifacts for years will suffer elevated blood sugar levels after meals. If such a person suffers a stroke or circulatory arrest after a meal, he will be like the monkey infused with glucose—much more apt to have brain damage and less able to withstand a long period of circulatory arrest.

The frequency of eating remains an individual matter. If you have no food allergies, your personal preference is an adequate guide. Three meals a day seems best for most people, but some may get along well on two or even one. Others will be more comfortable with five or six smaller meals each day. If you have hypoglycemia and it is impossible to eliminate the foods that cause an allergy, more frequent meals may be the best.

The importance of good nutrition must be emphasized. Many people feel that if they have been eating certain things for so many years, these items could not be harmful to them. They are more apt to change their view if they accept the idea that food artifacts made them ill.

Many people want to eat well and know what they should eat, but have a deficiency in their sense of taste and smell. This may be due to a lack of zinc. We have seen several patients who could not taste food properly and found their food to be unappetizing. It required a heroic effort on their part to eat what they knew they must. After several months of zinc supplementation, their sense of taste and smell became normal.

Finally, even the best advice on nutrition will not be heeded if there are anatomical or physiological factors that make it impossible to follow this advice. All these factors should be determined. Even fatigue may lead to malnutrition from starvation.

Several years ago, Dr. Hoffer was asked to see an elderly patient in the medical ward because he would not eat and was starving to death. When Dr. Hoffer first saw him, he weighed under eighty pounds. A few months earlier he had been suspected of having cancer of the stomach. He had suffered from an ulcer-type pain and had been losing weight rapidly. When his stomach was examined during surgery, a suspicious thickening was found, and a section of his stomach was removed. Later it was found the lesion was not cancer. His post-surgical recovery was poor, but after a while, he was discharged anyway. A few weeks later, he made emergency return because he was unable to eat and was suffering continuous weight loss.

In the hospital, in spite of intravenous transfusions and good care, the man continued to lose weight. When Dr. Hoffer saw him, they spoke together very quietly, and it was discovered that the patient was normally hungry, but was too weak to feed himself. When he did get some food down, the poor fellow was so exhausted that most of it came back up. Dr. Hoffer also discovered that the patient could retain fluids but not solid food.

The patient was immediately started on a milk preparation that was fortified with milk powder and contained banana and raw eggs. The nursing staff fed him one ounce of this mixture each hour. Niacin, ascorbic acid, and a few other vitamins were added to his intravenous fluid. In a few days, the man was able to sit up and feed himself. Within a few weeks, he went on to solid food and for a while gained one pound each day. He was discharged a few weeks later on a sugar-free, high-protein diet that required frequent meals, and he has remained well.

The medical intern on the case illustrates the nutritional ignorance of most recent medical graduates. After Dr. Hoffer had written his hospital orders, he received an irate phone call from the intern indicating his worry and concern. The diet he had ordered was free of sugar. The intern reminded Dr. Hoffer on the phone that some weight had to be restored to the patient, and he could not see how a sugar-free diet could do so. He erroneously thought sugar was needed for weight gain. Fortunately for the patient, his surgeon accepted Dr. Hoffer's advice and not that of the intern. Dr. Hoffer tried to explain to intern, but he was too irate and hostile to listen. He never did call back after the patient recovered, having gained all the weight he required.

9. NIACIN,

CORONARY DISEASE,

AND LONGEVITY

> Eat a third, drink a third, and leave a third of your stomach empty; then, should anger seize you, there will be room for its rage.
>
> —Talmud

The finding that niacin lowers cholesterol was proven in a 1955 study by Altschul, Hoffer, and Stephen, as was discussed in a previous chapter.[1] Their report initiated the studies that eventually proved that niacin increases longevity. At the same time that they were examining the effect of niacin on cholesterol levels, Russian scientists were also measuring the effect of vitamins on blood lipids, but they used very little niacin and found no significant decreases (Simonson and Keyes, 1961).[2]

The finding that niacin lowered cholesterol was soon confirmed by Parsons, Achor, Berge, McKenzie, and Barker (1956) and Parsons (1961, 1961a, 1962) at the Mayo Clinic. That launched niacin on its way as a hypocholesterolemic substance.[3,4,5,6] Since then niacin has been found to be a normalizing agent, which means it elevates high-density lipoprotein cholesterol levels, decreases levels of low-density and very-low-density lipoprotein cholesterol, and lowers triglycerides. Grundy, Mok, Zechs, and Berman (1981) found that niacin lowered cholesterol by 22 percent and triglycerides by 52 percent. They wrote, "To our knowledge, no other single agent has such potential for lowering both cholesterol and triglycerides."[7]

THE CORONARY STUDY

The reason for concern about elevated cholesterol levels is that

163

they are associated with increased risk of developing coronary disease. The association between cholesterol levels in the diet and coronary disease is not nearly as high, even though the total diet is a main factor. The kind of diet generally recommended by orthomolecular physicians will keep cholesterol levels down in most people. This diet can be described as a high-fiber, sugar-free diet that is rich in complex polysaccharides such as vegetables and whole grains.

Once it became possible to lower cholesterol levels even without altering diet, it became possible to test the hypothesis that lowering cholesterol levels would decrease the risk of developing coronary disease. Dr. Edwin Boyle, a medical researcher then working with the National Institutes of Health in Washington, D.C., quickly became interested in niacin. He began to follow a series of patients using three grams of niacin per day. He reported his conclusions in a document prepared for the physicians of Alcoholics Anonymous by Bill Wilson (1968).[8] In this report, Boyle reported that he had kept 160 coronary patients on niacin for ten years. Only six of them died, as compared to a statistical expectation that 62 would have died with conventional care. He stated, "... from the strictly medical viewpoint I believe all patients taking niacin would survive longer and enjoy life much more."

His prediction was upheld when the National Coronary Drug Study was evaluated by Paul L. Canner, chief statistician at the Maryland Medical Institute in Baltimore. But Boyle's data spoke for itself. The continuous use of niacin will decrease mortality and prolong life. Perhaps Boyle's study was one of the reasons the Coronary Drug Project was started in 1966. Dr. Boyle was an advisor to this study, which was designed to assess the long-term efficiency and safety of five compounds in 8,341 men, ages thirty to sixty-four, who had suffered myocardial infarctions (heart attacks resulting in permanent heart damage) at least three months before entering the study.

The Coronary Drug Project was conducted between 1966 and 1975, supported by the National Heart and Lung Institute. It was conducted at fifty-three clinical centers in twenty-six American states, and was designed to measure the efficiency of several lipid-lowering drugs and to determine whether lowering cholesterol levels in patients with previous mycardial infarctions would be beneficial. Niacin, two dosage strengths of estrogens, clofibrate, dextrothyroxine, and a placebo were tested.

Eighteen months after the study began, the higher-dose estrogen group in the study was discontinued because of an excess of new non-fatal myocardial infarctions compared with the placebo group. The dextrothyroxine group was stopped for the same reason for patients with frequent ectopic ventricular beats. After thirty-six months dextrothyroxine was discontinued for the rest of the group, again because myocardial infarctions were increased. After fifty-six months the low-dose estrogen group study was stopped. There had been no significant benefit to compensate for the increased incidence of pulmonary embolism and thrombophlebitis and increased mortality from cancer.

Eventually only niacin, clofibrate, and placebo groups were continued until the study was completed in 1975.

THE CANNER STUDY

Dr. Paul L. Canner, chief statistician at the Maryland Medical Research Institute in Baltimore, later examined the data for the Coronary Drug Project Research Group. About 6,000 men were still alive at the end of the treatment trial in 1975. This new study was started in 1981 to determine if the two estrogen regimens and the dextrothyroxine regimen had caused any long-term adverse effects. High-dose estrogen had been discontinued because it increased nonfatal myocardial infarctions, low-dose estrogen increased cancer deaths, and dextrothyroxine increased total mortality, as compared to clofibrate, niacin, and the placebo. None of the subjects continued to take the drugs after 1975.

The 1985 follow-up study showed no significant differences in mortality between those treatment groups that had been discontinued and either the placebo or clofibrate. However, to the investigators' surprise, the niacin group fared much better. The cumulative percentage of deaths for all causes was 59.7 percent for low-dose estrogens, 58.3 percent for high-dose estrogens, 57.8 percent for clofibrate, 57.0 percent for dextrothyroxine, 58.2 percent for placebo, and 52.0 percent for niacin. The mortality in the niacin group was 11 percent lower than in the placebo group. The mortality benefit from niacin was present in each major category, or cause of death: coronary, other cardiovascular, cancer, and others. Analysis of life-table curves comparing niacin against the placebo showed the niacin patients lived two years longer. With an average follow-up of fourteen years, there were 70 fewer deaths in the niacin group than would have been expected from the mortality in the placebo group. Patients with cholesterol levels higher than 240 milligrams per 100 milliliters of blood benefitted more than those with lower levels.[9]

What is surprising is that the niacin benefit carried on for such a long period after the subjects stopped using it. In fact, the benefit increased with the number of years followed up. It is highly probable the results would have been even better if patients had not stopped taking niacin in 1975. Boyle's patients, who took niacin for ten years and received individual attention, had a 90 percent decrease in mortality. With the size of the Coronary Study, this type of individual attention for the majority of patients was not possible. Many dropped out because of the niacin flush; of these, many could probably have been persuaded to remain in the study if they had been given more individual attention. This is very hard to do in a large-scale clinical study of this type. In discussions with Dr. Hoffer, Boyle later referred to this as one of the defects in the Coronary Drug Study. It seems reasonable to conclude that the proper use of niacin for similar patients should decrease mortality somewhere between 11 and 90 percent after a ten-year follow-up, with the reduction in mortality increasing as the follow-up period becomes longer. Nevertheless, niacin is now established as a safe natural substance that will decrease mortality and increase longevity, especially in patients with elevated cholesterol levels.

In 1985 the National Institutes of Health (NIH) released the conclusions reached by a consensus development conference on lowering blood cholesterol to prevent heart disease, held December 10 through 12, in 1984. This was followed by an NIH conference statement, "Lowering Blood Cholesterol to Prevent Heart Disease," Volume 5, No. 7.[10] This statement reports that heart disease kills 550,000 Americans each year and 5.4 million are ill. The total costs of heart disease are $60 billion per year. Main risk factors include cigarette smoking, high blood pressure, and high blood cholesterol. The relationship of age and cholesterol levels to risk is shown in Table 9.1.

NIH recommends that the first step in treatment should be dietary, and their recommendations are met by the orthomolecular diet. But when diet alone is not adequate, drugs should be used. Bile-acid sequestrants and niacin are favored, while the main commercial drug, clofibrate, is not recommended "because it is not effective in most individuals with a high blood cholesterol

Table 9.1 Moderate- to High-Risk Blood Cholesterol Levels

Age Group	Moderate Risk	High Risk
20–29	Greater than 200 mg cholesterol per 100 ml blood	Greater than 220 mg cholesterol per 100 ml blood
30–39	Greater than 220 mg cholesterol per 100 ml blood	Greater than 240 mg cholesterol per 100 ml blood
40 and over	Greater than 240 mg cholesterol per 100 ml blood	Greater than 260 mg cholesterol per 100 ml blood

level but normal triglyceride level. Moreover, an excess of overall mortality was reported in the World Health Organization trial of this drug." Since niacin is effective only in megavitamin doses, 1 gram three times per day, NIH is at last promoting megavitamin therapy. The NIH asked that their conference statement be "posted, duplicated, and distributed to interested staff." Since every doctor has patients with high blood cholesterol levels, they should all be interested.

NIACIN COMBINED WITH CHOLESTEROL-LOWERING DRUGS

Familial hypercholesterolemia is an inherited disease in which plasma cholesterol levels are very high. Illingworth, Phillipson, Rapp, and Connor (1981) described a series of thirteen patients with this disease who were treated with ten grams of colestipol twice a day, and later fifteen grams twice a day.[11] Their cholesterol levels ranged from 345 to 524 and triglycerides from 70 to 232. When this drug, plus diet, did not decrease cholesterol levels below 270, they were given niacin, starting with 250 milligrams three times daily and increasing every two to four weeks until a final dose of three to eight grams (3,000 to 8,000 milligrams) per day was reached. To reduce the flush, patients took aspirin with each dose for four to six weeks. This dose of niacin caused no abnormal liver function test results. The combination of drugs normalized blood cholesterol and lipid levels.

The researchers concluded, "In most patients with heterozygous familial hypercholesterolemia, combined drug therapy with a bile acid sequestrant and niacin results in a normal or near normal lipid profile. Long-term use of such a regimen affords the potential for preventing, or even reversing, the premature development of atherosclerosis that occurs so frequently in this group of patients."

At about the same time, Kane, Malloy, Tun, Phillips, Freedman, Williams, Rowe, and Havel (1981) reported similar results with a larger series of fifty patients.[12] They also studied the combined effect of colestipol and clofibrate. Abnormalities of liver function occurred only when the dose of niacin increased rapidly. The first month, 2.5 grams per day were administered; the second month, the level was increased to 5.0 grams per day; and the third month, it was increased to 7.5 grams. The niacin remained at 7.5 grams per day thereafter. In a few participants, blood sugar went up a little (from 115 to 120 milligrams), and uric acid levels exceeded 8 milligrams percent in six. None developed gout. All other tests were normal. They concluded, "The remarkable ability of the combination of colestipol and niacin to lower circulating levels of LDL and to decrease the size of tendon xanthomas suggests that this combination is the most likely available regimen to alter the course of atherosclerosis." The combination of colestipol and clofibrate was not as effective. For the first time it is possible to extend the life span of patients with familial hypercholesterolemia.

Fortunately, niacin does not decrease cholesterol to dangerously low levels. Cheraskin and Ringsdorf (1982) reviewed some of the evidence that links low cholesterol levels to an increased incidence of cancer and greater mortality in general.[13] Ueshima, Lida, and Komachi (1979) found a negative correlation between cholesterol levels between 150 and 200 and cerebral vascular disorders. Mortality increased for people with cholesterol levels under 160.[14]

Hoffer and Callbeck (1957) reported that the hypocholesterolemic action of niacin was related to the activity of the autonomic nervous system.[15] Earlier in this book, we referred to a study by Altschul and Hoffer on healthy volunteers (medical students) that found a linear relationship between the effect of niacin in lowering cholesterol, initial cholesterol levels, and body weight. The decrease in cholesterol could be shown by a straight line graph. This equation showed that for a 200-pound man, the optimum cholesterol level was 176 milligrams, while for a man weighing 150 pounds, the optimum level was 156. This is remarkably close to the optimum values recommended by Cheraskin and Ringsdorf many years later, that is,

180-200 milligrams per 100 milliliter. Hoffer and Callbeck found that niacin also lowered the cholesterol levels of schizophrenic patients, but the response of schizophrenics was represented by a different equation. At higher levels niacin decreased cholesterol levels less in schizophrenic subjects; at lower levels niacin did not increase the level of cholesterol in schizophrenic patients.

HOW DOES NIACIN WORK?

Niacin lowers cholesterol levels but niacinamide does not, even though both forms of vitamin B3 are anti-pellagra and are almost equally effective in treating schizophrenia, arthritis, and a number of other diseases. Niacin also differs from niacinamide because it causes a flush (to which most people adapt readily), while niacinamide has no vasodilation activity in 99 percent of people who take it. For reasons unknown, about 1 in 100 people who take niacinamide do flush. They must be able to convert niacinamide to niacin in their bodies at a very rapid pace. It is believed that niacin causes a flush by a complicated mechanism that releases histamine, interferes in prostaglandin metabolism, may be related to a serotonin mechanism, and may involve the cholinergic system (Rohte, Thormahlen, and Ochlich, 1977).[16] Histamine is clearly involved. The typical niacin flush is identical to the flush produced by an injection of histamine. It is dampened, if not prevented entirely, by antihistamines and by tranquilizers. The adaptation to niacin is readily explained by the reduction in histamine in storage sites such as the mast cells (which produce histamine). When these are examined after the administration of a dose of histamine, these cells contain empty vesicles (that previously contained the histamine) and also heparinoids (naturally occurring substances that act to prevent blood clotting). If the next dose is spaced closely enough, there is not enough time for the storage sites to be refilled and, therefore, less histamine is available to be released. Similarly, after there is complete adaptation to niacin, taking a break for several days will start the flushing cycle again. This decrease in histamine has some advantage in reducing the effects of rapidly released histamine. Boyle found that guinea pigs treated with niacin were not harmed by anaphylactic shock, which is a severe, sometimes fatal, allergic reaction to a foreign substance. Because the flush is relatively transient it cannot be involved in the lowering of cholesterol, which remains in effect as long as medication is continued. Prostaglandins appear to be involved in the flush mechanism, which is probably why aspirin (Kunin, 1976) and indomethacin (Kaijser, Eklund, Olsson, and Carlson, 1979) reduce the intensity of the flush (Estep, Gray, and Rappolt, 1977).[17,18,19]

Dr. Hoffer suggested in 1983 that niacin lowered cholesterol because it releases histamine and glycosaminoglycans. Niacinamide does not do so.[20] Glycosaminoglycans are biochemical compounds that have been implicated in the absorption and redistribution of lipids in the body.[21] Boyle (1962) found that niacin increased basophil leukocyte count.[22] These are cells that store heparin as well as histamine. He suggested that the improvement caused by niacin is much greater than can be explained by its effect on cholesterol. "Possibly," he wrote, "it is due to release of heparin from the mast cells simultaneously with the release of histamine and also to the eventual marked diminution in the intravascular sludging of blood cells."

It is possible the beneficial effect of niacin is not due to the cholesterol effect but is due to a more basic mechanism. Are elevated cholesterol levels and arteriosclerosis both the end result of a more basic metabolic disturbance still not identified? If it is entirely an effect arising from lowered cholesterol levels, why does clofibrate not have the same beneficial effect? An enumeration of some other properties of niacin may one day lead to the identification of this basic metabolic fault.

Niacin has a rapid anti-sludging effect. Sludged blood is present when the red blood cells clump together. Because the red blood cells must traverse the capillaries in single file, clumped cells cannot pass through as easily. This means that tissues will not receive their quota of red blood cells and will suffer anoxia (lack of oxygen). Niacin acts very quickly and changes the properties of red cell surface membranes so that they do not stick to each other. Tissues are then able to get the blood, and the oxygen, they need.

ACUTE CORONARY DISEASE

Altschul (1964) reviewed the uses of niacin clinically where it is used as soon as possible after an acute event. Goldsborough (1960) used both niacin and niacinamide in this way.[23] Patients with a coronary thrombosis were given 50 milligrams of niacin by subcutaneous (beneath the skin) injection and 100 milligrams by sublingual (beneath the tongue) injection. As the flush developed, the pain and shock subsided. If pain recurred when the flush faded, another injection was given, but if pain was not severe, another oral dose was used. Then Goldsborough used 100 milligrams three times daily. If the flush was excessive, he used niacinamide.

Between 1946 and 1960 he treated sixty patients, twenty-four with acute infarction and the rest with angina. Of those twenty-four patients, six died. Four of the angina patients also had intermittent claudication, which he relieved. Two had pulmonary embolism and also responded.

Niacin should be used before and after coronary bypass surgery. Inkeles and Eisenberg (1981) reviewed the evidence related to coronary artery bypass surgery and lipid levels.[24] There is still no consensus that this surgery increases survival. In most cases the quality of life is enhanced and 75 percent get partial or complete relief of angina. A major problem not resolved by cardiovascular surgery, however, is how to halt the arteriosclerotic process. Inkeles and Eisenberg report that autogenous vein grafts implanted in the arterial circuit are more susceptible than arteries to arteriosclerosis. In an anatomic study of ninety-nine vein grafts in fifty-five patients who survived thirteen to twenty-six months, arteriosclerosis was found in 78 percent of the hyperlipidemic patients. Coronary bypass grafting accelerates the occlusive process in native vessels.

If patients were routinely placed on the proper diet and necessary niacin long before they developed any coronary problems, most, if not all, of the coronary bypass operations now being performed could be avoided. If every patient requiring this operation were placed on the diet and niacin following surgery, the progress of arteriosclerosis would be markedly decreased. Then surgeons would be able to show a marked increase in useful longevity. One would hope to have the combined skills of a top cardiac surgeon and a top internist using diet and hypocholesterolemic compounds.

Studies show that niacin increases longevity and decreases mortality in patients who have suffered one myocardial infarction. The *Medical Tribune* properly expressed the reaction of the investigators by heading their report, "A Surprise Link to Longevity: It's Nicotinic Acid."[25] Had they taken Dr. Boyle's finding seriously, they would not have been surprised and would have gotten even better results.

10. TURN BACK THE YEARS WITH EXERCISE

I keep myself in puffect shape. I get lots of exercise—in my own way—and I walk every day. . . . Knolls, you know, small knolls, they're very good for walking. Build up your muscles, going up and down the knolls.

—Mae West at 61

Little Hulda Crooks was raised on a farm in Canada's Saskatchewan province, where her German parents had a large family, and she ran three miles every day. She climbed 14,494-foot Mount Whitney, the highest point in the contiguous forty-eight states of the United States, seventeen times after she first challenged a mountain in 1962—at age sixty-six. Hulda was a jogging, hiking, mountain-climbing great-grandmother of eighty-three.

Since starting to hike Mount Whitney, she backpacked the 212-mile John Muir Trail in five summer segments, descended to the bottom of the Grand Canyon, and crossed the Sierra mountains eighty miles from west to east.

In 1978, Hulda ran in the Orange Grove Marathon held in Loma Linda, California, completing the quarter-marathon of six and one-half miles in 1 hour, 28 minutes and 55 seconds. Later, that same year, the spry great-grandmother set a world standard for the eighty- to eighty-five-year-old age group in the Senior Olympics, staged in Irvine, California.

At 5-foot-1 and 115 pounds, this physical fitness enthusiast kept in hardy good health that sometimes surprised even her. She kept herself fit by following a lactovegetarian diet and austere lifestyle, and a sense of mission about spreading the message of healthy habits and continuous movement. She says, "Exercise you enjoy does you more good than exercise that you do because you think you have to do it. You say, 'I'm going to do this. I have to do it. I'm going to do it if it kills me.' And maybe it will if you do it that way."[1]

An enjoyable physical fitness program can be started at any age and at any level of fitness. And it's an important program to follow faithfully, because physical fitness promotes longevity.

Being physically fit means:

- You are not overweight or overly bulky. Very little of the body's bulk should come from fat tissues.
- Your muscles, bones, and cardiovascular system remain in tone.
- You feel more relaxed, active, and not fatigued, except when it's appropriate to be fatigued.

The result of being physically fit is improved health, one of the best ways to turn back the years. The process of becoming and remaining fit is primarily one of using your body in exercise or work. There is no set form of exercise, although some are more accessible than others. The main thing is to keep the body moving. Where many people spend fortunes trying to ward off the ravages of age with such surface improvements as makeup, hair dyes, toupees, face lifts, and smart clothes, in reality it's exercise that does the best job. You can delay or reverse many of the deteriorating effects of aging through regular exercise.

WHAT KIND OF EXERCISE PROGRAM IS RIGHT FOR YOU?

Machines steadily break down from wear and tear. The human body works just the opposite way; it improves its functions by working. Exercise maintains the flexibility of the joints, improves blood circulation, increases breathing ability, and builds up the strength of muscles necessary to keep the spine in an upright position. It keeps in tune the harmony of all moving parts working together. Most of all, exercise helps the heart to stay in good shape.

Illness can impose some limitations on normal daily activities and the regular "workout" your body gets even without engaging in a special exercise program. But there are ways around illness restrictions, too. Exercises are designed to make an elderly person feel less disabled.

Elderly people may have problems with balance, with lower reflex reaction time, and with osteoporosis. This only means they have to start slowly, but the end result can be just as good. No age should be considered a bar to improving one's physical fitness.

An overweight person may require a longer time to reach the same level of fitness as a person of normal weight, but once weight begins to decrease, this handicap decreases as well. Being overweight means that bones are under greater stress, muscles have to work harder, and the cardiovascular system has a greater burden. The overweight person shouldn't conclude that there is no point starting on an exercise program until weight is normal, however. Rather, begin right away and you will find that the program increases weight loss by increasing the consumption of body fat for energy. The program will also decrease your appetite for excess food.

An older person already in a fairly healthy state can start a more strenuous program and expect to reach his goal more quickly. However, it is important to be realistic about your condition. Too many people grossly overestimate their own level of fitness. This can be determined by a personal test of walking fast, jogging, running, or swimming to see how you become tired, pant, and develop a rapid heartbeat. If you have any question about your fitness to do these simple tests, then you should have a special fitness test done by a reliable expert in the field.

Take note that exercise and overexertion are two different things. Overexertion is bad not only for the elderly; the young don't fare so well with it either. The purpose of any exercise is to get rid of muscle pain, not to increase it; to create relaxation, not anxiety; to train the lungs, not to exhaust them; to improve circulation, not to tax the heart. Therefore, in answer to the question: What kind of exercise program should I begin? follow these ground rules:

- Do your exercises daily, preferably at the same time each day. It is a matter of building up your capabilities, not putting them to a test.
- Exercises are best done two times a day: on arising in the morning and before going to sleep for the night. The morning exercises can begin while you are still in bed with prone position movements. These go along well with "morning stretching" to take the stiffness out of the joints and the sleepiness out of the muscles. Evening exercises will put a little fatigue into the muscles, which enhances relaxation and helps set the stage for a restful sleep.
- Don't rush your efforts. Set no time limits and just follow your

own comfortable pace—feeling *comfortable* while exercising is the key.

- Set yourself a range of motions that can be accomplished in a range of minutes. You may allow yourself fifteen minutes to an hour to do your bit.
- A little heart pounding and panting after an exercise is normal, as long as it doesn't continue for longer than a couple of minutes following the exercise.
- Start out with a level and duration of exercise that causes just moderate fatigue. This is the level to pursue patiently. After weeks and months, the amount and variety of exercises will gradually increase as you adapt to the steady pursuit of fitness. This principle of gradualness applies whether you are using a single exercise or a combination. (A combination is preferred so that all the musculature is made to work.) If this principle is not followed, you can expect to suffer from strains, sprains, or swellings. A beginning walker or jogger who starts too enthusiastically may have sore, swollen ankles or knees. It is necessary to start slowly to allow the bones, ligaments, and muscles proper time to build up their strength. From steady and gradual movement, weakened or osteoporotic bones will calcify and areas of stress will be reinforced. Ligaments will toughen and muscles will firm up.
- Always engage in a warming-up period. This greatly diminishes the chance of pulling a muscle or ligament. Warming up is simple; merely pursue the exercise at a slow pace and gradually increase the tempo. When you are breathing easily but slightly more rapidly, and your muscles feel warmer, increase the intensity of the exercise until the desirable fatigue stage is reached for that day. If walking, start slowly and gradually increase the pace until eventually the walk is as fast as possible. It would be prudent to walk for a long time before jogging and to jog for a long time before running.

Among the attitudes toward becoming fit are the two extremes: being so fearful you don't start; or being so overly confident you do great damage to yourself from overzealous exercising. The first group of people won't be harmed by the exercise since it will never be started, but they won't benefit from a fitness program either. The second group must be cautioned not to begin too precipitously, and this applies even to those who have already been very fit and are familiar with fitness programs. They must be just as careful as a novice, but it is likely they will be able to accelerate their program. It is a process of reconditioning, which can be done with maximum advantage and little discomfort.

TYPES OF EXERCISE TO DO

We won't describe any exercises in detail, as these are available in a large number of useful books or can be obtained in a variety of fitness programs that are available. Exercising objectives should be to develop a good but not too bulky musculature; to have an efficient cardiopulmonary system that responds rapidly to increased demand and works efficiently at rest or work; to keep your bones dense, properly calcified, and reinforced at the stress points; and finally, to retain your sense of balance and orientation with respect to gravity and space.

To develop, muscles must be considered as functional groups, each requiring its own particular type of exercise. Let us make some exercise recommendations for conditioning different parts of the body.

The Legs

Walking, jogging, running, swimming, and bicycling will all tone leg muscles, as well as improve cardiovascular function.

Abdominal Muscles

This area involves any exercise that tightens the abdominal muscles against some tension. One example is to start from a position lying on your back with arms on chest or behind your head and sitting up while keeping knees rigid. We suggest a target of X situps, X equaling the age of the individual. Remember, each person approaches this target very slowly. There are also a number of useful twisting and rotation exercises for the hip and side muscles.

Back Muscles

The back muscles have the job of holding our heads up and keeping us erect. They are potentially the strongest muscles in the body and when not working right—too tense or too flaccid—they may give a lot of pain. Low back pain is a common affliction. All back exercises consist of bending or arching the back backwards. A useful exercise is going from the prone position on the floor (lying on one's stomach) to elevating the trunk with both hands on the floor. The back is arched more and more. This exercise also strengthens the arm muscles.

Arm and Shoulder Muscles

Swimming and pushups are the best forms of exercise for arms. Pushups also strengthen back and abdominal muscles. Bulging biceps are not necessarily the best criteria of healthy arm muscles.

Neck Muscles

Simple rotation of the head will strengthen these muscles. Attempt to make the largest possible circle in the air with the tip of the nose. This is done both clockwise and counter clockwise.

Bone Exercises

Bones bear weight and are attached to muscles. They are as light as nature can make them, consistent with the necessary strength and rigidity. To make them light, they are hollow; and to make them strong, they contain *trabeculae*, which are reinforced tissue sections that buttress the bone in areas most exposed to stress and strain. The main result of disuse is loss of calcium—osteoporosis. There are no specific exercises for bone strength. The groups of exercises we've already described will also help keep bones fit, but the best are exercises like walking, jogging, running, and swimming.

Balance

Balance is learned and retained by a variety of exercises. These include assuming various positions from standing on one's foot to standing on one's head. The latter requires a good deal of fitness and muscular development, and elderly people who can't do this should not feel they have failed to become fit.

We have not described exercises that require any gadgets such as rowing machines, exercise bicycles, trampolines, bars, swings, and so forth—not because they are not helpful, but because they are not available for the majority of people. We have drawn attention only to those forms of exercise that require a floor, a mat to lie on, a walking surface (beach, road, street) and you. We also have avoided referring to unnatural exercises. A natural exercise is one that has developed during evolution; as an extreme example, dragging a weight by one's teeth is not a natural exercise.

Health and physical fitness are both the result of a way of life that must include personal hygiene, nutrition, as described in this book, supplements of vitamins and minerals when needed—in optimum amounts—and a continual program of exercise and activity that involves all the elements of movement, muscle, bone, and balance. Using just one of these components alone will not result in health. We define health as the optimum possible feeling of well-being in a person who is not ill by any medical standard. We do not suggest that this feeling will lead to happiness, but it will certainly make it more probable that the individual will be happy, contented, or both.

There is no direct evidence that being physically fit will prevent senility, but old people who are not senile generally tend to be more physically fit, perhaps because they are more independent and mobile. It seems a prudent hypothesis that being physically fit will decrease the rate of senility development. There is pretty good evidence that it will prevent coronaries in people who have already suffered them, and should decrease the tendency to even have the first. What is good for the heart is good for the circulation, and what is good for the circulation should be good for the brain in retaining its normal function. But a program of physical fitness that ignores good nutrition and supplements is only a partial program. Unfortunately, too many physical fitness educators and leaders do ignore good nutrition.

HOW EXERCISE IMPROVES AN AGED BODY

Organic efficiency and muscle function are both enhanced by regular exercise. The result is that an aged person will get greater physical and mental health and fitness from his or her program of activity.

We could make an extensive listing of the various body functions that improve in the aged body as a result of endurance exercises like jogging, walking, swimming, and others. Instead, we will outline just a few of the more significant changes you may witness from routine training. Remember, we're talking here about a regular, gradual, and progressive load on the action of the muscles. Get them moving!

The large leg muscles have more than just locomotion as their job. They also aid total body circulation by massaging the blood back to the heart. Working with the diaphragm—also a muscle—the thigh muscles, and calf muscles minimize the stress put on the heart muscle by acting as auxiliary heart pumps.

If you exercise routinely—appointing the same time each day for yourself to work out—you can expect some excellent cardio-respiratory changes to take place in your aged body. First, you'll increase your vital capacity and have your lungs handling more oxygen. Your lung capillaries will pull more oxygen into the blood for spreading around to the 60 trillion cells in the body, including what's left of the 12 billion cells you started with in your brain. You'll be able to incur and repay any oxygen debt with ease. There will be more rapid gaseous exchange within the lungs.

Your chest wall will become more flexible, too, aiding respiration. The peripheral circulation far away from the central cardio-vascular system will have less resistance to bringing all that good blood to the outlying cells. You'll be providing more effective tissue oxygenation.

During the exercise period itself, the rate and depth of respiration increases as does the rate and force of the heartbeat. However, your resting heart rate will come down, and your resting blood pressure, if elevated, will also come down. Steady physical fitness procedures are known to lower high blood pressure.

Small blood vessels in your skin and muscles will function better, and your red blood cell count will increase. The result? Your skin will take on a glow, and the look of aging will fade.

Your heart stroke volume will increase so that more blood can be pumped with each stroke of the heart muscle. Your heart won't have to work so hard. There will be a lowering of the resting heart rate as well as more efficient heart function, in general.

Collateral circulation, where it is needed, will build up. In some cases, doctors have noted that patients' occluded coronary arteries open up as a result of a program of proper diet and exercise. Nathan Pritikin, the famed nutritionist, reported excellent results from his clients following a strict diet and exercise regimen.

The cortisone hormone balance of your adrenal glands will be enhanced. The adrenals themselves will be conditioned and fortified also, so that more severe stress may be adequately handled by your body and brain. You won't be so easily distressed by life's stressors.

We've mentioned before that elevated blood cholesterol levels tend to go down as a result of steady exercising, provided that no saturated fats are taken. There is some evidence to show that by minimizing your animal fat intake and supplementing your diet with vitamins and minerals, you'll be adding to the benefits of physical activity.

Exercise helps to maintain an adequate supply of cortisone. This doesn't just aid the adrenals, but also reduces calcium loss. Bones don't get brittle but are kept strong by your physical effort. The more you move the better.

As circulatory efficiency increases, the total organic efficiency of the body, including the kidneys, liver, lungs, and gastrointestinal tract, tends to go into action. You get rid of wastes more effectively. Furthermore, there will be less fatigue as well as pain related to body movement.

In general then, regular exercise improves the use your body makes of food: improves elimination; helps digestion; lessens constipation; helps prevent kidney stones; and even reduces the symptoms of diabetes. You'll be preventing fatty degeneration of the heart, lungs, blood vessels, and brain, which might otherwise occur, as it often does in sedentary people.

In short, the brief amount of time you appoint yourself to exercise daily is certainly well spent. The rewards in terms of better health and fitness will compensate you many times over for your effort.

EPILOGUE

Fortunate are those who actually enjoy old age.

—Talmud

By now, you are aware that we have not offered you the elixir of perpetual youth. We have described a new way of maintaining good health that will help most people fortunate enough not to have been hit by serious accidents or degenerative diseases such as cancer. The secret to preventing senility is to stay well until the end of life.

We have presented a general set of guidelines for staying at a high level of wellness through good nutrition and food supplementation. We have focused particular attention on techniques for the aging population.

Perhaps by now we have convinced you that health while aging is not something that can be done *for* you. It is a way of life that only you are able to adopt and follow diligently. We have not offered a pill prescription or medicines that require no effort on your part, except to remember to swallow them. Rather, you have been provided with our views and how we arrived at them. But you must begin this new way of life while you are still able to do so, for once senility begins, you may no longer have control over your own thinking. The longer you have been in a presenile state, the less apt you are to respond to the program designed to prevent senility discussed here.

Our program is a combination of no-junk nutrition, supplemented by vitamins and minerals in optimum quantities when needed, and combined with exercise for optimal physical fitness at any age. It requires dedication and effort, but it is a simple daily regimen that will reward you if you make it part of your routine each day.

NOTES

Chapter 1
Aging Is Inevitable, But Senility Isn't

1. Kaufmann, W. *Common Form of Niacinamide Deficiency Disease: Aniacinamidosis* (New Haven, CT: Yale University Press, 1943.)

2. Kaufmann, W. *The Common Form of Joint Dysfunction: Its Incidence and Treatment* (Brattleboro, VT: E.L. Hildreth and Co., 1949.)

3. Kraus, A.S.; R.A. Spasoff; E.J. Beattie; D.E.W. Holden; J.S. Lawson; M. Rodenburg; and G.M. Woodcock, "The Health of the Very Aged," *Canadian Medical Association Journal* 116:1007–1009, 1977.

4. Heston, L.L. "Alzheimer's Dementia and Down's Syndrome: Genetic Evidence Suggesting an Association in Alzheimer's Disease, Down's Syndrome, and Aging," *Annals of the New York Academy of Sciences* ed. E.M. Sinex and C.R. Merrill, 396:29–37, 1982.

5. Turkel, H. "Medical Amelioration of Down's Syndrome Incorporating the Orthomolecular Approach," *Journal of Orthomolecular Psychiatry* 4:102–115, 1975.

6. Harrell, R.F.; R.H. Capp; D.R. Davis; J. Peerless; and L.R. Ravitz, "Can Nutritional Supplements Help Mentally Retarded Children? An Exploratory Study," *Proceedings of the National Academy of Sciences* 78:574–578.

7. Smith, G.F.; D. Spiker; C. Peterson; D. Cicchetti; and P. Justice, "Failure of Vitamin/Mineral Supplementation in Down's Syndrome," Letter to *The Lancet* 2:41, 1983.

8. Rimland, B. "Vitamin and Mineral Supplementation as a Treatment for Autistic and Mentally Retarded Persons," Presented to the President's Committee on Mental Retardation, Washington, D.C. September 20, 1984. Copies available from Dr. Bernard Rimland, Autism Research Institute, 4182 Adams Ave., San Diego, CA 92116.

9. Turkel, H. "The Medical Treatment for Down's Syndrome," Ubiotica, 19145 West Nine Mile Road, Southfield, MI 40875, 1985. Copies available from Dr, Bernard Rimland, Autism Research Institute, 4182 Adams, Ave., San Diego, CA 92116.

10. Hoffer, A.; H. Kelm; and H. Osmond. *The Hoffer-Osmond Diagnostic Test* (Huntington, NY.: Robert E, Krieger Publishing Co., 1975.)

11. Hoffer, A. and H. Osmond, "A Cardsorting Test Helpful in Making Diagnostic Pyschiatric Dignosis," *Journal of Neuropsychiatry* 2:306–330, 1961.

Chapter 2
Normal Aging, Premature Aging, and Pseudosenility

1. "Retirement by Senility," *The New York Times*, May 8, 1977.
2. "Research News," *Science* 224: 1325–1326, 1984.
3. Goleman, D. "Don't Be Adultish!" *Psychology Today* 11:46–50, August, 1977.
4. World Health Organization. *World Health Statistics Report* 25:430–442, 1972.
5. Selye, H. *Journal of the International Academy of Preventive Medicine* II:1–21, 1975.
6. Altman, L.K. "Senility Is Not Always What It Seems to Be," *The New York Times*, May 8, 1977.

Chapter 3
Hypotheses of Senile Pathology

1. Calvert, P. "Senility Roll Call," Letters to the Editor of *The New York Times*, October 14, 1977.
2. Szent-Györgyi, A. *Life Sciences* 15:863, 1974.
3. Laki, K. and J. Ladik, "A Note on the 'Electronic Theory' of Cancer," *International Journal of Quantum Chemistry* 3:51–57, 1976.
4. Myers, R.E. Report to the Second Joint Stroke Conference, Reported in *Medical Post*, March 29, 1977.
5. Walsh, A.C.; C. Melaney; and B. Walsh. Paper presented to the American Psychiatric Association meeting in Toronto, 1977.
6. Walsh, A.C. and B.H. Walsh. "Presenile Dementia: Further Experience with an Anti-Coagulant Psychotherapy Regimen," *Journal of the American Geriatrics Society* 22:467–472, 1974.
7. Bjorksten, J. "A Common Denominator in Aging Research," *Texas Reports on Biology and Medicine* 18:347–357, 1960.
8. Bjorksten, J. "Aging Primary Mechanism," *Gerontologia* 8:179–192, 1963.
9. Bjorksten, J. "Chemical Causes of the Aging Process," *Procedures of the Scientific Section of the Toilet Goods Association* 41:32–34, 1964.
10. Bjorksten, J. "The Crosslinkage Theory of Aging," *Journal of the American Geriatrics Society* 16:408–427, 1968.
11. Bjorksten, J. "The Crosslinkage Theory of Aging," *Finska Kemists Meds* 80:23–38, 1971.
12. Harman, D. "Aging: A Theory Based on Free Radical and Radiation Chemistry," *Journal of Gerontology* 11:298–300, 1956.
13. Harman, D. "Role of Free Radicals in Mutation, Cancer, Aging, and Maintenance of Life," *Radiation Research* 16:753–763, 1962.
14. Harman, D. and L.H. Piette. "Free Radical Theory of Aging: Free Radical Reactions in Serum," *Journal of Gerontology* 21:560–565, 1966.
15. Bjorksten, J. "The Crosslinkage Theory of Aging," *Journal of the American Geriatrics Society* 16:408–427, 1968.
16. Bjorksten, J. "The Crosslinkage

Theory of Aging," *Finska Kemists Meds* 80:23–38, 1971.

17. Bullough, W.S. "Aging of Mammals," *Zeit. fur Alternsforchung* 27:247–253, 1973.

18. Hoffer, A., and H. Osmond. *The Hallucinogens* (NY: Academic Press, 1967.)

19. Hoffer, A, "Dopamine, Noradrenaline, and Adrenaline Metabolism to Methylated or Chrome Indole Derivatives: Two Pathways or One?" *Journal of Orthomolecular Psychiatry*, vol. 14, 4:262–272, 1985.

20. Dhalla, K.S.; K.G. Pallab; R. Heinz; R.E. Beamish; and N.S. Dhalla, "Measurement of Adrenolutin as an Oxidation Product of Catecholemines in Plasma," *Molecular and Cellular Biochemistry* 87:85–92, 1989.

21. Matthews, S.B.; A.H. Henderson; and A.K. Campbell, "The Adrenochrome Pathway: The Major Route for Adrenaline Catabolism by Polymorphonuclear Leucocytes," *Journal of Molecular Cell Cardiology* 17:339–348, 1985.

22. Rudin, D.O. "The Major Psychoses and Neuroses as Omega-3 Essential Fatty Acid Syndrome: Substrate Pellagra," *Biological Psychiatry* 16:837–850, 1981.

23. Rudin, D.O. "The Dominant Diseases of Modernized Society as Omega-3 Essential Fatty Acid Deficiency Syndrome: Substrate Beri-beri," *Medical Hypotheses* 8:17–47, 1982.

24. Horrobin, D.F. "Schizophrenia as a Prostaglandin Deficiency Disease," *The Lancet* 1:936–937, 1977.

25. Horrobin, D.F. "Schizophrenia: Reconciliation of the Dopamine, Prostaglandin, and Opoid Concepts and the Role of the Pineal," *The Lancet* 1:529–530, 1979.

Chapter 4
Senility From Subtle, Chonic Malnutrition

1. "Nutrition Experts Urge Study of Elderly's Needs," *The New York Times*, June 7, 1978.

2. Stieglitz, E.J. *Geriatric Medicine*, 2nd Ed. (Philadelphia, PA: W.B. Saunders Co., 1949.)

3. Stieglitz, E.J. "Nutrition Problems of Geriatric Medicine," *Journal of the American Medical Association* 142:1070–1077, 1950.

4. Droller, H. and J.A. Dossett, "Vitamin B_{12} Levels in Senile Dementia and Confusional States," *Geriatrics* 14:367–373, 1959.

5. Kral, V.A. "Senescence and Forgetfulness: Benign and Malignant," *Canadian Medical Association Journal* 86:257–260, 1962.

Chapter 5
The Role of Food Artifacts

1. King, S.S. "Agriculture Department Proposes New Limits on 'Junk' Food in School," *The New York Times*, July 6, 1979.

2. Shine, I. *Serendipity on St. Helena* (NY: Pergamon Press, 1970).

3. Altschul, R.; A. Hoffer; and J.D. Stephen, "Influence of Nicotinic Acid on Serum Cholesterol in Man," *Archives of Biochemistry and Biophysics* 54:558, 559, 1955.

4. Hoffer, A. *Vitamin B_3 (Niacin) Up-*

date (New Canaan, CT: Keats Publishing, 1989), 8–9.

5. Altschul, M.D. "What Causes Your Arteries to Harden?" *Executive Health* 10:9, 1974.

6. Alschul, M.D. "Is It True What They Say About Cholesterol?" *Executive Health* 12:11, 1976.

7. Hoffer, A. and M. Walker. *Orthomolecular Nutrition* (New Caanan, CT: Keats Publishing, 1978.)

8. Mann, G.V. "Diet-Heart: End of an Era," *New England Journal of Medicine* 297:644–650, 1977.

9. Cleave, T.L. *The Saccharine Disease* (New Canaan, CT: Keats Publishing, 1975.)

10. Hegsted, D.M. *Dietary Goods for the United States* (Washington, D.C.: United States Government Printing Office, The Select Committee on Human Needs, February, 1977).

Chapter 6
Risk Factors of Senility

1. Beebe, G.W. "Follow-Up Studies of World War II and Korean War Prisoners, II, Morbidity, Disability, and Maladjustments," *American Journal of Epidemiology* 101:400–422, 1975.

2. Negsfer, M.D. "Follow-Up Studies of World War II and Korean War Prisoners, I, Study Plan and Mortality Findings," *American Journal of Epidemiology* 91:123–138, 1970.

3. Jacobs, E.C. "Residuals of Japanese Prisoner-of-War Thirty Years Later," *ExPOW Bulletin* 35:15–18, 1978.

4. De Wied, D. "Behavioral Effects of Intraventricularly Administered Vasopressive and Vasopresser Fragments," *Life Sciences* 19:685–690, 1976.

5. De Wied, D.; M.A. Van Wimers; T.B. Greidanus; B. Bohus; I. Urban; and W.H. Gispen, "Vasopressers and Memory Consolidations, Perspectives in Brain Research," *Progress in Brain Research.* Ed. M.A. Corner and D.F. Swaab. Elsevier, Holland: Orth Holland Biomedical Press, Vol. 45. 1976.

6. De Wied, D. "Peptides and Behavior," *Life Sciences* 20:195–204, 1977.

7. Legros, J.J.; P. Gilot; X. Seron; J. Claessens; A. Adam; J.M. Moeglen; A. Audibert; and D. Bercher, "Influence of Vasopressers on Learning and Memory," *The Lancet* 1:41–42, 1978.

8. Oliveros, J.C.; Landali, M.K.; Timsit Bethier, M.; Remy, R.; Benghezal, A.; Audibert, A.; and Moeglen, J.M. "Vasopressers in Amnesia," *The Lancet* 1:42, 1978.

9. Rowe, D.J.R. "Salt and Sugar in the Diet," *Canadian Medical Association Journal* 119:786–790, 1978.

10. Angel, A. "Pathophysiologic Changes in Obesity," *Canadian Medical Association Journal* 119:1401–1406, 1978.

11. O'Keefe, S.J.D. and V. Marks, "Lunchtime Gin and Tonic, A Cause of Reactive Hypoglycemia," *The Lancet* 1:1286–1288, 1977.

Chapter 7
The Antisenility Vitamins

1. Pauling, L.,and M. Rath, "An Orthomolecular Theory of Human Health and Disease," *Journal of*

Orthomolecular Medicine, vol. 6, 3,4:135–138, 1991.

2. Bowerman, W.M. A review of Korsakoff's three papers on Korsakoff's syndrome, Personal communication, 1978.

3. Centerwall, B. "Put Thiamine in Liquor," *The New York Times*, February 12, 1979.

4. Altschul, R. *Niacin in Vascular Disorders and Hyperlipidemia* (Springfield IL: Charles C. Thomas, 1964.)

5. Siegel, B.V. "Enhancement of Interferon Production by Poly (RI) Poly (RC) in Mouse Cultures by Ascorbic Acid," *Nature* 254:531–532, 1975.

6. Horwitt, M.K. "Vitamin E: A Reexamination," *American Journal of Clinical Nutrition* 29:569–578, 1976.

7. Stampfer, M.J.; C.H. Hennekens; J. Manson; G.A. Colditz; B. Rosner; and W.C. Willett, "Vitamin E Consumption and the Risk of Coronary Heart Disease in Women," *New England Journal of Medicine* 328:1444–1449, 1993.

8. Rimm, E.B.; M.J. Stampfer; A. Ascherio; E. Giovannucci; G.A. Colditz; and W.C. Willett, "Vitamin E consumption and the Risk of Coronary Heart Disease in Men," *New England Journal of Medicine* 328:1450–1456, 1993.

Chapter 8
Dietary Minerals and Other Aspects of Good Nutrition

1. Leisner, P. "He Slept Through Part of His Life," *The Advocate*, September 28, 1978.

2. Myers, R.E. "Lactic Acid Accumulation as a Cause of Brain Edema and Cerebral Necrosis Resulting from Oxygen Deprivation," *Advances in Prenatal Neurology*, Ed. R. Korobkin and C. Guilleminault. (New York: Spectrum Publishing, 1977.)

Chapter 9
Niacin, Coronary Disease, and Longevity

1. Altschul, R.; A. Hoffer; and J.D. Stephen, "Influence of Nicotinic Acid on Serum Cholesterol in Man," *Archives of Biochemistry and Biophysics* 54:558, 559, 1955.

2. Simonson, P.K. and A. Keys, "Research in Russia on Vitamins and Atherosclerosis," *Circulation* 25:1239–1248, 1961.

3. Parsons, W.B.; R.W.P. Achor; K.G. Berge; B.F. McKenzie; and N.W. Barker, "Changes in Concentration of Blood Lipids Following Prolonged Administration of Large Doses of Nicotinic Acid to Persons with Hyperlipidemia," *Proceedings Mayo Clinic* 31:377–390, 1956.

4. Parsons, W.B. "Treatment of Hypercholesterolemia by Nicotinic Acid," *Archives of Internal Medicine* 107:639–652, 1961.

5. Parsons, W.B. "Studies of Nicotinic Acid Use in Hypercholesterolemia," *Archives of Internal Medicine* 107:653–667, 1961.

6. Parsons, W.B. "Use of Nicotinic Acid to Reduce Serum Lipid Levels," *Journal of the American Geriatric Society* 10:850–864, 1962.

7. Grundy, S.M.; H.Y.I. Mok; L. Zechs; and M. Berman, "Influence of Nicotinic Acid on Metabolism of Cholesterol and Triglycerides in Man," *Journal of Lipid Research* 22:24–36, 1981.

8. Wilson, B. "The Vitamin B3 Therapy: A Second Communication to A.A.'s Physicians," Bedford Hills, NY, February 1968.

9. Canner, P.L. "Mortality in Coronary Drug Project Patients During A Nine Year Post-Treatment Period," *Journal of the American College of Cardiology* 5:442, 1985.

10. National Institutes of Health. "Lowering Blood Cholesterol to Prevent Heart Disease," Consensus Development Conference Statement, vol. 5, no. 7, 1985.

11. Illingworth, D.R.; B.E. Phillipson; J.H. Rapp; and W.E. Connor, "Colestipol plus Nicotinic Acid in Treatment of Heterozygous Familial Hypercholesterolemia," *The Lancet* 296–298, 1981.

12. Kane, J.P.; M.J. Malloy; P. Tun; N.R. Phillips; D.D. Freedman; M.L. Williams; J.S. Rowe; and R.J. Havel, "Normalization of Low-Density-Lipoprotein Levels in Heterozygous Familial Hypercholesterolemia with a Combined Drug Regimen," *New England Journal of Medicine* 304:251–258, 1981.

13. Cheraskin, E. and W.M. Ringsdorf, "The Biologic Parabola: A Look at Serum Cholesterol," *Journal of the American Medical Association* 247:302, 1982.

14. Ueshima, H.; M. Lida; and Y. Komachi, "Is It Desirable to Reduce Serum Cholesterol As Low As Possible?" *Preventive Medicine* 8:104–105, 1979.

15. Hoffer, A. and M.J. Callbeck, "The Hypocholesterolemic Effect of Nicotinic Acid and Its Relationship to the Autonomic Nervous System," *Journal of Medical Science* 103:810–820, 1957.

16. Rohte, O.; D. Thormahlen; and P. Ochlich, "Tierexperimentelle Versuche zur Klärung des Mechanismus des Nikotinsäure-flush," *Arzneim. Forsch.* 27:2347–2352, 1977.

17. Kunin, R.A. "Manganese and Niacin in the Treatment of Drug-Induced Dyskinesias," *Journal of Orthomolecular Psychiatry* 5:4–27, 1976.

18. Kaijser, L.; B. Eklund; A.G. Olsson; and L.A. Carlson, "Dissociation of the Effects of Nicotinic Acid on Vasodilation and Lipolysis by a Prostaglandin Synthesis Inhibitor, Indomethacin, in Man," *Medical Biology* 57:114–117, 1979.

19. Estep, D.L.; G.R. Gay; and R.T. Rappolt, "Preliminary Report of the Effects of Propanolol HCL on the Discomfiture Caused by Niacin," *Clinical Toxicology* 11:325–328, 1977.

20. Hoffer, A. "Why Nicotinic Acid Lowers Blood Lipid Levels," *Canadian Medical Association Journal* 128:372, 1983.

21. Mahadoo, J.; L.B. Jaques; and C.J. Wright, "Lipid Metabolism: The Histamine-Glycosamino-

glycan-Histaminase Connection," *Medical Hypotheses* 7:1029–1038, 1981.

22. Boyle, E. "Types of Elevated Serum Lipid Levels in Man, and Their Management," *Journal of the American Geriatric Society* 10:822–830, 1962.

23. Goldsborough, C.E. "Nicotinic Acid in the Treatment of Ischaemic Heart-Disease," *The Lancet* 2:675–677, 1960.

24. Inkeles, S. and D. Eisenberg, "Hyperlipedemia and Coronary Atherosclerosis: A Review," *Medicine* 60:110–123, 1981.

25. "A Surprise Link to Longevity: It's Nicotinic Acid," *Medical Tribune*, April 24, 1985.

Chapter 10
Turn Back the Years With Exercise

1. Kendall, J. "Eighty-Two-Year-Old Granny Still Jogging, Hiking, Climbing," *The Advocate*, December 20, 1978.

SUGGESTED ADDITIONAL READING

Abrahamson, E.M. and A.W. Pezet. *Body, Mind and Sugar*. New York: Jove, 1971.

Adams, Ruth and Frank Murray. *Body, Mind and the B Vitamins*. New York: Larchmont Books, 1975.

————. *Megavitamin Therapy*. New York: Larchmont Books, 1975.

Airola, Paavo. *How to Get Well*. Phoenix, Arizona: Health Plus, 1974.

Altschul, A.M. *Proteins, Their Chemistry and Politics*. New York: Basic Books, 1965.

Bailey, Herbert. *Vitamin E: Your Key to a Healthy Heart*. New York: Arc Books, 1968.

Bieler, Henry G. *Food is Your Best Medicine*. New York: Random House, 1973.

Blaine, Tom R. *Mental Health Through Nutrition*. New York: Citadel Press, 1974.

————. *Nutrition and Your Heart*. New Canaan, Connecticut: Keats Publishing, Inc., 1979.

Bricklin, Mark. *The Practical Encyclopedia of Natural Healing*. Emmaus, Pennsylvania: Rodale Press, Inc., 1976.

Cheraskin, E., W.M. Ringsdorf, and A. Brecher. *Psychodietetics*. New York: Bantam Books, 1976.

Cheraskin, E., W.M. Ringsdorf, and J.W. Clark. Diet and Disease. New Canaan, Connecticut: Keats Publishing, Inc., 1977.

Clark, Linda. *Know Your Nutrition*. New Canaan, Connecticut: Keats Publishing, Inc., 1973.

Davis, Adelle. *Let's Get Well*. New York: New American Library, 1965.

Fredericks, Carlton. *Eating Right for You.* New York: Grosset & Dunlap, 1975.

Fredericks, Carlton and Herman Goodman. *Low Blood Sugar and You.* New York, Constellation International, 1976.

Goodhart, Robert S. and Maurice E. Shils. *Modern Nutrition in Health and Disease*, 5th ed. Philadelphia: Lea & Febiger, 1973.

Hill, Howard E. *Introduction to Lecithin.* New York: Jove, 1976.

Hoffer, Abram, and Humphry Osmond. *How to Live With Schizophrenia.* New York: University Books, 1966.

Hoffer, Abram, and Morton Walker. *Orthomolecular Nutrition.* New Canaan, Connecticut: Keats Publishing, Inc., 1978.

Hunter, Beatrice Trum. *The Natural Foods Primer.* New York: Simon and Schuster, 1973.

———. Revised edition. *Additives Book.* New Canaan, Connecticut: Keats Publishing, Inc., 1980.

Jacobson, Michael F. *Eater's Digest.* Garden City, New York: Doubleday Anchor, 1972.

Kirban, Salem. *The Getting Back to Nature Diet.* New Canaan, Connecticut: Keats Publishing, Inc., 1979.

Kirschmann, John D., Nutrition Search, Inc. *Nutrition Almanac.* New York: McGraw-Hill, 1975.

Kugler, Hans J. *Dr. Kugler's Seven Keys to a Longer Life.* New York: Fawcett, 1977.

Lappé, Frances M. *Diet for a Small Planet.* New York: Ballantine Books, 1975.

Moyer, William C. *Buying Guide for Fresh Fruits, Vegetables and Nuts*, 4th ed. Fullerton, California: Blue Goose, 1971.

Newbold, H.L. *Mega-Nutrients for Your Nerves.* New York: Berkeley, 1975.

Null, Gary and Steve Null. *The Complete Handbook of Nutrition.* New York: Dell, 1973.

Page, Melvin E. and H.L. Abrams, H.L. *Your Body Is Your Best Doctor.* New Canaan, Connecticut: Keats Publishing, Inc., 1972.

Passwater, Richard A. *Supernutrition.* New York Pocket Books, 1976.

―――. *Cancer and Its Nutritional Therapies.* New Canaan, Connecticut: Keats Publishing, Inc., 1978.

Pauling, Linus. *Vitamin C and the Common Cold.* New York: Bantam., 1971.

Pfeiffer, Carl C. *Mental and Elemental Nutrients.* New Canaan, Connecticut: Keats Publishing, Inc., 1975.

Pinckney, Edward and Cathy Pinckney. *The Cholesterol Controversy.* Los Angeles, California: Sherbourne Press, 1973.

Rodale, J.I. *The Complete Book of Vitamins.* Emmaus, Pennsylvania: Rodale Press, 1975.

―――. *The Complete Book of Minerals for Health.* Emmaus, Pennsylvania: Rodale Press, 1976.

Rosenberg, Harold and A.N. Feldzaman. *The Doctor's Book of Vitamin Therapy.* New York: Berkeley, 1975.

Stone, Irwin. *The Healing Factor: "Vitamin C" Against Disease.* New York: Grosset & Dunlap, 1970.

Taylor, Renée. *Hunza Health Secrets.* New Canaan, Connecticut: Keats Publishing, Inc., 1978.

Wade, Carlson. *Hypertension and Your Diet.* New Canaan, Connecticut: Keats Publishing, Inc., 1975.

Walker, Morton. *Total Health.* New York: Everest House, 1979.

―――. *How Not to Have a Heart Attack.* New York: Franklin Watts, Inc., 1980.

―――. *Chelation Therapy: How to Prevent or Reverse Hardening of the Arteries.* Seal Beach, California: '76 Press, 1980.

Williams, Roger J. *Nutrition Against Disease.* New York: Bantam, 1973.

Winter, Ruth. *Beware of the Food You Eat,* rev. ed. New York: New American Library, 1972.

Yudkin, John. *Sweet and Dangerous.* New York: Bantam, 1972.

INDEX

Keats, John, 6
Keyes, A., 163
Kidneys, function of, 17, 30, 37
Komachi, Y., 168
Korsakoff, Dr. S.S., 112
Kral, V.A., 61
Kraus, A.S., 6, 7
Kunin, R.A., 170

Lactic acid, 49–51, 159
Lactose, 86
Ladik, J., 48
Laki, K., 48
Lawson, J.S., 6, 7
Laxatives, 121
LDLs. See Low-density lipoproteins.
Lead, 53
Learning disorders, 50
Legros, J.J., 102
Lida, M., 168
Life Change Scale, 96–97
Lignin, 87
Lipids, 70
Lipochrome, 28
Lipodystrophies, 39
Lipofuscin, 28
Liver, function of, 17, 168
Low-density lipoproteins (LDLs), 103
Lungs, function of, 17
Lymph, 36

McComb, Marshall F., 23–24
McKenzie, B.F., 163
Magendie, F., 66
Magnesium, 129–130, 145–146
Magnesium orotate, 28
Malloy, M.J., 168
Malnutrition, 36, 98–100
Manganese, 151–152
Marks, Dr. V., 104
Mast cells, 169
Melaney, C., 52
Memory loss, 19–20, 116
Mercury, 53
Metabolic diseases, 39

Metals, toxic and heavy, 53
Methionone, 66
Mineral deficiency, 128
Mitosis, 24, 49, 55
Mok, H.Y.I., 163
Molybdenum, 155–156
Monosaccharides, 87
Montagu, Ashley, 32
Muscle conditioning, 177–178
Myers, Dr. R.E., 49–50, 159–160

NAD. See Nicotinamide adenine dinucleotide.
Nails, functions of, 54
National Institutes of Health (NIH), 166–167
Neocortex, 31
Nervous system, 30–31
Neurofibrillary tangles, 10
Neuromelanins, 31
Neurons, 9, 24–26, 55, 56
Niacin. See Vitamin B3.
Niacinamide, 67, 169, 170, 171
Niacin flush, 2, 119, 167, 169
Niacin in Vascular Disorders and Hyperlipidemia (Altschul), 117
Nickel, 155
Nicotinamide. See Niacinamide.
Nicotinamide adenine dinucleotide (NAD), 56, 114–115, 118
Nicotinic acid. See Vitamin B3.
Niflumic acid, 119
NIH. See National Institutes of Health.
Noradrenaline, 31, 53, 56
Noradrenochrome, 52
Nottebohm, Dr. F., 24–26
Nutrition, for elderly people, 59–60, 61

Obesity, 36, 102–104
Ochlich, P., 169
O'Keefe, Dr. S.J.D., 104
Oliveros, J.C., 102
Olsson, A.G., 170
Orthomolecular nutrition, 111–112